The Day Ain't Over Yet

A CF Dad's Journal

TODD MICHAEL GENT

First Edition

PAGE PUBLISHING, INC.
Conneaut Lake, PA

First originally published by Page Publishing 2021

ISBN 978-1-6624-5228-4 (pbk)
ISBN 978-1-6624-5229-1 (digital)

Printed in the United States of America

Acknowledgment

Todd Gent would like to acknowledge his daughter, Casey, for her help editing his journal.

February 21, 1992
Friday, Post Send-Off

Part of Day 1. Arrived at Raleigh/Durham Airport at 6:20 p.m. EST, 5:20 p.m. back home in Texas. Scheduled for 6:14 p.m., not bad. It was an easy flight. Coby got to sit by the window and seemed to be pretty excited. I think his cousin Dale helped a lot with getting such good seats. Cousin Dale also helped Coby's departure a little more exciting when his best therapy buddy, Billy, got to come on the plane before we left for Chapel Hill, North Carolina.

The American Airlines flight attendants were very nice. They frequently asked if there was anything they could do to help Coby feel more comfortable. They served us Coke and peanuts before the main meal. Coby had a grilled chicken, of which he ate about half. I had a club sandwich and ate all of it.

I had not eaten before then, didn't have much of an appetite.

Coby slept for a little while, and I listened to the plane radio stations. The landing was smooth and easy as the pilot banked the plane for the final descent. We both looked out the window and saw God's sunset reflecting off a lake. I knew God had sent us to the right place. I felt easier.

After landing, the plane taxied down the runway, and a flight attendant told us that the ambulance service had made contact and was waiting at the terminal. Coby and I waited until the other people departed from the plane. He seemed to be tired but still excited.

The ambulance guys were great. They helped me with all our stuff. They put Coby on a stretcher. We got the usual looks on the terminal. I had become used to it. Coby definitely had. One of the ambulance attendants gave Coby a Duke keychain which helped him relax. The ride was smooth and enjoyable in the back of the ambulance. It took about twenty-five minutes to arrive at UNC Memorial Hospital. We were taken directly to the seventh floor in our temporary home, Room 7303.

It is not as nice as Presby, but I didn't think it would be. It's livable.

After the ambulance attendants left, a medical team came in and started asking questions. After they left, Coby began to tear up. He was upset because he did not know anybody and it wasn't Presby.

The transition period had started, but I knew it would be coming. I wanted to cry also. I told Coby it was good to cry, and once he was a little more composed, we would call Mom and Casey. We did, he talked, and then he fell asleep for a while.

Coby was awakened by the lab crew that would perform the dreaded blood gas. It took two sticks. We both fell asleep then.

"Daddy, I love you," Coby said.

"I love you, too, Coby. Good night," I told him as I laid down in the hospital chair that makes into a bed.

Day 1
Saturday, February 22, 1992

I slept pretty good, next to Coby who must have been tired because he was still asleep. Much better than he had slept the last two nights. I looked out the window. The view was of another building. I could also see a water tower and trees. No clouds in sight.

After doing some push-ups and sit-ups, I shaved and showered. Medical people were constantly coming in and out to ask Coby questions. As they poked and prodded, they listened to him about his feelings on his disease. Everyone seems to be thorough.

Coby woke up and asked for a headache pill and a Coke. I did his treatment.

I have yet to leave his side, except to go to the nurses' station to get whatever he might want or need.

More medical folks come by. The talk is about the UNC/NC State basketball game this afternoon, here at the Dean Dome just down the street. Last night I did talk to Doug Whitt. Later today he is going to take me out to a store so I can buy a fan and some other necessities such as M&M's peanuts, Coke in a can, etc.

Doug Whitt was our superintendent of school's son who I coached at Wylie from the eighth grade up. He received a bachelor's degree from Texas A&M and got into the business school for his master's at UNC. He and his wife, Kelly, lived not far from the UNC campus. His dad had told him to expect a call from me and to help out where he could, since Coby and I had flown up to North Carolina and had no vehicle. Having Doug and Kelly was another part of God's plan, just like Cousin Dale working for American Airlines at the time.

Coby and I watched some TV, and then X-ray came to get us. Coby had a routine chest film, and we asked if we could go back by ourselves. They complied, and Coby and I began our sightseeing adventure of the hospital instead of going straight back to the room. Coby was in a wheelchair and on liquid oxygen at the time.

I wheeled Coby outside. It was a gorgeous day, about 70 degrees. We noticed people walking one direction. They were headed for the Dean Dome and the game. It was like ants going to a picnic. I saw later on TV that there were twenty-three thousand–plus people at the game. State upset number four UNC, 99–94. People at the hospital sure were disappointed. Everyone knew all the players' names and what cities and towns they were from.

Coby's spirits seem to be better after going outside. We both miss Tricia and Casey.

Doug called. He had been studying all day. We decided to go shopping for the fan and other items at six o'clock, five o'clock back home. It was good to see him. We made it a quick visit because Coby did not want to be left alone too long. Sure enough, when we returned, Coby had been crying. I told him it was all right, get that frustration and loneliness out.

While Doug and I were out, a pretty funny thing happened. I got in the wrong car. This girl said, "Pardon me." "You're not Doug!"

I told her, shut the door, and looked behind her car to see Doug in his exact model car.

Doug, Coby, and I got a much-needed laugh out of that story.

I called Tricia and Casey, and it was good to hear from them. Coby and I watched Saturday Night Live and then fell asleep.

Day 2
Sunday, February 23, 1992

I woke up before Coby and went running, which we had talked about the night before. It was nice to be out. I ran to the Dean Dome and back, shaved and showered, and then ate a bran muffin off Coby's tray. I drank some water and felt pretty good.

Coby finally woke and was in a funny mood, joking with the nurses and doctors. He was beginning to be Coby. He seems to be eating good, for him. We watched it rain all day.

Playing Ping-Pong on the ninth floor was fun. It really is nice to see him smile and do things.

Doug and Kelly came by and brought some homemade oatmeal raisin cookies, fruit, popcorn, and lasagna. We had a fun visit. It is really nice that Doug and Kelly are here. Coby really misses his mom, sister, and the Presby gang. So do I.

Day 3
Monday, February 24, 1992

Coby woke up homesick. I think it got worse when the teacher came by. She said she would be in contact with Mrs. Lawson back in Texas. Coby would not lose any ground. He cried and said he wanted me to teach him. He and I had a good talk about how this would be structured for one hour a day, and I would help him. I thought it would help keep his mind occupied.

"Man, Dad, ain't CF enough? Then I gotta go to another state and do school?" Coby said as we both laughed.

It is really nice here how every medical student comes by and visits. At one time today, there were nine soon-to-be doctors and maybe a pizza delivery boy. I do not know who everyone was. Coby had an echo-cardiogram and a pulmonary lab visit. They worked with him pretty well. When he finished, we went outside and saw a lot of coed joggers. Coby kept using his binoculars. He has to wear a face mask when outside the room, mainly for his protection.

We played Ping-Pong again, came back to the room, Coby took a TYLENOL and laid down. Headache as usual.

Oh, I almost forgot. Coby and I met a twenty-year-old who was back for her year anniversary—lung transplant, that is. I was pretty excited. She was not wearing oxygen, does not have to. Going to college in South Carolina and says she feels just fine. I felt really good talking to her. Her mother said she also has an eighteen-year-old brother with CF, who weighs 180 pounds, but is doing fine. It was my first double-lung transplant patient to meet ever. This is definitely where we should be.

When Coby starts getting homesick, I remind him that everyone wants him to feel good, and it would be letting the Presby gang down. It seems to help.

Just had a visit from a boy and his roommate from Terrell, Texas, who graduated with Trisha Blanton. They both attend Duke and left a T-shirt and a cup for Coby. Molly, Trisha's mom, is something else. The boy's name is Craig Davidson. Then night ended with me scratching Coby's back with a straw.

Day 4
Tuesday, February 25, 1992

Hadn't said much about Coby's nurse. The first one we met when arriving was Ruth Ann Wheeler, not related to the ambulance attendant. She was at the end of her shift when we got to the floor. She helped us get situated though. Ruth Ann, who I figure was around twenty-five, has a nice smiling face that makes you feel not so uncomfortable. A Kalamazoo, Michigan, girl who did missionary work for one year in Africa, contracted malaria, overcame, and wants to go back one day. She was back on Sunday, but off Monday.

The evening nurse is Sue Baker, in her fifties, from Iowa; a lot like Miss B's sense of humor and Mrs. Huxley's; trained at TCU in Ft. Worth, Texas. She is a very likeable straight-shooting gal, or lady. Leslie on Monday day shift, constant smile, gentle with Coby. Talked about how she is a Christian and prays for these CF kids who have transplants. All I know is they are twenty for twenty on CF double-lung transplants here. Leslie may be the inside track. Nice girl.

A couple more whose names I never got straight, and one from Massachusetts.

There is one more late-night nurse, a nice black lady, whose last name happens to be Dukes. I told her she might ought to change her name to Tar Heel around here. She just laughed. She works nights and goes to school at UNC Nursing School, studying for her BS in nursing. We talked Sunday night, about 2:00 a.m., about CF kids. She said they seem to be different—brighter and more mature.

Maybe Coby didn't have CF!

Then there is the senior nursing student, Kami, from Wake Forest. She kids a lot and wants Coby's Dallas Cowboys' cap. "That's my team," she'd say. When she finishes in three months, she hopes to stay here, but there is not an opening right now. She has a job lined up in Charlotte, North Carolina. Cammie and Ruth Ann would fit right in with the Presby gang.

We also met the teacher provided by the state. This way Coby won't be too far behind. Of course, Coby panicked, but he got over it. The medical student has been in already, getting his report ready for the morning rounds with the CF team. He is a super nice guy. The team of nine followed about twenty minutes later.

Ruth Ann is back today. She told us she went shopping on her day off. She is getting ready for her brother's wedding in about three weeks. Coby had a blood-pooling test today. When we got back, Dr. Egan, one of the surgeons, came to see us. He stayed about thirty minutes, a real thorough guy. He used to be in Canada on a lung transplant team.

He asked Coby, "Are you scared?" Coby replied, "Yes." He then told us all the bad things that can happen.

It is scary.

Coby said he still wants to try.

Dr. P called Coby while Dr. Egan was here. Coby let them both talk with each other. I just felt the timing was great. I feel we should be here. Coby called the therapy bunch today at Presby back in Dallas. He enjoyed talking with them. Coby had his six-minute walk test and did fine. The therapist was really nice. She said her oldest boy is Coby's age, born July 5, 1979, a few days before Coby. A child life person came by today. Coby liked her. Also, school may start for Coby tomorrow.

"This ain't going to the movies," Dr. Wood told Coby. Dr. Wood is the doctor who Dr. P and Dr. Brown communicated with. He told us the procedure Coby would go through. "The main thing is between the ears," Dr. Wood pointed toward his head. "Attitude is the main thing that will get you through," he told Coby. Dr. Wood is impressed with what he heard about Coby. He stayed about thirty minutes and answered questions. A nice guy.

Coby and I talked after Dr. Wood left. We talked about attitude, not going into a ball game to lose. I told him to keep scratching, clawing, and fighting. Do whatever it takes. Believe in God. "It is all right to be scared," I told him.

"Daddy, I believe in God, but I am still scared," Coby told.

"Just know he will take care of you," I replied with tears on my face.

We then hugged, held each other, and cried. I love him so much. Coby then read *This is Paul*, a book about a boy with CF. Coby then started reading a book, *Heaven*, that Margot sent with him. Molly, Jeannie, Grandma, Poppie, and his mom called. Coby and I always look forward to when Tricia, my wife, called.

Doug called to check in and see if there was anything he could do.

"Maybe tomorrow night we can have a pizza party," Doug and I decided. Coby ate all the food on his tray. The food was not really bad. We settled in to watch the *Grammy's*. Coby's feeding pump went bad, so the nurse replaced it.

"I love you, Daddy," Coby said as he fell asleep. I prayed for strength and courage and then fell asleep too.

Day 5
Wednesday, February 26, 1992

The feeding pump ended at 5:00 a.m. EST, 4:00 a.m. back home time. I flushed it and laid back down. Today Coby starts a twenty-four-hour urine collection. The lab came in and drew eighteen vials of blood. Coby didn't complain. Had to sign a release for him to be tested for the HIV. Ruth Ann came in with that pretty smile and took his vitals. A medical student came in and also took vitals, and then twenty minutes later, there was the parade of interns and residents.

Coby went back to sleep.

I was watching *The Maury Povich Show* this morning. The girl that was on *Diff'rent Strokes* was on from the drug rehab hospital, talking about her problem. "It is a disease," she said. I thought, *No, sweetie, it was a choice for you.* Coby did not have a choice about cystic fibrosis.

I prayed, "God, please be with us."

Ten o'clock, apple juice delivery. Brother Wayne called this morning, and it was very good to hear from him. I ran the stairs again as Coby slept. Showered and ready for the lung scan. Coby woke up, and I did his treatment. He seemed to be in a pretty good mood.

Seems to be another cloudy morning, I observed as I looked out at the psych hospital across the way. The routine of meeting different transplant team members continued. A psychologist stopped by and left some forms for both Coby and I to fill out.

It is some kind of psychological makeup. It asks Coby things like does he play with his sex organs, etc. Real interesting things for Coby. He answered, "Yes, but twice on Sunday." We both laughed for five minutes. It was as good as having a treatment for Coby as much as he coughed.

As usual, they talked down to Coby in those sweet little voices. At least they have a job. They will eventually learn.

The social worker stopped by for about forty minutes, and we talked about the ups and downs we would go through. If we get accepted, she told us about places we might stay after leaving the hospital and waiting for the transplant. She told us the waiting would kill us, no matter how positive we might be.

When she left, Coby said, "Heck, Dad, we're funny. We'll just laugh our time away!"

Lord knows, Coby is something else.

We kept waiting for the lung scan. Cindy Stone called, and it was nice to hear from her. Diane also talked with Coby. They updated us on who was in the hospital and who was going home back to Presby. They said Brian was in again. The school teacher left a computer. Coby really looks forward to lunch. He and I both are amazed at how right on time they are with the trays. There are some things Coby may not know, but he knows the trays come at 8:00 a.m., noon, and 5:00 p.m.!

We are looking forward to Doug and Kelly coming up tonight with pizza. Ruth Ann ordered Coby another bowl of vegetable soup. He sucked it down with a straw.

Another treatment, four *Honeymooners* in a row on TV, and then we went to the coffee shop. That was a pretty good outing. Coby bought a TV crossword puzzle, pencil, Jolly Rancher, and Sweethearts. When we got back to the room, we were told that a lung scan would not be needed. Although a cardiac catheterization would be done Friday.

I then canceled our flight with American Airlines. The little boy next door's dad stuck his head in the doorway. He asked if Coby would like to play with his remote-control car. Coby agreed. They were going out for a while. The little boy has leukemia.

Coby answered the weak ring of the telephone.

"Yes, my dad is here. Wanna talk with him?" Coby said. "Some lady from Lovejoy, Dad."

I took the phone receiver, and it was Cassie Roop. Her husband was being evaluated also for a lung transplant. Lovejoy is only about fifteen miles from Wylie. Wayne Roop was a forty-five-year-old doctor with cystic fibrosis. He ran the emergency room at Plano General, which is about fifteen miles west of Wylie.

She asked, when we had time, for us to come visit. Coby and I loaded up the wheelchair and went down to visit our Texas neighbors. We met Dr. Roop's wife, who said they heard about us in Lovejoy. Dr. Roop said Mrs. Janie Kauffman and Mrs. Roebuck had talked with him about us at the Plano Hospital. We had a nice visit and returned to our room. Kelly and Doug would be arriving with the pizza soon.

We had another fun visit, watched *Unsolved Mysteries*, and went to bed.

Kelly took Coby's PJs and some of my T-shirts to wash. I have been washing our underwear and socks in the sink. "Kind of like camping," Coby said.

Day 6
Thursday, February 27, 1992

Coby seems to be resting really well. They have changed some of the antibiotics. The usual parade of doctors came by. Coby kept sleeping. Another psychologist came by. Coby woke up and made her laugh. Leslie is our nurse today, but Ruth Ann checked in on us. Diana, the recreation therapist, stopped by and left some crafts. The social worker stopped in and said, once the final decision is made, she will give me the apartment list.

The person from dietary came by. Coby told what he wanted for snacks. The teacher will be back at one o'clock, and then we are going out in the pretty sunshine, take the camera, and film some memories.

We are both looking forward to going outside.

At one o'clock, the hospital teacher was coming to have school. I thought I would take this opportunity to go visit Dr. Roop and see how his test came out. Sure enough, at one o'clock the teacher came to see Coby. I walked down the stairs to the third floor and over to Dr. Roop's room.

I peeked through the door, and he was sitting up. He motioned for me to come in and asked how things were going. Cassie, his wife, was sitting in the chair next to him. He was waiting to go for his heart catheterization. Just as he was telling me, they arrived to take him.

I walked with him to the elevator, wished him luck, and walked outside.

I decided to walk around the campus. I walked a little ways and came upon a football stadium. It was hidden in the trees, and it was beautiful.

The gates were open, so I went in, looked around a bit, and then headed back to Coby's room. His door was still closed, so I waited in the hallway. After about ten minutes, the teacher came out smiling and said that everything went fine.

Coby walked out to the hall with his twenty-foot oxygen line then informed me that he was going to have a lung scan after all. His IV had stopped running, so they were going to have to stick him again. Coby asked them to do it then so the nuclear medicine folks would not have to stick him. They agreed that that was pretty smart on Coby's part.

I got to go with Coby when he had his lung scan. Coby had his mask not only on his face but also his shark feet house shoes and oxygen. We finished with the lung scan, went back to his room, and prepared to go outside. He put his blue sweatpants over his PJs with his Wylie letterman jacket. He added the Dallas Cowboys cap as a finishing touch, and off we went to roam around through the campus.

Coby said it was nice to feel the outside air. I took him to the football stadium. Coby was holding the VCR camera in his lap with the green oxygen bottle between his legs. Mask on and shark shoes, and off we went.

Coby and I really liked how the stadium was hid in the trees. They had fake owl statues hanging around to scare pigeons off and ceiling fans above the elite seats at the fifty-yard line. The field grass was beginning to turn green.

We took some pictures and headed toward the Dean Dome.

We followed the path of a par course. I stopped and did some pullups, and we watched coeds walk to their destinations. We came to the four-way red light. I showed Coby the Dean Dome, and suddenly behind us I heard the ding of a bat hitting a ball.

It was the Tar Heels baseball team working out. We decided to go watch. We went down a hill, across a dormitory sidewalk, and then down a hill to the ballpark. We watched a while and then decided we better head back to 7303.

We had been from the hospital building only about fifty minutes, but it was a great escape.

I decided to go and get a book at the volunteer library. We stopped at the coffee shop and got Coby some punch and a muffin—blueberry, of course—and headed back to the room.

After being back about ten minutes, a doctor who would be doing Coby's heart catheterization visited with us. Dr. Franny told us Coby's test would be around 8:00 a.m. on Friday.

Coby was not too excited, but he will, as always, do what he is told to do.

Coby's tray came, he ate, and was then ready to take a shower. Actually, Coby fills the tub and lays in the water.

I prayed as Coby was bathing to not let him worry. It made me feel better.

Doug called and said they would be up to watch *The Simpsons.* Coby really enjoyed hearing that news. Kelly and Doug did come and watch *The Simpsons.* Coby fell asleep sitting up after the show, and Doug and Kelly could not believe it.

They visited with me until around midnight.

I could've talked all night, but they needed to go. They were getting ready to head back to Wylie for spring break. They have been very helpful for Coby and me.

I kissed Coby, said a prayer for him, and went to sleep.

God, I love him.

Oh yes, Tricia called with the update from back home. Miss her and Casey a lot. Mom and Dad called. Card from Nanny and Molly.

Day 7
Friday, February 28, 1992

They came for Coby at 7:30 a.m. for a CAT Scan. He hopped up and went to the head. The nurse gave him a gown that swallowed him. It would have swallowed Too Tall Jones!

I took a shower, and off we went to cath lab. I stayed with him as long as I could and then went out in the hallway. There was a little window I could watch through before they took him in. He was sitting up, just waiting. My mind went back to where I first saw him, lying in an incubator, sleeping with that big chest. I couldn't keep my eyes off of him. I watched as he just sat there, talking with the techs. I'm really proud of him and the way he goes along with whatever is happening.

I thought of other kids back home just complaining because they might have to write, read, or run some laps. Coby has been stuck, poked, yanked, tugged, turned every way but loose, and he keeps going.

They finally took him away, so I went out a different door and roamed around on campus. I found the medical student bookstore and looked around. Then I went back to the waiting room. It was small, and there was no place to sit, so I roamed around and found another one. I wrote a little and kept a close watch on the time. After about an hour and a half, I went back. I was there for about ten minutes when the tech told me to come back with her.

"He did great," she said. "He is so polite."

"I'm with Coby Gent," I said. She smiled.

The doctor came out and said there were some problems due to CF, but no surprise. The doctor, by the way, has a brother who lives in McKinney, Texas.

"Keep him down for about four hours, then he may get up," he said.

A young black girl and I then took Coby back to his room. She said he was the sweetest thing.

Again, I said, "I'm with Coby Gent."

She was telling people on the elevator how he said, "Yes, ma'am" and "No, ma'am." To say the least, she was impressed. We made it back, and Ruth Ann was waiting. Coby was worried about his underwear. Ruth Ann was looking at his wound to make sure there was no bleeding as he was pulling the gown down.

I told her a funny thing, that he's afraid somebody may see him.

I told her, "Later in life he will be trying to show himself, but he won't find anybody who will look!" She laughed.

We settled down, and he is presently sleeping real easy.

People keep stopping by; he just keeps resting.

Jan Sumeal stopped by and brought him some paper, a pen, candy, and a toothbrush. She stopped and talked to Coby yesterday on the sidewalk and said she fell in love with his shark shoes. She told me if I need to step out to call her, and she would stay with him. She told me about the Carolina boys swim meet this weekend, close to the Dean Dome. Maybe Coby will want to go. Whatever Coby has, he netted another friend.

These people are super nice. His mom and sister will be proud when I tell them.

By the way, back to Jan. She works in oncology; that is where you hear the hospital operator announce, "If you are parked in front of oncology, please move your vehicle." It is heard throughout the day.

1:4 5EST, 12:45pm back home. Dr. Egan came in and said Coby's CAT scan showed damage to the left side of his heart. Either by infection or CF, a biopsy needs to be performed. It will be done again in the CAT scan department by the same people on Monday. If there is damage enough, a heart-lung transplant will be necessary.

"The heart needs to be strong to keep the lungs dry," Dr. Egan explained.

I asked, "Will that be done here?"

"It depends on Cigna, the insurance company," he replied. "With our success in lung transplants, they may consider us. They have centers that do heart-lung transplants."

Coby is still sleeping. He won't be happy about another cath department visit, but we will do whatever it takes. That's what troopers do. Just another hurdle.

Coby woke up about 2:20 p.m. EST and was ready for something to drink. I went to the coffee shop and got him a fruit punch drink, which we had discovered the day before. When I returned to the room, Coby told me Ruth Ann had ordered him a lunch tray. He took a drink and said it was great. We spent the rest of the day in the room.

Coby's right leg was sore from the exam, but overall, he was doing good. Waldron Garriss, a third-year medical student, came by to say goodbye. He was rotating to Greensboro, North Carolina, starting next week. He said he would check in and hoped things would be okay. He left his phone number if I needed anything. He was the first medical student we met a week ago tonight.

Chris Stanley stopped by to see us. He was a medical student from Tyler, Texas—premed university of Texas, medical school, Baylor. He was an upbeat guy. "Just heard there were some Texas folks up here," he said. We talked football, CF. It was nice to talk with someone about football. Coby was really not that down about having to go back to the cath lab. He just said, "It always happens to me." In other words, what's new?

Coby colored a little in his *Mad* magazine. We would laugh at some of the top-page cartoons. He really enjoyed them as much as I did, and still do really.

During Coby's treatment, I went to run. It is really nice running out here. I found out why it's called Chapel Hill and not Chapel Flat. Got back, showered, and Coby and I ate supper. He liked the club sandwich they prepared.

He got a card from Nanny, Nancy and Richard Johnson, and magnetic earrings from Trisha Blanton. Grandma and Poppie called, John Hartley, Miss B, and Tricia and Casey. She told me both Marks were told they would not be back coaching at Wylie next year. That is two good friends I will miss. Just another example of politics. I feel both will land on their two feet and move forward with their lives.

We watched a show about ghosts and *Cheers* reruns and then went to sleep.

I prayed for the best. "God, I love Coby so much."

One more thing, I talked to Dr. Roop. He may be going home tomorrow, and he thinks he will make the list.

Day 8
Saturday, February 29, 1992

9:00 am EST. Coby is still asleep. Just met a different nurse, Lisa. Coby is sleeping upright, comfortably. It is something how day to day it seems our lives have become. I've been thinking about both Marks. These guys were always prepared, organized, and liked competing. They were always at work and very dependable unlike some who are unorganized, sloppy, and anytime after a track meet or basketball tournament, they take off on Monday no matter what kind of effect it has on everyone. That is the way it usually goes, though. I like them all though.

Coby woke up and had a treatment. Dr. Harris stopped by with another doctor. We talked about how pretty the Dallas skyline was at night. Dr. Harris had attended a CF convention there in the fall and was impressed with the city.

They listened to Coby's lungs and asked what we were going to do today.

Coby told them we were going to the state swimming and diving meet close to the Dean Dome. "Have a good time," they said and left.

I think Dr. Harris gets a kick out of Coby. No surprise to me.

Coby ate a little something and took a bath. We started getting ready to go out and look around. Coby put on his blue sweat bottoms and the T-shirt Brother Draper brought and his Bo Jackson tennis shoes. We took his Wylie jacket, loaded his oxygen tank, and then headed out the room with his mask on his face.

Dr. Stanley, the doctor from Tyler, stopped us in the hall and grabbed Coby's cap bill. Then we met this lady from Raleigh who grew up in Georgia. Her ten-year-old boy, Ben, was down the hall with leukemia. Boy, does she talk that great Southern talk. I love listening. She made comments to Coby about his cap. She, being from Georgia, talked about "them dawgs." We visited a little while and then headed toward the elevator.

When we walked outside, it was pretty brisk but enjoyable. We went east, toward Manning Drive and the Dean Dome, talking about how nice it was to be out. It was obvious spring break was here as there was not much traffic.

The beauty of the pine tree-lined brick sidewalks leading up to the dorms even had Coby talking about how nice it looked. Coby said after he gets his lungs, he just might come to college at UNC. "I never really ever wanted to go until I saw how pretty this school is," he said. I thought how nice it would be if his mom and I taught here. It was our kind of place.

We started down the steep hill as we headed to the Koury Natatorium. I mean steep. This made the packing house back home in Kaufman, Texas, an anthill. Not bad going down the sidewalk. It was pretty smooth. I pushed Coby into the natatorium and immediately smelled the chlorine. That smell always makes me want to jump in and get wet. I love the water.

I asked the man selling tickets if we could stay a while because we were just passing through. "No problem," he said. I pushed Coby through the double door into the stand area. It was packed with people and very hot. I knew Coby couldn't take the heat, as after a while, it would bother his breathing.

Banners displaying women and men's ACC championships were hanging everywhere. Just like inside the Dean Dome, it was an impressive facility. Not as nice as UT in Austin but all right.

We watched some of the girls' diving. I know I am a little biased, but Casey looked like she could compete with some of those girls. Oh yes, this was the state of North Carolina swimming and diving championships. We stayed a little while then headed back up the hill we had previously descended.

It is pretty neat seeing the basketball courts at each dorm. I have noticed all the nets are intact on the rims. That contributes to the respect basketball has here. It was like taking a stroll in the woods, but the paths happened to have brick sidewalks. Coby wanted to find more of the parcourse that we had discovered Thursday. I stopped and did some pullups and knee curls.

We then went around the football stadium, down a steep hill toward the bell tower. The trees and the pretty buildings were nice views to witness. We came upon the art department. I told Coby this was where he would spend most of his time if he came to school here. He agreed.

We got to go into the museum and saw some neat and strange old stuff. We then found the main town of Chapel Hill on Franklin Street. It is a street of nothing but stores, little shops, etc. We went into a couple and decided to come back the next day and just look around. We started back to the UNC Hospitals after I bought some chips for my hot sauce.

We went to the cafeteria after checking in at the nurses' station. We came back, I read some *Meat on the Hoof*, and we waited for *Saturday Night Live*.

Tricia and Casey called, as did Mom and Dad. We laughed a lot at SNL and went to bed.

I prayed for good test results Monday.

Day 9
Sunday, March 1, 1992

Coby and I slept really well. I looked outside, and it was beautiful. I went ahead and shaved and showered while Coby was still sleeping. The normal visitation of doctors took place, Molly and Archie called, and Coby talked to them first. He was telling them about going out yesterday and that we were planning on going out this afternoon. Archie told me the Kaufman girls basketball team was going to state. I felt good for Mark Harris and his team. Ben the boy with leukemia's mom stopped in and visited. They might get to go home today. Coby had made Ben a get-well card. Ben's mom is a talker. Coby made like he was asleep, so she left the room so he could rest.

When the door shut behind her, Coby said, "Is she gone yet?" I said yes, and then he said, "Great. Let's get ready and go shopping." He was excited. I signed the release form, and the respiratory therapist brought up a full tank of oxygen. Coby put on a shirt, sweat bottoms, letter jacket, Dallas Cowboys cap, Bo Jackson tennis shoes and sunshades, with his mask.

We left for Franklin Street of Chapel Hill.

I decided to take Coby a route I had run earlier—down by the football stadium, by the bell tower, and through the campus. We were strolling along, looking at the old buildings. Some had been built in the 1700s.

Coby told me he felt smarter being around the buildings.

We came upon the university's planetarium, went in, and looked around for a while. They had a coin gravitational bank in which Coby dropped a penny we had found at a parcourse. We watched it spin toward the bottom.

We then walked down toward the botanical gardens where people were sunbathing. Coby said they were probably street people. He is really funny, along with being brave.

We walked around a giant sundial. Coby guessed the right time. *Kind of like* Crocodile Dundee, I thought.

We came upon an old church that was one of the first buildings built on campus. President James Polk, UNC graduate, spoke on the building's dedication, a plaque read. Coby said it looked like Tia's Mexican restaurant. He was right; it did to me also.

We then kept heading for downtown and Franklin Street.

It was such a pretty day, and lots of people were out like us, enjoying the trees and pretty buildings. People were playing with their dogs, and there was a feeling that there were no problems in the world. I watched Coby. He took in everything he could see. He said when Casey and Mom come, they will like this place because we did.

I felt the same way. I thought we were pretty close, but it seems we are becoming closer. We walked far enough that we arrived at the main drag, Franklin Street. We went across and started window-shopping. Coby saw a sign about a card shop that was in the plaza of a bank building.

We went in but could not find it. Coby said, "Look outside that door." Sure enough, it was outside behind the bank. We stayed there about fifteen minutes, looking at posters and cards. It was nice. We then decided to go eat at Pizza Hut. We headed that direction, just window-shopping and stopping at different displays, enjoying ourselves.

We went across another street and discovered The Hut. It was an old filling station that had been transformed into a pizza restaurant. I rolled Coby in. There were five TVs and UNC banners hanging everywhere. They also had all the banners of the Atlantic Coast Conference schools on one wall. A real nice boy seated us in a room with two TVs. We watched the last ten minutes of the UNC/Maryland basketball game while we ate. We ordered half pepperoni and half burger with Pepsi, Dr. Pepper, and breadsticks.

The young boy took his lunch break in the same room, and we all had a nice visit.

People from the other end of the restaurant would holler when UNC made a big play. UNC was behind by twenty-two points, at the end took a two-point lead, but ended up losing by two points. UNC has lost four in a row since we have been here. That has not happened since 1964. Four losses ago, they were number four in the nation. Now they are barely in the top twenty. They are a very young team. Coach Dean Smith and his assistants will have them ready by next year.

Coby really enjoyed himself. I did too.

We paid our bill and started to Whims, a store Coby wanted to buy a cap at, along with some other things. He got what he wanted, except for the underwear with peace signs on them. They were a size 42. I told him we would come back and find some elsewhere his size.

We went back through the college campus and were doing fine until the humidifier on his oxygen tank broke. We had been gone about three hours, but I started rushing him toward the hospital. He said he was fine, but to hurry.

I did.

We were about ten minutes away. I went quickly, up hills and down hills until we arrived at the seventh floor of the hospital. Coby was starting to have a headache when we arrived at 7303. I told the nurses, and they were moving pretty fast. I hooked him up, and shortly he began to feel fine.

He was turning blue just before we hooked him back up to the wall oxygen, but he soon started to look better. He began telling everyone how much fun we had at Pizza Hut, shopping, and riding around the campus in his wheelchair.

Holly called, and he really enjoyed talking with her.

Tricia and Casey also called. As usual, it was good to hear their voices.

We finished the night by joking around with the nurses and watching whatever was on TV. We talked about the heart biopsy that was scheduled for tomorrow and how he didn't want to go through with it but he would, of course.

Talked about, if we stayed, getting an apartment. He finally fell asleep.

I watched him sleep, the retraction of the skin between his ribs. He fights for every breath, it seems.

I have a lot of respect for Coby Gent. I prayed for the best and fell asleep.

One more thing, Ben with leukemia went home to Raleigh. He left Coby a get-well card.

Day 10
Monday, March 2, 1992

I woke up just in time to see Ruth Ann's pretty smile. She had been off all weekend. Coby could not eat or drink until the biopsy, so I hoped he would sleep until the time of the test. Boy, was I wrong.

Doctors visited and a psychologist from Penn State talked with Coby and me. I really enjoyed her visit. Coby and she talked while I left the room. I went out in the hall and read some of the book I picked up at the volunteer's library.

When the psychologist left, Coby was in a great mood. I have no idea what they talked about.

Coby's school teacher came by, and he had school right up to his valium pre-op. I went walking out in front of the hospital. It was about seventy degrees.

I finished the book and went and picked up another one. I returned to 7303, and they came for Coby just as I sat down. We went to the cath lab. I waited until about 1:00 p.m. EST and then went back to the room to wait for Tricia's call. She called about 1:15 EST, 12:15 p.m. her time. She was on her lunch break. I could not give her any news. She will call back tonight.

Sandy Gonzalez called, but Coby was still sleeping. She will call back later. She is another Presby nurse.

I am currently in the waiting room at the cath lab. It just is not going fast enough for me, and I cannot imagine how Coby feels.

But it is not about me.

I just hope he is hanging in there. I pray and wait. Nothing more I can do.

The tech came in and said they are about completed. Coby had become a little anxious, and his heart rate increased. He has no reserve in his lungs, so his rate always gets up. I think it kind of shook up Dr. Franny.

What is strange is that I could sense how things were not going well.

I asked God to be with Coby. All of a sudden, I felt good.

About three minutes later, the technician came for me, and we took Coby to his room. The doctor was here, so I knew something must have happened. Coby saw me and said he loved me. I felt so much better. The doctor told me he hoped he got enough tissue sample and that only time would tell.

We were back at the room, and the technician, Dr. Franny, and I put Coby back in his bed. After everyone left, Coby wanted his PJs on, so I helped him put them on. I went down and got him some punch from the coffee shop, came back, and let him have some. He said it was good and then went to sleep.

I went and got my hot sauce from the refrigerator at the nurses' station, had some chips with it, swallowed it down with a coke, and sat next to Coby's bed. The female chaplain came by, and we had a good visit. I cried, but I felt better afterward.

I hadn't run today to let out my frustrations about the unknown. She said a prayer for Coby and wished us well. "I have been thinking of him and you being so far from home," she said. She asked me how I was doing. *Heck, I'm fine. Coby is the one who has to put up with all this testing,* I thought.

I just said, "I am doing okay."

After the chaplain left, the social worker came by to let me know her fingers are crossed. Hopefully, she will be able to give me the apartment list tomorrow. God, thank you for giving Tricia and me Coby and Casey.

5:00 p.m. EST. Ruth Ann just brought Coby fifteen pieces of mail. He will enjoy reading once he wakes up. "Keeping the postal service busy!" she said. I thought, *Well, Cliff Claven will go to Cheers when he is through.*

5:30 EST. Shirley Trewin just called from Cigna insurance and wanted to know how things were going. She said to hang in there and wished us well. Ruth Ann is on for twelve hours today. She has been checking on Coby regularly.

I read a little, but my mind kept wandering to what was going to happen with Coby. He was really sleeping good. For a second I thought if he didn't have CF how active he would be. I hope that the transplant goes as expected, and he will be able to play golf, run, play baseball, go to school, college, whatever he wants to do.

Coby finally started to wake up. Dr. Albert and Dr. Nash (I believe) are his pulmonary doctors for this month. He needed to go void, so I helped him go to the bathroom.

He came out and wanted to know when he could eat. His soup was still warm, so he slurped it up.

"Somebody needs to move their car from the oncology building," the operator said over the intercom.

We took it pretty easy the rest of the night. I got Coby some more fruit punch, and Chris's dad next door brought him some pizza. Coby was feeling good. Our night nurse was going to be Chip. He was a nice guy. We talked about Andy Griffith going to school at

UNC. We also talked basketball and other sports. Coby seemed to like Chip.

Other nurses are starting to stop by to talk to the kid from Texas.

They have heard how funny he is. Coby opened all his mail and read each piece. People back home have been good to write and call. Molly and Nanny send something just about every day. Mother and Daddy, Tricia and Casey, and also Molly called.

Lisa, one of the nurses, brought Coby a water gun so he is ready for battle.

We waited for Cheers and then went to sleep.

Day 11
March 3, 1992

Coby slept a little restlessly, but overall, not bad. I think his leg was still bothering him from the femoral stick. Two sticks in three days bruised him a little. I got up and went running for about thirty minutes around the campus. I had it pretty much to myself with spring break going on.

I got back, and Coby was hungry. I went and got him some punch and a ham and cheese sandwich.

I shaved and showered.

The regular parade came through to see Coby. The chaplain visited. Coby's IV had to be taken out again and would be restarted this evening. We went to UNC Hospitals' version of the CF clinic and had PFT (Pulmonary Function Test) done. It was just like Children's in Dallas with people everywhere.

We came back to the room, and the teacher said she would be back at one o'clock.

Coby's respiratory therapist gave him the aerosol and talked about NASCAR racing, along with her internal digestive tract problems. It's nice listening to her talk.

Coby ate lunch, bathed, and waited for his teacher.

The psychologist came by to talk with "The Cobe." His teacher came at 1:00 p.m. to tell us she would be back at 1:30 p.m. I went outside to write, and it was beautiful.

The Carolina sky is really blue today.

Oh, by the way, Coby wrote a nice story the teacher assigned. He really is good. If he would just apply himself more, I think he could write for a living.

The mother of Ben with leukemia called and checked on Coby. I must say again how nice this place is and how nice everyone is to us.

The research here for CF is really aggressive. They are developing their own PT jacket for a cheaper price than $20,000. After school today, I am going to take Coby outside.

A lady stopped by and talked with Coby and me. Her eleven-year-old daughter, April, was at the CF clinic from Charlotte. She told me Coby is one of the happiest kids she has ever been around. She hopes everything will work out for him. Just another person Coby has touched.

He is something else. His mom, sister, and I love him so much.

I stayed outside for about an hour, enjoying the warm sunshine. People seem to be even more friendly with the weather being so nice.

I went back to the room, and the door was still shut, so I found a waiting room and read some of the book I picked up from the volunteer's library. The teacher was coming down the hallway, so I knew Coby was finished with school. I went to his room, and the door was still closed because the psychologist was talking with him.

I decided just to wait in the hall. The recreational therapist saw me, and we visited for a while. Annie, the respiratory therapist that did the six-minute walk with Coby, stopped to talk as well.

The psychologist walked out of Coby's room, just laughing and shaking her head. "He is funny," she said. Annie stayed for a little while and then left.

Coby and I were going to Franklin Street again, and I told him it was nice enough to wear shorts. "Great," he said. He started getting ready when Connie, the physical therapist, stopped in for a treatment. "Shoot," Coby said, jumped back in the bed, and received his treatment.

Connie and her friend were going to Charlotte that night to attend a U2 concert, about three hours away.

She finished with the treatment. Coby hurried and got dressed before any other obstacles could detain him from getting outside. We loaded up the oxygen tank and took an extra humidifier and then headed for the strip. The weather was fantastic. We just took our time and took in the sights.

Coby wanted to have pizza at Pizza Hut before he bought his peace sign underwear. It is really easy getting around with twenty thousand students gone on spring break.

We arrived at Pizza Hut and got the same waiter and room. It was as nice as before. Coby really seemed to enjoy being there. He told me all his friends were in school, and he was at Chapel Hill, eating pizza. "That's wild."

I thought, *Not as wild as having a double-lung transplant!*

We finished and started our journey to Whim's, the store with the Carolina-blue peace-sign underwear. We were at the corner light where earlier, Annie, the respiratory therapist, yelled at us from her car just smiling.

We purchased the undershorts, keychain, and pen, and started back to UNC Hospitals. I kept a close eye on the oxygen tank and made sure everything was intact. It was one of the nicest afternoons I have ever spent, just walking. No wind, pretty scenery, squirrels running around us fearlessly, and Coby enjoying every second.

I will never forget this afternoon.

I was pushing Coby, and we were both looking across campus when, all of a sudden, a German shepherd came running toward us. Thank goodness he was tame. He was just out with his owner, who had released him from his chain. Coby was funny. He squealed and said, "Oh my god, that scared me! Was that a horse?"

Ever since he got bit when he was smaller, he is a little edgy when it comes to big dogs. I don't blame him. It was a strange feeling seeing that big dog come straight for us, but a nice feeling when it passed us!

Right before the dog episode, we watched a couple of guys on top of a church steeple, repairing and painting it. They must have been 150 feet in the air, just hanging by ropes. A lady told us they had even been up there singing last week in the rain. She told Coby she would see him up there tomorrow. He laughed, and we went on our way.

We arrived back at the room just in time for Coby's IV to be restarted and his six o'clock medicine to begin. Dr. Wood stopped by to tell us pathology was still studying Coby's sample, but things were looking pretty good. There was still a possibility he would have to have a heart-lung transplant.

I thought, *God, please just lungs.*

It is amazing how a few weeks ago, I didn't want to hear about a lung transplant, and now I am praying for one over a heart-lung transplant. I keep telling myself that whatever happens is God's will. It is all I can do.

Life is really a ride.

Dr. Wood left, and Coby said, "He's funny."

Tricia called earlier because of open house. Esther was there and said I would do anything to get out of open house. I really wouldn't mind being there getting that free soda. Tami and I always get a kick out of what parent goes with what sixth-grader. Mother and Daddy called as well as Jeannie. News is about the same, although storms are supposed to arrive tonight in the metroplex.

Coby finished his homework. Waldron Garriss, the medical student from Texas, stopped by to visit Coby and see what was happening with the transplant. He is really concerned, and we have made a good friend. He helped Coby with a math problem.

Thank goodness he came by.

Nurses not assigned to Coby came by to visit, and he joked with them.

Molly and Tricia's aunt sent Coby some LEGOs, and he enjoyed putting those together. Monica Rose sent Coby a card and some pizza money. Freshmen athletics also sent him a card. I really miss those nuts. Brent Baker, a kid I coached a few years ago, sent a card with a note that said to let him know if there was anything he could do. That was really nice.

We watched the *Happy Days* reunion, *Cheers* rerun, and went to bed. Leslie would be our all-night nurse, and she would be checking in on us.

We prayed and went to sleep.

"I love you, Daddy," Coby said.

"I love you too. Good night," I told him.

Ben's mom called. They are probably coming back.

Day 12
March 4, 1992 (Ash Wednesday)

I woke up when Leslie gave the six o'clock medicine. Man, Coby has this room cold, but he likes it that way. I laid in bed, dozing off and on. I was thinking about the coaching situation back home. Coach Ard will be gone, Spann, Mazzon, possibly Wilbanks. It will be like changing jobs, but I never moved. I'm going to miss those guys, but time will go on. I must look forward, not backward.

Joe, Peters, and I will have an interesting year, that is for sure.

Daylight appeared, but it looks like it is going to be cloudy. Ruth Ann came in just a-smilin' and said good morning. I was sitting in the chair with a blanket on, trying to keep warm. Ruth Ann said her boyfriend saw a young boy in a wheelchair with a green tank and a Carolina cap on his head yesterday on Franklin Street. There was a guy pushing him down the sidewalk.

"That bes us!" I said. She said she figured.

Wayne called this morning. They are going on the train to Seattle during spring break. He said they would be checking in regularly.

Coby is really zapped out this morning.

I hate CF.

The waiting is something else. CF really could make one paranoid, if they let it. I haven't showered yet. I think I will go on a run during Coby's school time.

Dr. P just called to check in and said, "We are thinking about y'all. Don't wake Coby up." He told me to tell Coby to get those folks organized! It was good to hear from him. I told him if UNC did not win this week in basketball, Coby might be the next coach. He laughed and said, "They may change the name of the arena!"

Chris is really crying next door. Leukemia doesn't look like much fun either. I think of the hurdles God puts in our lives. There is a reason, I keep telling myself.

Coby gives me strength to keep going.

His fight and willingness to have this lung transplant is motivation for me to do the best I can every day without complaints. Yesterday when I was heading out for my run, a young black woman with only one leg was walking into the hospital on crutches. I dedicated that run to her and Coby. I will run for the ones who can't.

God always, if you let him, will help us get over the hurdles. Just believe.

Dr. Black, the medical student, informed me that Dr. Egan was doing a transplant at this moment. She said he would let us know later today if Coby would be listed. Things aren't looking that bad, she told me.

A clown was in Coby's room, performing magic tricks, while I was talking to Dr. Black. I decided to go and run before lunch. I felt anxious about the news. I was riding the elevator down, thinking, *Please God, let him be a candidate.* When I got outside, the weather was cooler than yesterday. This is a very busy place with people coming and going.

It struck me, which I was already aware of, how many elderlies there were walking around. I thought maybe Coby will get a chance to be old. Man, would he be able to tell some stories. I started running at a good pace. I wasn't even getting tired.

I ran around the Dean Center, back around the football stadium, did some dips and pushups, and went back to room 7303. When I got to the room, two doctors were with Coby. They told us the same as Dr. Black did earlier. Coby and I had lunch, and then he went to school.

I think school is good to occupy his time. Tricia called and said Casey made the tryouts for the talent show. I was glad to hear that.

Jan Sumeral stopped by from oncology. She has nothing to do with Coby or his transplant. Just another one of those people that met him outside the hospital one day and became interested in what was going on. Coby had to come back and get more oxygen in his tank, so she was able to visit with him. Coby left back for school, and Jan told me that when she was in the fourth grade, doctors in Winston-Salem Hospital removed a thirty-pound tumor from her liver. She told me to call if there was anything she could do. She and her husband have six and two-year-old girls, which keeps them busy, of course.

The psychologist stuck her head in and said hi. Coby returned from school and did his homework. I am really proud of him for that. He is waiting to go walk on the treadmill. Pat Thomas from respiratory came and did Coby's treatment. Connie Johnson from PT took Coby to do his treadmill work.

Afterward we went to the coffee shop and bought a drink and a sandwich. Ben with leukemia was back in the hospital, and his mom came by to tell us. Dr. Albert came by and said the pathology report was normal. The left side of Coby's heart is the way it is because of the lungs working so hard against the right side. The septum pushes a little toward the right. In other words, if Dr. Egan is satisfied with the results, we should be a candidate.

Thanks, God!

Sue Baker is Coby's nurse tonight. He likes her a lot. Sue is also a member of the Chapel Hill school board. We have talked a lot about schools when she has been on duty. She just flushed Coby's IV. He has fallen asleep during the clapping of the treatment.

Mother called, and I told her I was relieved about the report, but still a little anxious awaiting Dr. Egan's decision. Dr. Wood stopped by and said the same as the other doctors, "Just waiting on Dr. Egan." Dr. Mann came by, and we talked SEC football. He's all right.

If the word is *go*, I am going to buy some cards and send them to the afternoon and freshmen athletics, thanking them for their concern and to keep working hard.

The helicopter just left again. Three or four times a day it comes and goes. Coby slept until about eight o'clock EST, and I woke him to give him six enzymes for his feeding. He was a little groggy, but *Unsolved Mysteries* was beginning to come on, so he perked up a bit.

I went down and got him a fruit punch from the coffee shop, another twenty ounces.

Jeannie called, Mother called, Molly called, Tricia and Casey called. It is always good to hear their voices.

We watched all the *Unsolved Mysteries* and then watched the Tar Heels break their losing streak by defeating Georgia Tech. I looked out the window, and all I could see were many Tar Heel taillights leaving the parking lot.

We watched Cheers, some Dick Van Dyke, and then we were off to sleep. We were both ready for that.

Coby said, "Another day gone by, Daddy. I love you, Daddy."

"I love you, too, Coby," I said and kissed his head.

I have been doing that for over twelve and a half years. I said my prayers and sleep began.

I forgot Jon Peters called. "It is a mess here, Todd," was about the call in a nutshell.

Day 13
Thursday, March 5, 1992

I heard Leslie, our night nurse, come in and hook Coby up to his medicine. I never remember her disconnecting it. I must have been pretty sleepy. This waiting puts some kind of stress on that makes the body tired. I have even more respect for Coby. He goes with the flow well. I was lying in bed, looking at the poster Dr. Roop and his wife left, when the phone rang.

"Dean Smith, please," the caller said. I knew it was ole Spann. It was good to hear his voice. "Is there a job up there?" he asked.

"If Dean didn't win last night, there would've been one," I responded.

He said just about what Peters had told me last night; it was a complete mess. I told him to go forward and to hang in there. It was nice of him to call.

Operator: "Would whoever belongs to the Ford Escort move it please. It is blocking the main drive."

The workday has started at UNC Hospitals. The operator made it official. Dr. Mann stopped by. "Nothing new from Dr. Egan," he reported. Ruth Ann came in and took Coby's vitals. He took a TYLENOL and went back to sleep, upright across his pillows, naturally.

Looking out the window, I can see it is a cloudy morning. Maybe it will clear up, and we can go outside later. I am going to wash tonight. There is a washeteria in the motel lobby connected to the hospital. Chris next door sure has been quiet this morning, but I know it won't last long.

Hospital operator: "Anyone who has their car parked in the fifteen-minute parking area, please remove." Times two.

I forgot to write that Ronnie and Kyle Johnson called last night. Kyle will probably be going to Presby soon as he is not doing well. Coby really likes Kyle, and it was nice they called. Kyle told Coby that Lisa was fired from Continued Care—attitude. I know Lisa was just standing up for what she thought was right. It just doesn't make sense sometimes. She will find a job soon. "She's a good one," I told Coby. He agreed.

I visited with Ronnie about how nice they were here and about the research they had going on with the PT vest. Coby said he wished Kyle could be here. That would be nice, I thought. I know the Johnsons must hate CF also.

Operator: Times two, same song and dance.

Coby received some books and a video from Mrs. Marks at the middle school library yesterday. We are going to look at it today. Coby got up, took a bath, and went to school.

Dr. Egan and part of his team stopped by and told us Coby will be listed if he wants to be. Coby and I were really happy. Coby was pretty excited.

People stopped in and congratulated Coby all afternoon. Dr. Egan had talked to doctors in England, and they all agreed with Coby's findings. A double-lung transplant should be fine. When they left, Coby said, "I knew I would get listed. God helped me."

I feel relieved. Now I must find us a place to live. I will start tomorrow because Coby, Dale, Jeannie, and I will be out running around. Oh yes, Dale and Jeannie are flying in this afternoon. Coby does not know yet, and I am not going to tell him.

Coby's doctors started stopping in and giving him high fives. They were shaking my hand. The nurses were excited as well. It was really great. It is nice to know everyone was pulling for us to get over another hurdle. It wasn't but about twenty minutes later when Dale and Jeannie walked in the room.

Coby almost fainted.

He was so surprised and happy to see them. I was too. It was great to see some kinfolks. Everything seems to be going our way. Dale and Jeannie were sharing Coby's being listed with us, and they were having fun too.

I think just a month and a half ago, I really did not want to talk about Coby having a double-lung transplant, but now I think it is the best thing for him. He is so happy to be a candidate. It is just like he made a ball team of some kind. I have a lot of confidence in these people after being here for a while. I hope the wait is not long.

Jeannie and Dale were a little thirsty, so I took them down to the coffee shop while Coby was taking a breathing treatment. Dale was so funny about saying how confused he was in this place. "Man, what a lot of hallways!" We got their drinks and returned to 7303.

Coby was scheduled for a treadmill workout. Jeannie stayed with him while Dale and I walked to the Dean Dome. Dale couldn't believe how beautiful the campus was and all the hills. We went into the natatorium and watched some of the diving team work a little while. Then we went into the Dean Dome. Dale looked at the banners and sat in the seats. He was loving it.

We walked back and found Coby and Jeannie in the treadmill room. Afterward Coby wanted to give them a tour of the campus, so we headed out. They seemed to enjoy the walk. We went back to the room so Coby could have his treatment, and then we were going to eat at Chili's in Durham.

While Coby was taking a treatment, Jeannie and I went to wash his PJs in the hospital laundry room. It took about forty minutes. We loaded up Coby's wheelchair and oxygen and headed for the parking lot to get the Alamo rental car Dale and Jeannie had picked up.

It took about ten minutes to get to Chili's. We laughed all the way at crazy Dale. He is a hoot!

We walked into Chili's just like we were at home. Coby and I went to the restroom when I heard, "Hi, Mr. Gent." I turned around, and it was the Davidson boy from Terrell. He is the boy that brought Coby the Duke shirt and cap. It was nice seeing him again.

We ate. Coby had chicken, of course, and then we headed back to the hospital. Jeannie and Dale went to their room at the Holiday Inn, and Coby and I waited for Cheers. It was one wild afternoon for the Cobe.

Life is definitely a ride.

Day 14
Friday, March 6, 1992

I told Coby last night that we are going to get up early and do some sightseeing with Dale and Jeannie. They were going to have to be back at the airport at two o'clock to turn in the car. He said that was fine with him.

I got up, showered, and got ready. I let Coby sleep until they arrived. About 8:30 a.m., Jeannie walked in. I got Coby up and signed a release. Dale was waiting outside at the patient pickup parking lot. We rode around and decided to check out Ramsgate Apartments. We had to stop and ask for directions.

Dale stopped at a convenience store and asked a guy wearing only a bathrobe and no shoes where Ramsgate might be. "Dang," he said, "I think they are, uh, thataway." He pointed.

We found out later he was wrong. We did do some laughing though.

We finally stopped when we saw a postman and asked him for directions. He told us right where to go. The apartments were just right. There was an indoor pool, racquetball court, tennis court, and most all the patients waiting for transplants lived there.

The manager was very nice. I called her later and told her I would be back Monday. She said that would be fine. We then rode over to Duke. Man, what a beautiful school. We came across a bunch of tents with folks camping out. There were 115, we found out later at the information tent, waiting for Sunday's Duke versus UNC basketball game. They had been camping out for two weeks! Yeah, I'd say basketball is pretty big here.

We couldn't believe it. Dale said, "I think I will watch it on channel four instead of camping out." We took the eight-mile drive back to Chapel Hill and then to Franklin Street to Coby's Pizza Hut. Right off the bat, he saw his friend Craig Jones coming to work. He said hi to Coby who really liked him. Jeannie and Dale couldn't get over how many people we knew in such a short amount of time. We ate and went to the drug store, baseball card shop, and Whim's. It was then time for Dale and Jeannie to drop us off at UNC Hospitals. It was a little sad, but Coby was so happy to see them he was okay. I was also.

Coby told me, "Daddy, the apartment is going to be great. We won't be bored, will we?" I told him that no, we wouldn't. I called the phone company and the apartment to verify that we could be there Monday.

Coby went for his treadmill walk. I am now washing our undies and shirts. It is raining, and Jeannie and Dale should almost be back to Dallas. Coby and I will settle down and watch some Friday night TV. Just a week away from Casey and Tricia. We miss them. I finished washing and went back to the room. The phone rang, and it was Jeannie. "Well, ya'll made it," I said. Actually no, there was a plane problem, and they were still at Raleigh-Durham Airport. She didn't think they would have to wait long. Coby said, "Go back to the Holiday Inn, and we will have more fun tomorrow!"

Coby and I talked about the transplant some more. He said, "I'm really scared." I told him I was too. I told him he is the bravest person I have ever known. He said he wasn't because he was scared. I told him there was nothing wrong with being scared and hugged him. "Just look forward, don't look back," I told him.

God, I asked as always, please be with Coby. It always makes me feel better.

Jeannie called back and said they should be leaving in an hour. Dale talked to Coby for a while, and as far as Coby and I know, the two-headed West. I strawed Coby's back, did a treatment, talked to Tricia, watched *20/20*, *Cheers*, and went to sleep.

Coby is really tired. He had a lot of fun with Jeannie and Dale visiting and seeing the new apartment and all. "Daddy, the apartment is just like I thought it would be," Coby said.

Also, Mom and Dad called. The Kaufman girls lost.

"I love you, Daddy," Coby said.

"I love you too, Coby," I said and kissed him on the head.

We both went to sleep.

Day 15
Saturday, March 7, 1992

As far as I could tell, it had rained most all of the night. I got up and went running. I found the old gym, practice football fields, one Astroturf and one natural grass, the blue track, and a swimming center. *New places to push Coby today*, I thought. I got back to the hospital, and Coby was still asleep. I showered, got some ice water, and started reading the book I had checked out.

Dr. Mann stopped by. Kami Moore, the student nurse, is back from spring break in Florida. She reminds me of a girl we called Tree in x-ray school. I like them both very much. They kid around all the time. Chris next door is hollering. Must be time for his medicine.

The boy two doors down, Sean Diaz, is one of five people in the world that has some kind of spine disease. He is fourteen and runs track when he is able.

The sun is coming out. It should be a great day.

Gary Larson's *Far Side* for the weekend is great. Coby started stirring around when the doctor started listening to his lungs. Ben was his nurse today and brought in his medicines. Coby was ready for lunch. It came, and then he took a bath, followed by us going out for a push and stroll. I took him toward the track. Coby brought his Super Soaker to squirt at squirrels. It was a partly sunny day with the temperature around seventy-five degrees. It was enjoyable.

Coby couldn't believe how pretty the Carolina blue track was. "Looks like a swimming pool," he said. I pushed him around a soccer field, and we went to other places we hadn't seen until now. We came upon the Astroturf practice field, and the field hockey team was working out, so we watched for a little while. I looked on a practice field schedule that was posted and read where football starts the twenty-third of March. I told Coby we would come and watch a while.

We looked through the gates of the baseball field. Maybe we can make a baseball game or two. We had been gone about two hours, so I started pushing Coby back to UNC Hospitals. Coby was shooting water at the squirrels as I pushed him up the hill on the brick pathway. We got back to the room, and I asked Coby if he wanted to order out pizza for the night. He said yes and that he was looking forward to *SNL* tonight.

The phone rang, and it was Billy back in Irving. It was good talking with him, and Coby enjoyed talking with his old therapist. Everyone is really excited around here about the UNC/Duke game tomorrow. I visited with Ben's dad, and he is doing a little better.

It is a bit quieter around here, since Chris next door is gone. No remote-control car hitting the walls and doors. Tricia called. She worked in the yard and pool all day. I don't worry about her because I know she will keep busy. She is a player. I can't wait to see her and Casey next week.

We ordered pizza, watched *Cheers* and *SNL*. It goes off late here. We finally fell asleep. Coby is getting excited about the apartment. I will enjoy the room. Billy is our night nurse.

Day 16
Sunday, March 8, 1992

Dr. Mann looked in and listened to Coby. Kami took his vitals. Ruth Ann is his nurse. Things are pretty normal. I went out for a run not wearing sweats. It is really warm today. I ran on the track. I believe it is a new surface. I came back, showered, and gave Coby a treatment.

Molly called. We are just waiting on the basketball game. Coby is eating turkey and dressing for lunch. I am thinking of chips and hot sauce. I wrote down things I must do tomorrow. Should be busy.

We watched the UNC/Duke basketball game. Duke won, but it was a good game. The ACC tournament starts this coming weekend.

Kami and Ruth Ann kept coming in to watch the game. They really enjoy the basketball here. It is very easy to get caught up in the excitement.

After the game, Coby and I went outside for about an hour. We stopped once and just looked up at the pine trees swaying back and forth with the wind. We saw a lot of kids back from spring break. It is really nice just taking our time. I keep thinking what I am going to do when the call comes for the lungs.

I hope Coby does not worry much about things.

We returned to the seventh floor, and Kami introduced Coby to his new neighbor, Lauren. She was a six-year-old leukemia patient. She has a cap with a ponytail attached to it. Pretty clever, Coby and I thought.

Coby's supper tray had just arrived. We watched a James Taylor concert on the public station, and I found out he was from Chapel Hill. His dad was supposedly a professor. Kami kept coming and going, laughing at Coby. You can tell she likes him, just like everyone else. Ruth Ann and Kami got off work at 7:30 p.m.

Coby and I watched *America's Funniest Home Videos* followed by a *James Bond* movie. Coby fell asleep and missed Tricia and Casey's call. She was pretty busy again today, but that is good. Billy is Coby's nurse again tonight. He came in, sat down, and talked fishing. He said when we get settled, he would take us fishing.

Coby finally roused, and I started his feeding through the G-tube. He went back to sleep quickly. He seemed to be tired. I laid down and thought about what I needed to do tomorrow about the apartment. The next thing I remember was the feeding alarm going off. I flushed Coby's tube and went back to sleep.

Could this be the night? I thought before falling asleep.

One more thing, Lisa brought Coby another water gun.

Day 17
Monday, March 9, 1992

I got up and showered. Dr. Mann caught me shaving again. He listened to Coby's lungs and headed on his way. "Poor officiating," he said about the UNC/Duke game. Coby stayed awake because the eight o'clock breakfast tray arrived.

I called the apartment and made arrangements to be there at 11:30 a.m. Coby's teacher stopped by and said she would be there at one. Theresa, the psychologist, stopped by and said hello. I did a treatment on Coby, and then he took a bath.

Kami and Ruth Ann came in to harass Coby a bit. Ruth Ann is his nurse today. I called for a cab and went down to wait. It was something to see, all the people coming and going. The temperature was about seventy-five degrees, and the sky was Carolina blue.

The cab arrived, and a young black girl, her son, and an old black man got in. The driver took me to my destination first. Everyone was very nice. Everything went fine at the apartment. We can move in Wednesday if we are out of the hospital. The manager showed me around. Just like everybody else around here, she wished us good luck.

I called the same taxi driver, and he was there in about five minutes. I sat in the front seat. We talked about the Dallas Cowboys, UNC, and Coby. He was a trip. I got back and then talked to the telephone company. This lady was so nice I could not believe it.

Coby had lunch, school, and a treadmill walk. He was still pretty tired, so I went running. I stopped and watched two innings of the UNC/Appalachian State baseball game. People were in their shorts, sunbathing. Some girls were in their swimsuits.

It was a great day.

I came back, and Coby's five o'clock tray arrived. I got him a fruit punch, showered, and then had some black-eyed peas. Coby's IV came out again. It is his sixth or seventh one. *Honey, I Shrunk the Kids* is on the hospital station. We are just going to kick back. I need to go to Hillsborough tomorrow, about twelve miles, to get our electricity turned on.

Coby wanted more punch. I got in the elevator with a funny black woman. "I hate these things," she said. "I always think of movies where they stop between floors, and people are crawling out the roof!" I told her always make sure you go to the restroom before getting on an elevator. She laughed just like my friend Joyce Jackson back in Kaufman.

Doug called. We made arrangements to use his car tomorrow to go to Piedmont Electrical in Hillsborough, North Carolina, so our power would be turned on in our apartment. I popped some corn, Coby is watching *Fresh Prince of Bel-Air*, and I started his feeding. Coby cannot wait to get into our apartment.

We waited for *Cheers*, but it didn't come on, so we just went to sleep. Coby slept fine until about 3:30 a.m. He could not stop coughing. I called down for medicine to go in his nebulizer, and he took that and finally fell back to sleep. I thought how nice it will be for him not to struggle for each breath; how nice it will be when he laughs and does not throw up his guts.

I prayed to God to give him some relief and fell asleep after I kissed him on top of his head.

Oh yes, Tricia and Casey called earlier.

Day 18
Tuesday, March 10, 1992

I didn't run this morning. I wanted to be here when Coby woke up. I shaved and showered, read some of the week-old *Dallas Morning News* that Dr. Stanley from Texas brought me. I read where Sandy Dennis, the actress, died. Just watched her and *The Out-of-Towners* with Jack Lemmon. She died of cancer.

It is cloudy this morning. Dr. Mann stopped in to check on Coby. "Maybe next week," I told him. "Maybe this weekend," he said. He would see…hope by at least Saturday, but whatever.

Coby is pretty tired and sleeping, for him, pretty easy. I read his poem every morning. I feel the determination the words express. I wish I could do more for him, but at times like last night when he was coughing, I felt so helpless.

CF never lets you put your guard down. It is the pits.

The floor is really busy this morning. A lot of new leukemia kids have been admitted. The little girl in Chris's room was diagnosed on Super Bowl Sunday. That is one day, I guarantee, her parents won't forget. The mother is still in denial to me. She talks on and on about things and doesn't seem to listen when I talk to her. That doesn't bother me, but she asks me things and answers for me.

Heck, but what do I know? I am just a coach.

Ruth Ann was really busy but kept checking in on Coby. He woke up, and I gave him a treatment. I then went down to the coffee shop to get him a fruit punch. I was waiting for the elevator when the doors opened, and a girl pushed out a portable x-ray unit. My mind regressed to my hospital days. I thought, *Stat chest in pedi, routine chest, maybe upright KUB*. The girl was nice looking in her hospital-issue scrubs. It reminded me of Baylor Medical School of Radiology Technology.

I returned, and Carol, the social worker, was in Coby's room. Then Ruth Ann, and then Deanne. The day has officially started for Coby. The phone rang, and it was Kelly. We made an arrangement for her to bring me her and Doug's car so I could go to Hillsborough and get our electricity turned on in the apartment. She came by around 11:20 a.m. and had a suitcase Tricia sent with Coby's books, more clothes, and mainly, Girl Scout cookies. Also, a bottle of km, potassium mineral. Kelly and Doug had gone back to Texas for spring break and met up with Tricia. I took the suitcase to Coby's room and hurried back to take Kelly to work. She told me how to go to Hillsborough, and after she got out, I headed north on Highway 86.

It was a very pretty drive. It reminded me of when Tricia and I would go to Arkadelphia, Arkansas, with the winding pine-tree-lined roads. I could see us living here. It took about twenty minutes, going the speed limit.

Just as I got into the city limits, a news bulletin came over the radio. "Hillsborough, NC: A man has been charged with burning body parts," the announcer said.

I still think it is pretty here, I thought.

I found the electric company without any problems. I went in and paid a five-dollar hook-up fee and started back to Chapel Hill. The TV electric company had faxed our credit reference the day before that saved me $130.

I stopped by the apartment and made arrangements to have everything turned on Thursday. I then stopped at Food Lion and bought some Mountain Dew and chips and then headed back to the hospital.

When I got to Coby's room, he was doing his homework. I am really proud of him doing his work on his own, without me telling him. He also read his assigned reading.

We went to the treadmill and met Suzanne Nutt, a twenty-seven-year-old recent transplant recipient from San Antonio, Texas. We had a good visit. We returned to the room by way of the coffee shop. Before we went to the treadmill room, Coby and I shot pool at the seventh-floor playroom.

Tar Heel football players were there visiting kids. Lauren next door was having a bad time with, what I found out later, a spinal tap. Heck, I would be hollering even louder than that.

All these kids put up with a bunch of stuff.

The nurses and therapists are special people.

It was time for me to take the car back to Kelly, and it began to rain. I am getting comfortable driving around Chapel Hill. It is nice.

Kelly got off work at 5:15 p.m., and she drove back to the hospital. She cut through the university. It is really nice. I can see my kids going here. Kelly seems to be really nice. I can see why Doug married her. She seems to listen and be sincere. Heck, she is from Texas! What else?

Kelly stayed and visited with us until Doug got finished with school. After she left, I popped some corn, and Lisa and Coby talked about art. Coby likes Lisa a lot. She seems to have a lot of interests. *Cheers* is not coming on late anymore, so I watched a James Taylor concert. He is a good one.

Tricia called and said Banks still has his coaching job. We lost both Marks, who are always where they are supposed to be. It is amazing. Tricia said Ken took the Dayton job with Larry Sherman. I will truly miss Ken. He is a good friend.

I am glad our lives crossed paths. His persistence is hard to find these days. I told Tricia to give Joe Stone a call and to hang in there. Time will go on.

Day 19
Wednesday, March 11, 1992

Coby slept better than the night before. Chip was his nurse all night. He's pretty funny, in an intellectual way. I woke up, read a little, and then shaved and showered. Chip said it was thirty-four degrees, a thirty-degree drop from the morning before.

I decided to run when Coby had school. I talked with the cable guy, and I will meet him Friday between three and five. Coby went for a chest x-ray and came back for a treatment. I bought him some punch and lasagna. Theresa stopped by just to visit. Leslie is Coby's day nurse. She told Coby she rides her bike to work from where we are going to live. Coby had school, so I went running on the track. It was pretty cool.

I came back, and Coby ate some lasagna. He did his homework and then went to first-floor occupational therapy. They had a treadmill just like Presby. It had a fan attached to it. I met Connie, who would work with Coby on a daily basis. He will work every day from four to five thirty. I don't know when he will go to school, but we will do whatever it takes.

Coby stayed on the treadmill seventeen minutes, and then he rode the bike for three. We stopped at the coffee shop on the way back. It is really motivating to me to see Coby working out on the treadmill. He is really working hard at getting in shape for the transplant.

When he got back to his room, he started reading Gary Larson's *Far Side* books that DeAnne brought him. He loves them. They are funny. The books belong to DeAnne's husband who collects them. She went home early because her little girl was sick.

When we were at the x-ray department, I flashed back to when I was working in one: all the clutter, but it has its place in the department; techs running everywhere; people waiting in wheelchairs; outpatients filling up the waiting room. It is just like when I was working in x-ray, never ending. Time goes on.

Dr. Waldon Garriss stopped by to see if we were on the list. He seems sincere about our transplant hopes. Coby asked him if his wife was still out of town. "Just one more week," Dr. Garriss sighed. Sue Baker is Coby's nurse. He enjoys her humor. We watched *Unsolved Mysteries* about ghosts. Coby said he would sleep with his feet under the covers tonight. He has a little *Far Side* in him also.

Doug called and said he and Kelly would be up tomorrow night to watch *The Simpsons* with us. "All right!" Coby said. Those two have really been a help for us while we have been here. Camille came on duty. Coby and she planned a pizza party for tonight at about nine EST. John Elzner called, and the pizza arrived.

Dr. Stanley from Texas came in and got a slice. We stayed up late. I gave Coby a treatment, and we went to sleep.

"We are going to have fun in our apartment, aren't we, Dad?"

"Every day, boy, every day!" I told him. You gotta love him.

Ben introduced a new nurse to Coby today. The phone rang, and Coby was talking to his mother. I heard Ben tell the nurse, "This is the neatest kid you'll ever see! Look at this poem he wrote."

Coby did it again! Be with us, God.

Day 20
Thursday, March 12, 1992

Coby slept through being hooked up to his medicine at six this morning. I woke up when Chip brought his aerosol at seven. Chip said everyone coming in said it was cold again, but clear sky. I got up, shaved, and showered. I'm going to run later this afternoon.

I decided to wash during Coby's schooltime today. Dr. Mann from Florida came in wearing a sweater.

"Man, it's too cold for me," he said. "Friday still looks good for discharge," he told us.

"Coby's ready!" I answered.

I asked him if he had looked at Coby's x-ray yet.

"The radiologist couldn't find it when I was down there, but I am going back this morning."

Flashback: I thought of Baylor's light side. "It's here in the hospital," we would tell the doctors.

Over twenty years ago I was in training, and they still can't come up with a system to keep track of films. It's great.

The telephone operator that pages over the intercom was warning the people to move their cars out front. *UNC Hospitals have officially started operations this morning,* I thought.

DeAnne from respiratory therapy just stopped by and said they want to film Coby at ten for a UNC video at the ninth floor. I got Coby up, and to the ninth floor we headed. We played Ping-Pong for the camera. Coby and another boy played pool and air hockey.

After we finished, we went back to the room, and Connie Johnson, who made Coby some chocolate chip cookies, was waiting for his CPT.

Today's school was at two o'clock. Treadmill at three. After the treadmill, I finished the laundry and went back to the room. Coby ate supper and was then ready for *The Simpsons.* Doug and Kelly showed up to watch. Everyone around here was waiting for the ACC tournament to begin.

We went to bed late, and I was thinking about what I have to do tomorrow. The move to the apartment began tonight as Coby was packing. Doug and Kelly and I put some things in their car. They have really been great, and I will never forget them for their help.

They are two special folks.

Maryland beats Clemson in the opening day of ACC.

Day 21
Friday, March 13, 1992

I got up, showered, and went downstairs to wait on Doug and Kelly to pick me up. The plan was to drop Doug at school and Kelly at work, and then I could use the car all day. I took some more sacks of stuff down with me as I was waiting for my "Whitt" rental for the day. The plan was working. After dropping Kelly off at work, I drove to Durham to Dial-A-Page. It was a short drive, and Wayne Suggs at the Dial-A-Page was a terrific guy.

Of course, all over the radio stations was talk of the ACC tournament. So was Wayne Suggs. We talked awhile. I found out he has an uncle who lives in Plano, Texas. He donates the beepers to families with medical needs. He wants to meet Coby sometime, so I will probably drive Coby over next week when we show Tricia and Casey Duke.

After getting the beeper, I headed west to Chapel Hill. I stopped at Roses, the department store, and bought sheets, blankets, pillows, and a phone. I then went to the apartment to sign the lease. I talked with Shannon about teaching. She has a degree and plans to get back into teaching. Sure is nice listening to her Southern drawl.

Shannon went with me to the apartment for a walk-through. After she left, I unloaded what I had in the car. I went back to the hospital, and Dr. Mann was in Coby's room. "Whenever pharmacy gets your scripts, you are free to go," he told Coby. I started loading things and taking them to the car.

It is about half a mile uphill to the car. I decided not to run this morning and decided this would be my workout. Each time I got back, Coby had more items ready. People stopped in to wish us luck. Doctors told us they would be thinking of us, and all the families we had met over the weeks stopped in.

Annie Downs, the PT who followed Coby on his six-minute walk, stopped in and gave us her phone number and said to call if we needed anything. She has a twelve-year-old who loves movies, so maybe we can get Coby and him together. She also has two younger kids.

Coby and I had the same feeling of sadness about leaving, but we knew we would be back every day for school and therapy and would see everyone then. Leslie Brock, our nurse for the day, went over Coby's medication with me. She told me Coby has really made an impact on everyone, and they will all miss him.

I thought of what Shannon at Presby told me before we came to Chapel Hill. "Wherever Coby goes, he will make a difference in people's lives. He will work that charm."

We loaded up the last of our stuff in Coby's lap as he was in the wheelchair with oxygen and headed out. We passed the leukemias, bone cancers, and CF kids to the elevator. I hit the Ground button, and suddenly Dr. Albers and Dr. Stanley rushed by and said, "See ya, champ!"

The doors closed, and we descended toward the ground floor. I had already gone by the pharmacy, so we were free to go.

I pushed Coby up the ramp toward the parking lot instead of leaving him to wait for me with the car. "Because we are Winchesters!" I said, and we both laughed. We drove out of the parking lot, and the radio announced, "Duke ahead by two." ACC tourney day, you know.

We stopped at Food Lion and then went to the apartment. Coby was really happy.

We unloaded, packed things away, and Coby arranged things just like his mom would have done. She will be proud Sunday on her arrival.

The phone rang, and we both looked up.

Coby said, "Our first call."

It was Tim the oxygen man.

"Everything all right?" he asked.

"You bet, buddy," I told him.

"ACC day, you know," he said. "Watch them Tar Heels!"

We were planning on Doug and Kelly coming over later with pizza to watch the Tar Heel game.

The cable guy called and won't be able to come until Saturday. We had about three stations, but it worked out, and the game was on one of them. I picked up the wrong sheets, so I went back and bought some more. When I got back, it was time to get Doug. I got to him in about seven minutes, we went to get Kelly, and then we headed back to our apartment.

They went home, Doug ran, and back they came with pizza and Pepsi. We had a good time. The Tar Heels won their first game and will play tomorrow.

Coby had bought the *Sports Illustrated Swimsuit Issue*, so that kept things going during timeouts. Doug and Kelly left around midnight, and we all had a great time. I took a shower, and then Coby and I went to bed.

Tricia called and said they were packed and ready. I know we are ready for them. Mom and Dad called and said they were surprised their phone bill was not bad. I had given Coby his treatment, so it didn't take long for us to fall asleep. It was the first time in three weeks that I could straighten my legs out while sleeping, and it felt pretty good.

Coby fell asleep pretty fast. I kept expecting Chip the nurse to check on us, but I realized we were at our temporary home.

Life is a ride.

Day 22
Saturday, March 14, 1992

I slept until about 8:30 a.m. EST. I haven't slept that long in a while. Coby is sleeping good. Got up, did some exercises, and wrote a while…just going with the flow.

Coby finally woke up at 10:30 a.m. EST. It was his first un-nurse molested sleep in two months.

"How did you sleep in your new apartment?" I asked.

"Fine," he said. "I like it."

I gave him his medicines and a treatment and then went to run and lift. I have not lifted in over three weeks. When I finished, I stuck my hand in the swimming pool, and it felt like bathwater.

Coby will like this, I thought.

When I got back, Coby was sitting on the couch, waiting for the cable man. I sat down with him, and we started having a rubber band gun-shooting contest. We lined Styrofoam cups on top of the TV and both had five shots apiece. Whoever knocks the most cups off wins. We called it our ACC Rubber Band Shooting Tournament.

We watched Duke beat the tar out of Georgia Tech. A magazine salesman stopped by, and Coby bought a hot rod truck magazine. The cable man came, so we were fixed up with more channels. The Tar Heel game came on, and they beat Florida State. They will play Duke tomorrow for the ACC championship.

I took a shower. Coby fell asleep for about an hour and a half. I wondered throughout the afternoon about Tricia, Casey, and Jeannie and where they might be on the road. I prayed they were making it all right.

Doug called and said he and Kelly would take us wherever by 7:30 p.m. That worked out fine because Coby needed to sleep. Alabama beat Arkansas with a last-minute shot. They will now face Kentucky for the SEC.

Coby woke up and said he wanted to go to the mall. He got a letter from Nanny today, so we knew the mailbox worked! Coby was having a good time. He was talking so fast I thought he wasn't going to get a breath in between city blocks as Doug drove. We went to the university mall, hunting for a small basketball goal for the apartment. Kelly said she would get Coby tomorrow and take him to Whim's after the UNC/Duke game and look for one.

Coby talked them into staying and watching *Saturday Night Live*. We watched Willie on Farm Aid Five, live at Texas Stadium, until *SNL* came on. That brought back a lot of memories for me. *SNL* was pretty funny, mainly Cajun Man. Afterward Doug and Kelly went home, and we went to bed.

Tricia had called and said they were 485 miles away and that everything was going fine.

Coby and I were pretty excited. I prayed for their safety.

Coby asked me, before we fell asleep, how bad it would be if Dr. Egan died suddenly. I told him UNC Hospitals would get someone else to keep the team going. What's strange about him asking me about the transplant doctor is that I had already thought of that situation.

God, please be with Dr. Egan. Amen.

Then we fell asleep.

Day 23
Sunday, March 15, 1992

I got up before Coby again and did some exercises. Wonder where the Texas bunch might be at this time. Coby was really excited about them coming today. They should be here around six or seven this evening. Coby got up, and I did the routine on him medically. We waited for the UNC/Duke ACC championship game. Kelly called and said she was still going to take Coby to Whim's after the game. She and Doug watched the second half of the game with us, we took Doug to school, and then we headed to Whim's.

After Whim's, we went to the grocery store with Kelly and bought a few things. Kelly made Coby a sandwich at the apartment, and then we went to Carrboro. We went a different way home and were sitting at a red light when Coby spotted our van.

"They're here!" he screamed. They made great time. It was nice to see them. It was just after five EST. That was the best-looking van I had ever seen. We pulled up to the filling station where they were, and Tricia was looking up Kelly and Doug's phone number when Coby said, "Hey, lady, need some help?"

Tricia turned around and was smiling from ear to ear. Casey came running from the other side of the van, showing me some Alabama shirt she had bought me. Jeannie appeared. They looked road weary but were glad to be here.

We went to the apartment and unloaded tons of items people had sent us, ate a snack, and went to bed. Jeannie was in one room, the kids were in another, and Tricia and I were sleeping in the living room on a mat. It was great to have them here.

The next few days are a summary of the Texas crew stay.

Day 24
Monday, March 16, 1992

Coby had the week planned, so we just went with whatever he wanted to do. It was just nice to be together. Coby had school at three o'clock and PT at four. After everyone got up, we went to the

Dean Dome, football field, track, and the student store—hangouts familiar to Coby and me.

Coby would be talking so fast he could not catch his breath at times. He wanted to do everything in one day. Casey would push him in the chair wherever he wanted to go.

She loves him very much.

She looked five years older to me. Tricia said she was doing good in her little world. She has high hope for the lung transplant.

Tricia met the psychologist, Theresa, today. She is nice, Tricia thought.

Day 25
Tuesday, March 17, 1992

Coby's school is going to be at two thirty today, so we got up and went to Hillsborough to the Walmart to get some things we needed for the apartment. It is a very pretty historic town. After Walmart, we bought some sandwiches and went to a park for a picnic.

Casey ran everywhere. Coby just watched. I know in time he will be running with her after his transplant. He seems to struggle for every breath, but somehow, he keeps going.

We went to Toys R Us and got a basketball goal for the apartment. It is a lot of fun. Jeannie bought it. She would not have it any other way.

Day 26
Wednesday, March 18, 1992

Coby's school is now at noon, and PT is from 1:00 p.m. to 2:30 p.m. This morning we went to Carr Mill Mall in Carrboro, a place with a lot of shops in an old cotton gin. It was pretty neat. After PT we went to Durham and ate at Chili's. We then went to Circuit City, and Jeannie bought Coby a Walkman. Yellow, his favorite color. It was for when he walked on the treadmill.

Jeannie is something else.

Afterward, back home, Tricia, Casey, and I went swimming. Not too bad of a day.

Day 27
Thursday, March 19, 1992

We took Jeannie to the airport. It was sad to see her go. She loves Casey and Coby so much. We are lucky and blessed to have her.

Kelly and Doug are going to eat with us and watch *The Simpsons*. Tricia is baking chicken. Coby, Casey, Tricia, and I played tennis. Tricia was really excited after meeting a girl at the laundry room who had had a lung transplant the month before.

I know how Tricia felt. It is nice to see a finished product. The girl came out to the tennis court with her little boy and husband. She talked and never once coughed. She looked great. They are moving back home to South Carolina next week.

I will be glad when we can go back to Wylie. We will do whatever it takes.

Day 28
Friday, March 20, 1992

This is Coby's and my one-month anniversary of living in Chapel Hill, North Carolina. We went to the mall, school, and PT for the celebration. The kids and I went to the racquetball courts at the apartments. Coby just cannot stand for too long. It has been a very busy week for him. He has introduced all the people to Tricia and Casey.

Dr. Garris even came by the apartment to meet them. Tricia and Casey saw how nice everyone is.

UNC is trying for the Sweet 16 this week, and I hope they make it. This has been too fast a week for me. I am going to hate this Monday morning, taking Tricia and Casey to the airport. But again, we must do whatever is best for Coby.

We watched a movie with Doug and Kelly and some basketball.

Day 29
Saturday, March 21, 1992

We went to Shoney's and visited the Duke campus. We walked around the football field, Cameron, the chapel where a wedding was taking place, and a courtyard. It was like being in London or some place, so nice. Coby and Tricia stayed in the apartment while Casey and I played tennis. She went swimming afterward, and I watched her and read. We enjoyed watching TV together as a family. UNC is going to the Sweet 16. Twelve years in a row.

Day 30
Sunday, March 22, 1992

We woke up to rain, but it didn't matter. I was just glad to have everyone here. After the rain, we went to the hospital and took some pictures of Coby for the Wylie paper. We then went walking around the campus. I believe Coby really likes doing this as much as anything.

It is really nice Casey pushing him, not wanting any help. She wants to do a lot for him.

We then went to The Hut. It started raining again, so we ate and went back to the apartment and watched *Dutch*. Tricia and I washed and dried some clothes.

Casey went swimming and said bye to the pool. It was getting to be night too fast for me. I really did not want them to leave. Time goes on.

Day 31
Monday, March 23, 1992

I did not sleep much. I kept looking in on Coby who was struggling. The alarm went off at 4:55 a.m. EST. Tricia got up and got ready. Then we got the kids up and headed for the airport. It rained the entire time. Rainy Monday morning.

I stopped at the bag check-in and let everyone out. I parked the van as Tricia got hers and Casey's boarding passes. They were boarding the airplane as soon as possible. We said our goodbyes and went our different ways.

Coby and I waited until the plane took off and went back to Ramsgate.

He was really tired, and I began to feel lonely.

We got back to the apartment, and I carried Coby into H-103. I kept waiting for Casey and Tricia to help me, but they were about twenty-five to thirty thousand feet up in the air. I turned the TV on and saw where a plane had crashed in Newark. I prayed for the families and prayed that Tricia and Casey's plane would get to DFW safely.

Coby fell asleep and slept until eleven o'clock. Tricia called, and everything was fine. I felt relieved. We went to school and PT. Coby was having a rugged day on his PT because he was really tired.

I wish I could do it for him.

After PT, we stopped at the store and got a few things. Coby stayed in the van. He was really tired. We got *Point Break* at the video store. Coby just wanted to go home.

I went to run and lift, and that took about an hour. I went back to the apartment and showered.

We then watched *Point Break*. Hollie called, and then we watched *Fresh Prince*, *Blossom*, and *Cheers*.

Coby went to bed. He was so tired. Molly called.

I really do miss Tricia and Casey. Coby slept pretty well, at times.

Day 32
Tuesday, March 24, 1992

I got up at about 7:30 a.m., or should I say I woke up at 6:30 a.m. I just laid back and thought about how wild Tricia's and my lives have been since we met.

Life is definitely a ride.

The phone rang, and it was Stan the Man from oxygen services just checking on us. Coby got up, and I gave him a treatment, fed him through his tube, and he did some school work. No PT on Tuesday, so we are going to see *Wayne's World.*

Don Swanson called from *The Sentinel,* a newspaper back home. Tricia called during her advisory time. She is learning a lot about our swimming pool. After talking with Tricia, Coby and I read some Dr. Peale. We then cleaned up the apartment and ourselves and headed to the movie theater to see *Wayne's World.* It was really funny to us. Coby is using more oxygen. I believe he is getting some lung infection.

He enjoyed the movie, though. We came back home and ate. On the way home, I got a library card and checked out a book on Steve McQueen. Kelly and Doug came over and watched *Terminator 2.*

Mother called, and Tray as well. I gave Coby a treatment, and we went to bed. He is struggling.

Day 33
Wednesday, March 25, 1992

Coby seemed to toss and turn all night. I feel we will be getting an IV soon. I did his morning feeding and went over his spelling words with him. Tricia called as did Carol, the social worker, and Stan, the oxygen man. Coby was tired, but we got ready and went to school and PT.

I had to play the waiting game for a parking spot. After letting Coby out at the PT door, I put the van in a No Parking spot. I hurried him to the seventh floor. I rushed back and was relieved there was not a wrecker hauling the van away.

I stayed in the spot until a legal spot opened up. That took about twenty-five minutes. As I was waiting, I watched all sorts of people step outside to smoke. It is still unbelievable to me that people still smoke, especially those who work in a hospital.

Of course, I like M&M's with peanuts, but I could go without them if I had to…maybe.

I watched a hearse from Walker's Funeral Home back up and take the old empty stretcher into the back of some old building. It had its custom spread on the cot. People were coming and going back here just like at the front of the hospital.

I saw a handicap bus pick up some patients in wheelchairs. I feel lucky that I can move around. I thought about my hospital days and counted my blessings again. I run for those who can't; that is what I try to get over to our ball players. It should be our duty to do what we can with what we have. Work hard to improve, and do not look for the easy way out.

I am proud of Coby on how he is working to get ready for the transplant.

After watching Casey this past week doing headstand push-ups with her feet against the wall, it made me proud about her work ethic. I just hope she continues that attitude the rest of her days here on earth. It will make things more enjoyable for her.

Tricia confirmed that Esther's cousin was killed in the plane crash in Newark. That is so sad to hear about, but somehow life will go on for her and her cousin's family. Difficult, but it will go on.

I hope they believe in God. He will be with them if they ask.

After school Coby went to PT. I went running during this time. I ran by the Dean Dome to see if practices were open or closed this week. The lady said they would be closed. I then ran toward the track and ran a couple of miles once I got on it. I then ran to see if the football team was working out yet. Apparently, they had some meetings going on and were not on the practice fields yet.

I then returned to the PT department. Coby was still going, just like that pink rabbit on the TV commercials. He looked pretty tired, but was still plugging along.

We made the six-minute trip back to Carrboro. Coby ate a little something and fell asleep. I went to wash something and use the universal machine. I'm trying to work as hard as Coby. It helps my mind, along with this diary.

I met a lady in the washroom who just moved here with her daughter and son-in-law. She is waiting for a lung transplant, another twenty-year-old CFer. They are from Windsor, Georgia, just outside of Augusta, where the Masters is played. She works for the Holiday

Inn in Augusta. They are booked in a year in advance for the Masters at double price rates.

I had put potatoes in the oven to bake, and they were just right when I returned to the apartment. I have been feeding Coby three times a day through his G-tube, plus whatever else I can get him to eat.

Tricia called, using her sister's 800 work number, and we had a good talk about the pool. It is really funny how everything she is telling I have lived through before, kind of like me on this end cooking she has lived through before.

I had to wake Coby up so we could go to the support group. It is really handy being here at Ramsgate because the support group meets here every two weeks. It was good for Coby and me to see all these people from different areas of the United States with the same medical problems Coby has. Some had already received their lungs while others, like us, were still waiting.

Annie Downs, the physical therapist, gave a presentation on the benefits of exercise pre and post-transplant. Recovery is quicker if you train for the surgery, it showed. It was a good slide presentation. Also, Will, the social worker, answered questions and told about the upcoming picnic that transplant awareness group is having. Will also talked about a Special Olympics for transplant patients, only in Los Angeles, this summer for three days.

Carl Lewis is spokesman for the event. Ellen Carines was also there, answering questions. She is the lung transplant coordinator; a very nice but busy person.

Afterward Coby and I went back to H-103 and watched *Unsolved Mysteries.* Coby went to bed after the show. I gave him his fourth treatment of the day as we watched the program. Esther called. Trisha Blanton called. I read some of McQueen, but could not go to sleep. Spann called. I'm really going to miss coaching with him. Maybe we can coach together in the future. Only the shadow knows.

Coby got up around one in the morning, and I gave him a treatment. I left him asleep on the couch, and then I watched the last of *Presumed Innocent.* I thought about calling Tricia, but I knew she would be asleep. I found out the next day that she couldn't sleep either. Maybe we are made for each other, huh.

Coby woke up at about 3:30 a.m. and went back to bed. He was very restless.

I heard rain hitting the window, and after praying for relief for Coby, I fell asleep.

Day 34
Thursday, March 26, 1992

We both woke up at 8:15 a.m. EST. I got up and gave Coby a treatment and started his morning feeding. He drank some milk, and I juiced some fresh oranges and apples.

Tricia called when we were about to go to school. She said the pool was looking good. She had spoken to Pat Ferguson's mother. Pat was a boy with CF who was also a guest at the Don Whitt roast. His mom kept him at home, so he didn't go to school.

Pat was thinking about a transplant, and his mother was asking Tricia some questions.

She said Casey still has not heard about oral reading for UIL. Mrs. Anderson is going to have a special meeting Friday. Casey told Tricia she was not going to miss gymnastics because they have been trying out for a month and a half, and Mrs. Anderson still cannot decide. They work every Tuesday and Thursday on oral reading. I do not blame Casey at all. That is the way I like her to be, standing up for what she thinks is right.

Coby went to PT afterward, and Dr. Wood stopped by to check on him. He will be starting home IVs tomorrow. Coby needs them.

We went grocery shopping. I am trying to get Coby to eat anything. He found some TV dinners he would try. I fixed rice for myself and a TV dinner for Coby. He ate the potatoes, corn, and apple cherry crumb dessert—more than I thought he would eat.

Tricia called, and I got to talk to Casey.

Kelly and Doug came over and watched *The Simpsons* and half of the Duke / Seton Hall game. Duke won. They are coming back tomorrow for pizza and the Tar Heel / Ohio State game.

Tricia called again. Her sister Linda Gayle is worried about using the phone line to call us. Tricia told her that was fine because she didn't want her sister to lose her job.

Funny, it was her sister's friend's idea in the first place, but whatever.

Tricia 6, Pool 12 today. She is learning, though.

Coby had his fourth treatment and went to bed.

I watched the rest of the Blue Devils and went to bed.

Jeannie, Mom, and Dale called. Everything is about the same. Jeremy is the big one-year-old.

Day 35
Friday, March 27, 1992

Coby slept better than he has in four nights. I feel this weekend, starting IVs and all, he will rest all of the weekend days. Coby did not have school, so I took him to PT at one o'clock EST.

There was not a parking space, so I left him at the PT department.

I decided to park at the Dean Dome and run from there. As I drove into the parking lot, I saw a lot of men walking into the Koury's swim center. They looked like football coaches to me. Sure enough, they were in town for Coach Brown's football clinic.

I talked to about four different ones, and they invited me to attend the clinic with them. I told them about Coby, and they all wished me good luck. They asked about the high attendance the 5A teams have at playoff games in Texas. They were amazed.

I went to run and then picked up Coby.

He did not have a good workout, but I know the IVs will help. While I was running, I listened to my headset. James Taylor's "Carolina" on my mind was playing. It was great.

We went back to H-103 and waited on the home care nurse to bring Coby's medicine. The nurse arrived at about four o'clock and brought us an Intelliject. It is a computer that automatically injects Coby's ticar, tobramycin. It even flushes with saline and heparin. Kami stopped by to visit with us, and Coby enjoyed that. Doug and

Kelly came by with pizza and watched UNC get eliminated from the tournament by Ohio State.

Coby was feeling really bad and went to bed earlier than usual.

Doug, Kelly, and I had a good visit. It is really nice having them here. I could not go to sleep right off as I was watching Coby struggle.

God, I hope the transplant is soon.

Tricia and Molly called.

Day 36
Saturday, March 28, 1992

Coby got up at eight and slept in the living room until 11:15 a.m. I read my McQueen book. When Coby woke up, he felt miserable. He stayed on the couch all day, sleeping off and on. I worked out in Ramsgate's weight room and met a kid by the name of Mills who was working on a movie set. May get Coby to watch if he can.

I made Frito pie. Coby ate some and said he liked it. Doug and Kelly came by to watch *Saturday Night Live* with Coby. Coby and I watched the Duke game. The Blue Devils won in overtime with no time left on the clock. It was the most exciting game I have seen in a while. We were glad Duke won.

Tricia called. She and Casey are doing better today, after Casey's experience at school Friday.

Mother and Wayne called, and I went to bed about thirty minutes after Doug and Kelly left.

Day 37
Sunday, March 29, 1992

Coby seems to be better, but not much. He stayed on the couch all day, until he took a shower. He ate a little bit and drank lots of milk. We watched *Home Alone* and the Michigan basketball game. Talked to Tricia, Casey, Spann, Myers, Mazzon, and Joe today. Nice to hear from everyone.

Coby went to bed early again.

We read some of his assignment.

I miss Tricia and Casey a lot. So does Coby.

But we are doing whatever it takes.

Day 38
Monday, March 30, 1992

Coby tossed and turned all night. I prayed that he would settle down. Every time I do something for him, he always tells me, "Thank you. I love you, Dad." I say, "I know."

I think the medicine will start kicking in, but it seems to be taking a while.

I wish we would get the call for the lungs so Coby can get some relief.

We both have become very confident that things will go fine after seeing some of the results they have had up here.

Coby got up, and I started his tube feeding. He watched a little TV after doing his treatment. He finished his homework, and we got ready to go to UNC Hospitals. I started taking things out to the van once I was shaved and showered. When it was time for Coby and I to leave, we met our neighbor across the hall.

Her name is Kaaren, pronounced "car-in." She is a graduate student in nutrition. We all left at the same time, Kaaren running errands, Coby and I school and therapy. It is a cloudy but mild temperature day. There was not much traffic on the 200 bypass today. The construction crews were working as usual. I started thinking about my alternate parking plans if there was not a space. I need to try and get a haircut today, maybe during Coby's PT.

I asked Coby what he might want to eat later, but he didn't know. I changed the radio station, trying to find him a rock station.

He just looks at the scenery and doesn't say much today.

I know he is really tired. Somehow, he keeps going. I keep telling him and myself that the new lungs will be worth the wait. As we drive on South Colombia, Monday has already been going on for a while on campus: people getting on buses, off buses, and the trolley transporting people to and fro, students hustling around, most in Carolina logo clothing.

I turned off S. Colombia onto Health Drive, slowing up for people to cross the street. I noticed the white Range Rover was not in its usual place, maybe on vacation. Then there it was. I couldn't believe it. Not one empty parking spot but two! What a break.

I waited for three people to walk across the street. Thought they'd never get across for fear of losing one of the two available spaces. They got across, and I pulled the van right into the space on the right. I found that if you park on the right instead of the left, closest to the building, people seem to not double park behind you.

Last week, I had to pull up on the sidewalk, over the curb, and back up very carefully.

Coby couldn't believe I got out without banging the side of the van. It was a good job, I must say. One does what one must have to do.

I unloaded the chair, placed Coby's oxygen behind it, got Coby out, and put the IV Intelliject behind the chair, his extra oxygen tube. I locked the van, and off we headed to the seventh floor for school. It is really a relief when there is a parking space available. As I left Coby with Mrs. Taylor, I met a new doctor. He had worked with Coby in the hospital. He played golf in college. I asked him if he could get some passes for the Kmart Greensboro Open in a few weeks from a detail pharmaceutical representative. I want them for Doug and Kelly. He said he would if he could, but they don't seem to hand them out too freely anymore. He asked about Coby and said for us to hang in there.

Later today, I am going to wash, but I must wait until the home care nurse drops by. Vicki and Dale will be here tomorrow, and that will help Coby's spirit. Mine too.

When Coby finished PT, we went home, and he got on the couch. He was really tired. He fell asleep and slept for about two and a half hours. Paula called, and they will see Coby tomorrow. As he slept, I did the laundry. His appetite has yet to pick up much. The antibiotics have not taken full control.

I ate some potatoes and began to read when Jeannie called. There had been some changes. She was coming instead of Vicki. Coby finally woke up.

The Oscars came on, and we watched the entire ceremony. We went to bed, and Coby just tossed and turned. I did not fall asleep until about 3:30 a.m. I thought Coby might have to go to the hospital.

I might have become a little paranoid. I prayed, and he seemed to be easier.

Day 39
Tuesday, March 31, 1992

The last day of March, and we are still in Carolina. Coby slept until about eight, and I then did his treatments. He was excited about going to the airport to get Jeannie and Dale. It was a little cloudy.

Paula called, and they would see us at four o'clock to check on Coby's arm. It seemed to be tender when it was touched.

We arrived at the airport, and the monitor showed their flight to be earlier. It wouldn't be but about thirty minutes, and Jeannie and Dale would be in RDU, Raleigh-Durham.

We looked in the gift shops, and I heard my name over the PA. I knew then that Dale was in town. We headed toward the baggage claim, I pushed the elevator door open, and there was Dale! I didn't mention that the people at the x-ray door, letting people in at the terminal, were getting to know Coby and asked how he was doing.

Pretty wild, the effect Coby has on people.

Found Jeannie, and we headed to Ramsgate in Carrboro. Dale was talkative and funny, as usual. Jeannie had brought a honey-baked ham, and that was all we focused on upon returning to H-103. We settled into the apartment. Dale and I were wanting to play tennis after our snack.

Paula and Michelle, the home care nurses, stopped by and discovered that Coby was in the beginning stages of phlebitis where the landmark catheter was placed. They pulled the catheter and inserted another in his right arm. The Intelliject worked fine, but the dose of tobramycin was so concentrated it irritated Coby's veins. We then went to the home care pump, where I became the computer. I will be responsible for flushes, inserting the needle housing, and heparin.

One every six hours. Ticar and tobramycin every twelve.

I now was using the nursing skills I learned in x-ray school once again. God has a purpose for our lives, and we must be responsible to work toward that purpose.

After Paula and Michelle left, Dale and I played tennis. Michelle came back later with the medicine pumps. Coby was doing fine.

Dale slept on the floor, Jeannie in one room, and Coby and I in the other. I got up during the night to do Coby's medicine. The window blinds were shaking by Dale's snoring. He said he would be getting up at 5:30 a.m., right? Not!

Dale and I kept talking about Willie B. in his bathrobe, giving us the wrong directions. We just laughed.

Day 40
Wednesday, April 1, 1992

Coby got his new lungs today… April Fools'.

I know, sorry, but we must try to stay sane.

Jeannie made some biscuits, which were very good. Dale finally woke up, and we played some tennis. I had to wake Coby up at 10:45 a.m. and get him ready for school. The medicine seemed to start working. The oxygen man called and was going to make a delivery today.

We took Coby to school and PT. Afterward we went to Circuit City, and Dale bought a radio. We then went to Drug Emporium and ordered PULMOCARE. At the mall, Coby found the cap he had been wanting. We had eaten at Darryl's, a fun place with good food. Coby even liked it.

His appetite was getting better.

We went home and watched *Unsolved Mysteries.* Dale and I watched Notre Dame get beat by Virginia in overtime baby! I did Coby's medicine and went to bed.

A fun day. Coby really enjoyed Jeannie and Dale. I did too.

Tricia, Mom, and Molly all called, checking in.

Day 41
Thursday, April 2, 1992

Coby slept good, finally. I listened to James Taylor's tape on Coby's new Walkman until around three o'clock. Easy listening.

We got up and got ready to tour the transplant ICU. Annie Downs gave a talk with pictures on what was going to take place during the surgery and afterward. Jeannie, Dale, and I were able to attend. Coby asked questions. He is really learning a lot about the transplant. So am I.

We then toured the ICU. We saw Michelle, who had had a transplant Sunday night, through the glass door. She waved at us, and we got pretty excited.

I wondered where she had been this week during PT. I just thought her times had changed. Heck, she had some new lungs! *That's great*, I thought.

Coby had PT afterward, and then we took Dale and Jeannie to the airport. We had some pizza at the terminal, said goodbye, and went back to Ramsgate. Coby had another sandwich, and I washed. Michelle checked in on Coby's arm. Coby showered and got ready for Doug and Kelly and *The Simpsons*.

Kelly brought some spaghetti and a small basketball with NationsBank on it. We had a good time with my juicer. Coby went to bed early, mainly due to the thirty-minute walk on the treadmill. Kelly and Doug left. I gave Coby his medicine and then went to bed.

I set the alarm to take the used pump out and went back to sleep.

Day 42
Friday, April 3, 1992

The alarm went off at 5:00 a.m. I set the medicine out to reach room temperature, went back to sleep, and then got up at 6:00 a.m. to start Coby's medicine. I set the alarm for 7:15 a.m. for the other meds, went back to my bed, and read McQueen.

The phone rang. It was Spann. He said the 180 applicants were now down to three. I feel Blake Cooper will get the job. Thirty-two years old, that's amazing to me.

When this transplant is over, I am going to work for the new coach and hope to eventually get me a head job. Time will tell.

Looking out the window, it looks like it will be a cool day. But the weather changes quickly here, just like back home. Coby is going to have school earlier today. Eleven instead of twelve. He got up, got ready. It is really a chore for him, but he keeps going.

Coby had school, and we then had an hour to kill before PT. He made a 100 on his spelling test, so he felt pretty good. We decided to go to the Kenan field house and check out the weight room. I pushed Coby out of the hospital through the shortcuts we have discovered going to the student health center.

We exit out right at the front of the stadium. I pushed Coby down the steep hill, actually holding the chair back. Coby always squeezes his handlebars as if he is going for a jet ride.

Kids were going all directions, living in their own worlds. I pushed Coby into the weight room. He was impressed by all the machines. They have Nautilus exercise equipment, free bar, and a treadmill room with stair steppers all on Tar Heel blue carpet. Even the Nautilus is Carolina blue.

We met Coach Tootsen, the strength coach. He used to coach at Florida and told us about Emmit Smith dehydrating his first day as a freshman. He had to stay in the hospital overnight. They were afraid he was going to leave and go home. He played with Jeff Bostic at Clemson and had talked with him yesterday. He told us the routine the players go through during the off season. I really enjoyed listening.

He invited us to the afternoon scrimmage at Kenan Memorial at 3:30 p.m. Coby said he would like to go watch them if it was not too cold. We went to PT and then home to eat. I ran while Coby ate.

I went to the mailbox and found a slip to go to the post office and pick up a package. We stopped by there on our way to watch the scrimmage. It was a poster of Cindy Crawford that Molly had sent.

Coby said, "Excellent!"

We then went to the scrimmage. It was a little cool up top at the stadium, so I took Coby down to the floor, where the wind was not as strong below. Coby had a blanket on along with his letter jacket and said he was fine.

It was nice to hear some leather poppin'! I really enjoyed watching. It made me want to coach in college again. Coach Bruce Hemphill, the recruiting coordinator, stopped by and introduced himself. Coach Tootsen had told him about us. He took us to the sideline, next to the players. He was really nice to us. He gave Coby a Starter Carolina cap, football T-shirts, and posters. He invited us to come back to practice in the Blue/White game next Saturday.

It began to get colder, plus it was time for Coby's six o'clock medicine. After we got home, we ate and watched an M. C. Hammer special. He was going to be at the Dean Dome on Saturday night. I was thinking of Casey and her talent show.

Coby was coughing a lot. I just wish he could get those new lungs soon.

He went to bed. I had checked out *Animal House*, and he enjoyed watching it but was tired. We put Cindy and the other posters on the wall. It looks like we have been here a while.

Tricia called. Casey won, third year in a row. She is a player. I went to bed.

Coby is still on night medicine, so I get up at different times. We are planning to go to the mall in Durham tomorrow and then watch Duke play Indiana with Doug and Kelly...pizza, ya know.

Day 43
Saturday, April 4, 1992

It was a cold, rainy day, but we went to the mall. Coby came across a man selling Coca Cola items, which he collected. He also gave Coby UNC and Duke Coke bottles, with their championship years on the bottle. We bought a radio and a phone cord extension so Coby wouldn't have to get off the couch to talk. We ate at Taco Bell and had a nice time.

Coby and I are taking each day as it comes. I know he misses Tricia and Casey, but he keeps going.

He is really physically getting worse. I know God will not let him get too down, though, for the transplant.

Doug and Kelly came. We watched Michigan and Duke win. I feel Duke will now win their second straight national title. They are tough.

Day 44
Sunday, April 5, 1992

Sunshine woke me up this morning. Actually, the alarm to do Coby's medicine, but I could see it is going to be a nice day. It really was nice. I fixed Coby a lunch, and then Kelly, Coby, and I went to watch the Tar Heels play baseball. Doug was studying.

It was such a nice day that I got sunburned. Clemson swept the three-day stand. They are winning the ACC baseball. They had a seven-run inning in the seventh to beat UNC.

Coby enjoyed going, and it was nice to be out.

We got home just in time for his medicine. Coby bought Casey some birthday cards to send. It is hard to believe I won't be there for her party.

We lost an hour because of daylight savings time. It kind of threw Coby off a little.

Day 45
Monday, April 6, 1992

Coby slept until 10:45 a.m. I had to hurry him for school and PT. We mailed Casey's cards and made it to school on time. Coby walked the six minutes test and then thirty minutes on the treadmill. He was so tired when I got him in the van.

He said how nice the weather was today.

When we got home, Coby ate and then fell asleep for about two hours. I ran while he was sleeping. He didn't mind. I love him so much I just wish I could go through the physical pain instead of him.

He is really one tough kid.

I came back home and ate. Coby never woke up until *Cheers* came on at six. I vacuumed the apartment, and then Kami called and said she was coming over. She did and watched half of the Duke game. Michigan was ahead 31–30 at half, but Duke showed why they are national champs and won 71–51, second straight year. First time in nineteen years, since UCLA, that someone has won back-to-back. That is very hard to do.

Tricia called and was concerned about how Coby was feeling. I had to give her a pep talk. I believe if it was just Tricia and Coby, he might talk her out of some of the things that must be done. It is very hard, but I know it must be done—hospital mentality, which I learned at Baylor.

Coby and I watched all the Duke game, and he was pleased that they won. It is hard to believe we are right in the middle of all this craziness.

"We will never forget this NCAA tournament," I told Coby.

Coby said, "I wish UNC would have won. Maybe next year."

I will never forget him saying when Duke was behind with 2.1 seconds in the Kentucky game, "Daddy, Duke is going to win!"

He was right.

Laettner put it in after Grant Hill made the three-quarter court pass. It was exciting. There's always time when there are ticks left on the clock.

I just hope we have some more ticks left before the lungs get here.

God, I love him so much. I am very blessed to have Coby, Casey, and Tricia. Thank you, God.

Day 46
Tuesday, April 7, 1992

Clinic today at 10:30 a.m. Our second in North Carolina. Coby got up at 9:30 a.m. and was very irritable. I didn't know if it was having to go to the clinic or if he was just feeling poorly.

We got into the van, and Coby became super restless. Luckily, the hospital is only five minutes away. I parked the van and hustled him to the clinic. When we arrived, they shuttled him into a room.

Coby's saturation was 50, 40 below what they should be.

They put him onto the hospital oxygen line, and he seemed to get better. Later he discharged a mucus plug out of his right nasal passage. He could breathe a lot better afterward. It was decided to admit and watch him for a few days.

I know he is really tired. I do not know how much longer he can go with these lungs.

I know God knows best, so we wait.

We both wanted to go back to H-103, but maybe we won't have to stay long. I went home after Coby got a room and got some of his things. I thought I might come home and sleep at the apartment, but Coby didn't really want me to. I should be with him anyway. I called the oxygen people, the home nurses, and Tricia. She said she was going to take Casey to the doctor. I hope she is not down long.

I stopped at the Model T next door to Ramsgate and got a burger; spaghetti for Coby. When I got back, Coby was really stressing to breathe. I did a treatment, and it seemed to help.

Sue Baker is his nurse, and she is getting him settled in. One of the respiratory therapists stopped in and gave him a Snickers bar. "Coby is one of my favorites," she said.

Coby thanked her. His doctors stopped in and are changing his medicine. I hope we do not have to stay long. I parked the van on the street. I must move it by 7:30 a.m., though, when I will put it in the parking lot. I shouldn't worry about parking fees; it's just the idea of paying to park that gets me. It is 10:20 p.m., and Coby is still restless. I definitely will stay all night.

I am doing fine. I just don't know how much of this struggling Coby can deal with. He told me he is really tired. I prayed to God to give him some relief. He still thanks the nurses and me when we do something for him.

I went down and got him some fruit punch. His IV is giving him trouble. It keeps the IMED beeping occult. They will probably change it tomorrow. Dr. Lever said they may put in a central line. They are different than four years ago.

Again, whatever it takes, I told Coby.

The Denison coach got the football job at Wylie. Offensive coordinator for eleven years. Maybe I will learn another system. I hope Lanny Pettit will come with him. Things are really changing, but time goes on.

The floor orderly and I talked about Duke's victory. Tomorrow Casey will be eleven. Time is definitely moving on.

Day 47
Wednesday, April 8, 1992

One heck of a night.

No sleep for Coby. He couldn't breathe and struggled all night until around six this morning. He kept telling me he loved me. I kept telling him not to talk to conserve his energy.

They put a mask on him with the nasal tube, and it seemed to bring up his saturations.

I moved the van while a nurse stayed with him.

When I got back, they asked me about putting him in the Pediatric ICU, just to stay on top of things better in case they had to put him on the ventilator. I agreed.

We have come too far to slide back.

Whatever it takes.

I called Tricia, and Casey answered the phone.

"Happy Birthday," I told her.

"Hi, Daddy," she said.

"Are you eleven yet?" I asked.

"No, not until 7:54 a.m.," she said. That's my girl.

Tricia got on the phone, and I told her what was going on.

"Let's see what a few more hours will do," I said.

"Maybe things will take a turn for the good. They are going to give him some steroids to bounce him back, hopefully like before at Presby."

"I still feel good about being here," I told Tricia. "I know things will be fine."

His teacher stopped by and said, "He is a fighter, he will be fine."

I just wish some lungs would come in soon. I want him to feel how great it would be to take in some air without coughing. His x-ray was different today than yesterday. More fluid. Hopefully, the Lasix would rectify the situation.

It is 10:53 a.m. EST. Coby is sleeping. I love him so much.

Theresa, the psychologist, stopped in and stayed quite a while. Everyone is really pulling for Coby, just like back home. He is sleeping sitting straight up because of the sensation of not getting enough oxygen. The Lasix are kicking in, so maybe relief will follow.

Pat Thomas, the respiratory therapist, along with Barbara, the nurse, are moving Coby to ICU. It is now noon EST.

I must make a decision within the hour whether to tell Tricia to catch the next plane to RDU or to hold up. The ICU staff jumped on Coby like ticks on a dog! People from everywhere, with all sorts of monitors, hooked Coby up. He is definitely getting the medical attention.

I get to stay with him until 7:00–8:30 p.m. He will be without Tricia or me for the first time ever on a hospital stay. I told him this will be good practice. This is how it will be after his transplant for a few days.

He seemed fine with the arrangements, although he asked me when he thought he would get out.

As the afternoon progressed, Coby seemed to get better, even his appetite. I called Tricia and told her he was doing better, so we decided that she could wait until next week, if not sooner (maybe the transplant will take place by then).

Coby watched some TV and then fell asleep. I went for a walk to PT and then to Kenan Stadium. I watched a few drills and then went back to the hospital. Coby was awake and wanting something to eat. The steroids were taking hold, it seemed.

A parade of people kept peeking in to see how he was doing. I went to get him some punch, heated him up some meatballs I had bought at Model T's the day before, and he ate them all quickly. I left at seven and went home to fix him a sandwich.

The apartment was very lonely without my roommate.

I made a sandwich for myself and spoke to Doug and Kelly about what was going on with Coby.

I went back to the hospital, parked out front, and headed to PICU 7. Coby introduced me to Robert Hawkins, his nurse for the night. He seems nice, no surprise.

Coby ate more—sandwich, cereal, whatever he could get!

I stayed until ten and left for the quiet apartment.

I talked to Tricia and Molly and then showered and went to bed.

I put Larry King's show on the radio. Ivana Trump was his guest. I remember three callers, and then I was a goner.

Day 48
Thursday, April 9, 1992

The alarm went off at 6:15 a.m. EST. I took Coby's and my clothes to the laundry room. It is not too crowded at this time. Sure enough, it wasn't. I put the clothes in. Colors on permanent press, whites on hot. I went back to the apartment, set the alarms for fifteen minutes, and caught a quick nap before going back to move the clothes to the dryer.

I set my stopwatch for forty-five minutes and then went back to get ready to go the hospital.

I arrived at the unit at 9:04 a.m., and doctors were in with Coby. I went to the lobby and began reading *The Daily Tar Heel.* Major Geer and Mrs. Taylor stopped by to visit along with DeAnne and another occupational therapist. They asked me to come into the unit because Coby was awake.

He then fell asleep at noon. He definitely needed the rest. I listened to all the ICU machine sounds. It is like a flowing brook. The alarms beeping are like birds chirping, just like being outside on a cool day.

Coby keeps the room cold.

He still struggles to breathe, but he is not fighting so much as the day before. Hopefully, he is on his way back. Sure do need some new lungs, though. Coby finally woke up and wanted to eat. He has so many wires, he looks battery operated!

He still does not have a potty chair. Coby said, "It is just like camping. No phone, no bathroom. I'm ready to get out of ICU, Daddy," he continued to say.

He is a hoot.

He took it pretty easy the rest of the day. Doesn't have much of a choice, as he is pretty much tied down. I had to go out on the floor to use the facilities. As I was walking by the ICU waiting room, the telephone was ringing. There was not anyone around, so I answered the signal.

It was Doug, wanting to know how things were going. I couldn't believe the timing. He invited me over for burgers at the seven o'clock change. I said yes.

The typical flow of traffic came by to see Coby. Kami was back today and wanted to know what Coby was doing in here. He hugged her. She said, "I didn't think he felt well Monday when I saw him at the apartment." She told Coby she would come by at seven when she got off of work.

I went on to the apartment to get the mail before I headed to Doug and Kelly's. The drive is getting prettier here. Spring is fast approaching now. Things are blooming, people are running, walking, and bike-riding. I believe we could live up here.

I got the mail. Had a nice shortcut to Doug's place as I am learning to stay off the main routes…just like a local. Kelly and Doug fed me well, and then I went back with the mail to Coby's latest hangout. It was a real nice night to be out. I arrived and we opened the mail. Coby didn't see *The Simpsons,* as this particular room does not get Fox. Kind of goes with not having a potty.

Coby used the bedpan. What an experience.

I bathed him, and he felt better. He told me he was going to sleep, so I left around ten. When I got home, it sure was lonely. It is really funny how it has become home. I look around, and Coby's spot was empty.

"Home is where you find it," said Willie Nelson.

Talked to Tricia, watched some of *The Masters*, read some Ali McGraw, and fell asleep.

Day 49
Friday, April 10, 1992

I got up, cleaned up, and went to the hospital.

Coby's night wasn't that great, but he was steadily getting better. It was good seeing him. I saw Leslie Brock, the nurse on the floor, and she said Coby was in a dream she had. He was getting his lungs. De Anne stopped in with her *Where's Waldo?* magic wand. The chaplain stopped by and said she would know that green pillowcase anywhere. Kami stopped by after her morning class.

The big happening, though, was the arrival of the potty chair. Coby could not wait to use it.

Coby's attitude is still upbeat. He has wires and IVs running everywhere. His CO_2 levels are beginning to level out. I hope they start being more constant.

I went out to get a drink. I noticed the little babies in ICU. I regressed to my Baylor days and taking portable films on the young'uns. These kids are really sick, but they are getting great care.

Coby fell asleep after his treatment. I went walking to Kenan Memorial. The field was ready for tomorrow's Blue/White game.

I walked to the football office to see Coach Hemphill and ran into Mr. Blanchard and told him about Coby. He wished us well.

When I got back, I found Coby awake. He ate. I came home, fixed some nachos, and returned to the hospital at 8:30 p.m. I bathed Coby, changed his sheets, and then he went to bed.

I came home, talked to Tricia, and went to bed. I read Ali's book a while and then fell asleep.

Day 50
Saturday, April 11, 1992

I didn't set the alarm, but I woke up around eight EST. I got cleaned up and went to see Coby. He was a little restless and seemed unsure. Then he threw up his guts. "I feel better, Daddy," he said.

Man, this kid's tough.

He now has an atrial line, IV in one arm for one medicine and an IV in his left thumb for another. I took his picture with the video camera. He is definitely battery operated.

I stopped by the post office and received a package from Tricia. It had the video of Casey's talent show. She looked good, even though she was sick with a cold. Coby enjoyed watching it. He talked about how good her flips were.

Coby let me go to the Blue/White game, and I enjoyed watching the football crowd. Everyone was relaxed. About four thousand people were in attendance. The band was playing, and the cheerleaders were dancing. You'da thought they were playing Duke or something.

I went back, and Coby was looking at the *Far Side* book De Anne had left him. We turned on the Masters. One of Coby's nurse's husband is on tour part-time. He is a pro at Prestonwood Country Club in Carey, North Carolina, home of Bobby Clampett.

Coby ate a good supper. I went home and ate a potato. Coaches Mazzon and Meyers called and said things were going along. I went back to the hospital

Coby was really tired and uneasy. I think the medicines make him sick at his stomach.

The doctor ordered some Benadryl IV.

Coby told me, "I love you, Daddy," and went to sleep.

I went home and spoke to Tricia. I called Lanny Pettit about Coach Brooks. He said I would like him. I'm trying to get Lanny to come to Wylie…maybe so.

We got a card from Brent Baker. He said to let him know what he can do and that we are in his prayers. He just said what he could do. The more prayers the better.

I love Coby so much. I am very proud of the way he is handling all this. Tricia and I are very fortunate to have Coby and Casey who have good attitudes toward adversity.

Life is definitely a ride.

Day 51
Sunday, April 12, 1992

I couldn't go to sleep until 2:00 a.m. EST. I was just thinking about a lot of different things: Tricia and Casey, how Coby was doing, next year's football season with a new head man, etc. I just seemed to be wide awake. If I could have got in a weight room, I would have done it.

I finally went to sleep and woke up at 8:20 a.m. EST. I cleaned up and went to the hospital. It is cloudy today and not much traffic out this morning. When I got to the ICU, I was greeted by Coby saying, "I had a terrible night. I want out."

Truth is, he threw up around 6:00 am EST all over himself and the bed. He actually had a good sleeping night. He just wants me around.

He got up more mucus plugs out of his nose. He said that was a lot better, laid down, and went to sleep. His saturations are doing good. His blood gases are more stable. He still has a lot of retraction when he is sleeping, I noticed.

I watch him as he sleeps and ask God to be with him and to give him comfort. I wonder if that is for me. I don't know. I just know God is in control, and I must wait the time with patience.

It is 11:55 EST. Coby is sleeping. He is so tired. I love him so much.

His fight is still going. I hope the transplant is soon.

I stared out the window, looking at another brick building. Pigeons were perched on the ledge. I wondered how long was there lifespan. I watched Coby lying on his back. It seems he is struggling for every breath, but for him, he is resting.

The wires, the tubes, the scars…I overlook all that and see the pretty boy whose mom, sister, and I truly love and selfishly want to keep.

Somehow, we must get over this hump. With God's help, we will.

3:20 p.m. EST. I just got back from UNC Bookstore. I went to get Coby a stamp pad for the smiley-face stamp that Tricia sent him. On my way, I stopped in the hospital chapel, and I had a visit with God. I know you can visit with him anywhere or anytime (even at school), but the overall quietness is nice.

I left a dollar and took some scripture notes that were available. The friendly orderly stuck his head in to ask how things were. Kami also stopped in.

I then left the hospital out the back way and headed to the bookstore. It is nice walking outside with the treelined brick pathways, squirrels running around, and birds singing.

Although it is not as nice as when Coby is with me. It is just more fun sharing nice things with him. He and I have become such a good team it really seems strange without his being with me.

I bought the stamp pad and went back to the hospital. Coby was awake when I got back. I had been gone thirty-three minutes. I had put my stopwatch on when I left.

Heather, his nurse for the day, said his latest CO_2 gas was not bad for him. His PO_2 was high, meaning his O_2 flow was better. He had gotten rid of more mucus plugs earlier, so his nasal oxygen flow was improved. I think the Benadryl he was given last night for queasiness is wearing off, although he is going back to sleep.

He needed an all-day rest day. I watched the UT girls get second behind Stanford for the national title in swimming. One of the diving champions had been a gymnast for nine years. She switched to diving, and the gymnastics had helped her well.

It seems like something Casey would like to do someday, but that's me. I'm not Casey. Whatever she wants, we will try to provide.

Coby continues to sleep. He must be coming down off the steroids. I watched Fred Couples win the Masters during the seven o'clock change at the apartment in Carrboro.

When I returned, Coby was semiawake. Randy was his nurse for the night. Randy got Coby up and changed his bed. The respiratory therapist was putting in Coby's breathing medicine in the nebulizer. She had told me earlier her husband had passed away two years earlier from CF at age thirty-three.

Coby told me he felt better and that he loved me. After the breathing treatment, I clapped on him and put him close to sleep.

I kissed him good night, told him I loved him, and he put his hand on my face and told me he loved me.

I then went to H-103 Ramsgate.

During the seven to eight thirty change, I called Coach Brooks. He told me not to worry and that family comes first. I felt good about calling and talking to him.

I talked to Tricia and then went to bed. Casey was asleep.

Day 52
April 13, 1992

I woke up at 7:30 a.m. and stared at the ceiling. For a second I thought I could lay in bed all day. Then I thought, *Get up and run for Coby*. I did. It was about fifty degrees, clear skies, and a little windy, but a nice run.

I came back to the apartment, cleaned up, and went to the hospital.

As I was getting dressed, I had the TV on one of those morning shows. The guests were Roy Rogers and Dale Evans. They were talking about the book she had written twenty-five years ago about their little girl who passed away with Down syndrome. They were telling about how they had been told to just put her in a home and pretend they did not have her. They both said God had sent her to them for a reason. They will never forget her.

I needed that. God works in timing ways.

When I arrived at the hospital, Julie was giving Coby a treatment. He had thrown up for the third morning in a row, but he said he felt fine. Dr. Wood came in and said he was going to try and get some DNase to try and get that deep, thick mucus out. "He is just not moving enough air around," he said.

I thought of how we needed the transplant soon.

I might get Tricia and Casey to come out now, but I do not know. I know God will give me a sign on what to do. We are definitely back in the hospital.

The operator asked people to move their cars from the front of the building.

Coby is sitting up on his pillows and sleeping. The doctors came in and said, blood-wise Coby is looking good. I told them it seems he has a virus. "Could be," they said.

Medicine is wild.

Coby's teacher is coming by at one for school. I think I will go get me a snack then. Kami stopped by and told Coby to get better. It was one, and Mrs. Taylor came in to work with Coby. I went and bought a Mello Yello and nuts. I went outside and ran into some of the mothers of the people who Coby works out with at the same time. They asked how he was, and I told them he was better. One lady said they had been fighting a virus all weekend. *Bingo*, I thought.

Connie was working them hard. Karen from Georgia looked really tired. Turns out, she does not have CF. She lost all of her cilia six years ago when she had the Asian flu. She needs a lung transplant to replace hers, which are deteriorating.

After visiting, I went back toward the ICU. One of the girls who had had a lung transplant was in for her check-up. She was running, not walking. She has CF. I just cannot wait for Coby's new lungs to arrive. I stopped and talked sports with Major Geer. He is really enjoyable to visit with.

Coby's teacher told me he listened to two stories. I went into his room, and he was almost asleep. He told me he loved me and nodded off. He was out for a couple more hours. I watched him as he slept. He seemed to be breathing easier. If we can get over this stomach thing, maybe we can bounce back.

He woke up, drank some ginger ale, and began to get restless once again.

It was getting close to time for me to leave. I tried to calm Coby down some. Kami stopped by and told Coby she was going to sneak him out to the floor. He laughed, which is a small sign of recovery, I hoped.

I left and felt very uneasy about the way Coby was doing. When I got to the apartment, I quickly put on my workout clothes and went to lift. When I got back, I cooked some rice. I asked God to give Coby some relief.

When I returned to Coby's room, Randy had him sitting up in the chair and was changing his bed. I was afraid Coby must have thrown up and soiled his sheets. That was not the case. Randy was just putting clean sheets on the bed.

I bathed and washed Coby's hair, and he brushed his teeth. He felt better, he told me. I was feeling better about the way he was progressing now.

God was working.

After getting Coby settled in bed, he ate half a Snickers candy bar, a pickle, and drank some ginger ale. He told me he loved me and he wanted to go to sleep. I left him, which is always hard to do. It was a cool walk to the van. The helicopter was at home on the pad.

When I arrived at the apartment, the phone rang. It was Casey. We talked, and then Tricia got on the phone. I sure miss them; it is hard being away, especially when Coby is not doing well. I keep telling myself things will be fine. I went to bed, reading myself to sleep. I thought, *Coby will be better tomorrow. Please, God.*

Day 53
Tuesday, April 14, 1992

When I arrived at Coby's room, he was getting a treatment by Julie. He had not thrown up, and I felt good about that.

Thanks, God.

When Julie left, Coby told me he might eat some Rice Krispies. He was a little depressed though. He cried because he was too spunky. Theresa, the psychologist, happened to come in, and she visited with Coby for a while. She told him how everyone was pulling for him.

It helped a lot.

She is coming back later. Coby ate a little, and that makes me feel better. The rest of the day was positive. Coby seemed to be getting better. He started eating little by little. He lost about five pounds in a week. I have been working his legs in a cycle motion to try and keep atrophy from totally taking over.

His SATs are holding pretty good. I am glad Tricia did not see him during this trying time. I am thankful for my hospital background. It is helpful for when times look bad. Patience is the name of the game; although, when my own is involved, things do not move fast enough.

The rest of the day went fine. I left at 6:30 p.m. and returned at 8:30 p.m. EST. Coby fell asleep about 9:45 p.m. EST. I returned to H-103. I told Tricia Coby was so much better. Still depending on O_2, but better.

Ali and I went to bed.

Day 54
Wednesday, April 15, 1992

Got up at 6:00 EST to do the laundry. The wash room is not too crowded at this time in the morning, I have noticed. After they were washed, I put the clothes in the dryer and went running. It rained on me halfway, but not for long. I returned, got the clothes, got ready, and went to the hospital.

Coby was up and having a breathing treatment. I clapped on him. His mood seemed to be a lot better. He had already had a chest x-ray. He looked to me that he was struggling breathing a bit, but his SATs looked tolerable.

I read him *Rip Van Winkle*. Dr. Theresa Pawlegoe stopped in and visited. She was going to leave tonight for the upper part of New York, a twelve-hour drive. Mrs. Taylor came in for school. I walked Dr. Pawlegoe to her office, and then I went out the student health center door and walked around campus. I went to Union Street and got a Mountain Dew and multigrain cheddar chips. I took my time going back to the ICU. When I got back, the teacher had just left. Coby was removing the waste caused by Lasix.

He felt better, he said.

Dr. Ken Ausloos from the transplant unit stopped in. He thought Coby's problem might be mucus-plug related. It is 11:00 p.m. EST. Treatment time. The thumb IV was removed today. Coby was happy about that happening. He told me earlier that he didn't think he could take it any longer being here. I told him, "It's okay to say it, but don't believe it."

Coby never took a nap today. Julie and I walked him for a total of about ten feet. It tired him out. I felt, when I left at six thirty, he would probably go to sleep.

When I returned at 8:30 p.m. EST, sure enough, he was asleep. Robert woke him to give him his pills, and I helped him with the urinal. Then Coby went back to sleep, not before he told me he loved me though. I told him I loved him too and left out the door.

Dr. Wood was at the nurses' desk. He told me they are trying to balance his electrolytes. He is still waiting to hear from Gentex about the DNase.

I left and went to the apartment, stopping for some peanuts and a Pepsi along the way for a bedtime treat. Tricia called and said things are falling into place for their visit. Johnny Murrey called. "Just keep me posted," he said. Molly called and said Coby's picture was in the Terrell paper.

Then the hospital called. They had moved Coby to 7303. He would be glad about that.

He was sleeping, so I stayed home.

Day 55
Thursday, April 16, 1992

I got to the hospital at 8:20 a.m., and Coby was still sleeping. He won't be for long because I saw the doctors' parade down the hall. He seemed to be struggling still, but that is CF. The doctor said he needs more salt, so maybe he could eat more chips.

It is Coby's first full day back on the floor. Everything is about the same except for all the monitors. Streams of people come by, wishing him well. Julie gave him a papier-mâché bunny rabbit with candy. Annie, PT, gave him a chick that cheeps when hands have moisture on them.

Overall, he had a good day.

He went for about an eighty-foot walk. Not bad after being in bed for a week.

Doug and Kelly came and watched *The Simpsons* and *Cheers*. All three of us left at the same time as Coby was ready for bed. Mail-wise, he got a good bunch of get-well cards, and a sorority from UNT sent him their pictures.

I know it will be better when I can get him back to the apartment so he can get some rest.

Spoke to Tricia and Casey. They will be here tomorrow. That will be great.

A peculiar thing happened as I was watching the news tonight. A bulletin came across about a little boy getting hit by a train, details later. I thought, *What if this is it?* I feel it will not be much longer, holiday weekend and all.

I finished Ali McGraw's book. What a headcase! Maybe she has got her life worked out, hope so for her sake. Tomorrow, of course, as they (whoever they are) say, is another day.

Day 56
Good Friday, April 17, 1992

I got up, vacuumed the apartment, showered, and went to the hospital. It was a nice four-and-a-half-minute, sunny drive. When I got to Coby's room, his chest monitor was screaming, and he was mad because it woke him up. Penny got it fixed, and he went back to sleep. Cynthia will be his nurse today. We are planning on getting him a bath sometime today. That means he will be free of the monitor chains.

His SATs are doing well, and things seem to be better. I will be leaving at 11:00 a.m. to get Tricia and Casey at the airport. I hope the flight is early. It looks like the start of a beautiful day, and seeing those two will just make it more gorgeous.

Coby got up and got ready. Bath, teeth brushed, and he was ready.

I left and got to the airport about forty minutes before the plane arrived. I walked around, bought some ice cream, and continued to check the arrival times on the TV. 12:04 p.m., it kept printing. Finally, the time had come, and the plane arrived at the gate.

Casey came out looking, and I caught Tricia's eyes. Casey still hadn't found me. I went toward them. She saw me and came a-running. It was good to hold them. We got their bags and went to the hospital.

On the way, we stopped and aired up some balloons Hollie had sent at Harris Teeter. We arrived, and I let Casey and Tricia out front. They went up to Coby's room, and I went to park the van.

We were a together family again.

Day 57 and 58
Saturday and Sunday, April 18 and 19, 1992

Casey stayed all night with Coby at the hospital. We had pizza together in Coby's room. We were all pretty happy. Tricia and I got to stay with each other, which was nice. We never have liked being apart.

Casey and I played tennis, swam, walked around the campus, waited for the helicopter, and just enjoyed talking with one another. Tricia stayed with Coby and cross-stitched. It was a fast but enjoyable stay.

Tricia got to see some of the hospital routine, UNC style. I am glad she did not see Coby last week with all his problems. She cut Coby's hair, and he looked a lot better.

Doug and Kelly came over Saturday night and stayed a while. They also stayed with Coby when I took Tricia and Casey to the airport Sunday. It was a tough thing to leave them at the airport, but I did. I went to the apartment and got some things, made a McDonald's stop for Coby, and headed to room 7303.

I went to bed and waited for day 59.

Day 59
Monday, April 20, 1992

I got up, fed Coby, ran, helped Coby with math, read some history, and visited with Carol. Dr. Lever and Dr. Henry say we are getting better. I took Coby for a walk. After his afternoon treatment, he slept for an hour and a half. I am going to take him for another walk later. I hope we can go back to the apartment soon. Tomorrow will be two weeks.

He had the parade of going-to-be doctors. He is like a monkey in a cage. They all look, some listen to his lungs, and others just grin. Betsy, his nurse, weaves through them, hooking his medicine to IMED 980c volumetric infusion pump. After they left, Coby did some math and read some Texas history. He is doing better at paying attention. Better airflow, I suspect.

Lunch, treatment, and afternoon nap.

When he woke from the nap, Coby wanted to eat. Cereal pacified him until I brought him two McDonald's burgers and an order of fries.

I went to the apartment, got the mail, and visited with Kaaren across the way. I lifted weights at the clubhouse and then went back to the hospital. Kami was there talking with Coby. She had told me earlier that Coby is a tough kid. I think he and all terminally ill kids are tough, mentally and physically.

Tricia called, and the rotary club has given her another plane ticket. People back home are really unbelievable.

I cannot keep up with who does what. We are really blessed.

Tricia has found Doug some Huaraches for $69.99. I will talk with him later.

The plane was delayed due to the weather, but Tricia and Casey did arrive, and that is the main thing. I talked with Doug about the shoes, and he is going to check his size for sure at the mall.

Coby finally settled down and went to bed. I went to the apartment and crashed pretty quickly. I thought how nice it would be to get Coby back to the apartment. Then I thought how nice it would be to get him back to Wylie, Texas.

Heck, if you're going to wish…wish big!

Day 60
Tuesday, April 21, 1992

I woke up to rain, got showered, and went to the hospital. The traffic was backed up on the 200 bypass because of the rain. When I got to the hospital, it was around 8:15 a.m. EST. Coby was eating his breakfast. He was in a cheery mood. The doctors stopped in and told Coby he needed more salt in his diet, so I got chips, pickles, and whatever down the boy.

He is getting off the concentrator. He seems to be doing all right. I think he is surprising himself on how well he can walk the halls. It has been exactly two weeks since we were admitted.

Coby is ready for H-103. Me too.

We finished the morning doing schoolwork. Ruth Ann came in to talk about her year in Africa. It was very interesting to hear about the primitive hospital conditions.

Coby said, "Sounds like ICU at UNC Hospitals!" We all laughed.

Coby ate his lunch, had a one o'clock treatment, walked again, visited with the psychologist, and I went to the apartment. There was no mail. I went to Kerr drugstore and bought cards for Tricia and Casey, birthday and I-miss-you cards, respectively.

I stopped and got Coby a burger at Mickey D's. I had some vitamin M&M's with peanuts. When I got back to the hospital, Coby was watching the end of *The Montel Williams Show*. Coby was doing a lot better.

His mom called, Wayne called, Spann called, and everything was about the same. I left Coby in a good mood, stopped at the post office and mailed the cards. It was pouring rain like crazy. When I got home, Mrs. Link called and talked about the card mix-up. Bryan is pitching again and is 2–0. Winthrop is in town tomorrow to play UNC.

I went to sleep listening to the Carolina rain.

Day 61
Wednesday, April 22, 1992

When I arrived at the hospital, Coby was finishing breakfast. He had a good night's sleep and woke up when they drew his blood for the electrolyte check. The usual parade of folks filtered in and out, doing their own occupational duties.

Coby was getting stronger. He went six minutes on the treadmill. It worked him, but he kept going. We met Misty Ferguson, the girl who had her transplant on Halloween. She looked good. It was her six-month evaluation, and her mother told me that if not for the transplant, she did not think Misty would have lived to see Christmas.

Tricia called earlier today. Rayvac is now fixed and working to clean the pool.

Tricia, 14; Pool, 10

I did not go and run until after *Cheers*. I ran on the track and showered in Coby's bathroom at the hospital, and we watched *Unsolved Mysteries*. I went to the apartment at 10:30 p.m., watched the news, and ate some Ben & Jerry's ice cream that I got at Merritt's, and then to bed.

Coby read some Texas history aloud. He wanted to. I have noticed him trying harder with his schoolwork. That is a good sign. He is talking about getting a climbing rope in the backyard when we get home.

I know God has a plan. That keeps me going.

I have been looking at our playbook the new coach sent. Looks fun to me. Heck, it's just football!

Day 62
Thursday, April 23, 1992

Stopped on the way to the hospital and got Coby some Lay's chips. I got myself a hot biscuit at Burger King. When I got to his room, Coby was visiting with the new chaplain. Betsy was giving him his medicine. The sun was shining through. It was a very nice morning.

A lady from Kaufman School District called about Keenan getting the baseball job. Her name was Mrs. Ramsey, I believe. I told her Keenan was ready for a high school job. He is still like all of us, in the maturing stage, but with good guidance, he will be fine. "He needs a wife," I told her, and she understood.

Coby is doing fractions. Boy, that is a struggle for me! The normal routine followed for the rest of the day and night. They said we go home tomorrow, early afternoon.

Kelly and Doug watched *The Simpsons*.

Oh, Kelly is going to have a baby!

Day 63
Friday, April 24, 1992

The phone rang about eight. "Daddy, Ruth Ann is going to get married." He was happy for her. I am too. Good person. I had been up since around six, did the laundry, and ran. I was thinking of Casey and UIL, so I called, wished her luck.

I was also thinking of Coby, yesterday around noon thirty when he started crying about why God has people die. He is afraid of not dying now or doing the operation but later, when all his friends are gone. I really did not know what to tell him, but I do know it was just good for him to talk. I told him God puts us here on earth to see what we will do with our lives. That is why I know God must like humor.

Anyway, it seemed to satisfy him. He deserves a depressed moment, that's how I felt about it.

He told me he loved me, and "I love you too, big man," I said.

Stan, the O_2 man, got here a little late, but we got both tanks filled. When I got to the hospital, Coby was fixin' to go to the treadmill with Connie Johnson. I went to the van with a load of stuff, spoke with Connie Arnold, and found out Coby's PT will be the same time. I then went back to his room.

Actually, I went to the Anderson PT room. Coby was on the treadmill. Fifteen minutes and fifteen seconds today. I am very proud of how he is working. I keep telling myself to focus on what we are here for. Not but two more parking lot loads.

Coby was discharged at three o'clock.

As we were leaving UNC Hospitals, the helicopter Tar Heel I was taking off. It was neat seeing the foot on the bottom of the copter. We got to the apartment, and girls were sunbathing. Coby was having fun. I was telling myself what we were here for.

Michelle was here from the nursing service with his medications. Coby had already had a landmark catheter put in place at the hospital. After she left, it was time to give him a treatment. I then went to the store for a few groceries and to Roses for a heating pad. It will help Coby's arm. I also needed one for my back.

5:00 p.m. EST. Medicine time—slow drip, of course. Coby and I tried to find the right position for his arm so it would drip in an hour.

Wrong.

It took two and a half hours. It is very frustrating. Coby would just like to have a heparin lock. It finally got all in. I spoke with the nurse, and she recommended flushing it with saline. I did it, but it was not much better.

I had Coby squeeze a stress ball, and the fluid went in faster.

Ain't science grand!

Doug and Kelly brought us some Mexican food, Carolina style. It was tolerable. They stayed and watched TV until *20/20* was over. I gave Coby his sixteen pills, then a treatment, and then started the Primaxin again. It dripped in about two hours. A lot better. It is supposed to drip in one hour.

Coby went to bed, and I followed an hour later.

4:50 a.m. EST. Get up and start the IV. We can never find the right position for Coby's arm. After three hours, I discontinued. Only half had dripped in.

He was fine.

Day 64
Saturday, April 25, 1992

I was frustrated. I get that way when fancy stuff does not work.

I called the nurse, and someone will be here later this morning to troubleshoot the problem. I feel the line is too long, and Coby's muscles pinch off partially at one end while another part is open, so it drips slow. But heck, I am just a coach. All I know is, a heparin lock seems to always work, but it is too basic for modern science.

Casey got second in UIL reading. I was very happy and proud for her.

Coby had to have another line put in, and it is a lot better. We went to the Transplant Awareness picnic. It was good for both Coby and me. The park is nice. Coby ate great and really enjoyed meeting others in the same situation.

People that we did not even know took his picture. Afterward we picked up Kelly and went to the ball game. Doug was studying.

NC State clobbered UNC, but it was fun to be at. Except for the outcome, Coby had fun.

We later rented two movies and watched them with Kelly and Doug. Doug was pretty tired from studying, and Kelly made some good spaghetti.

Coby and I watched *SNL* between treatments and medicine. We went to bed. I set the alarm for 4:50 a.m. to give Coby his medicine. The IV ran just great.

Tricia called.

Day 65
Sunday, April 26, 1992

Happy forty-third to Tricia. She called about 8:30 a.m. and wanted to know how things went with the IV. Afterward Coby woke up, talked to his mom a while, did a treatment, and ate breakfast that I made very good. I went running and came back to start another IV. It did not run as well, but it got in okay. I showered, Molly called, and then I went to meet Nick at the University Inn.

It is a cooler day than yesterday, cloudy but feels good outside. Coby and I have a lot of schoolwork to do. He is feeling better about doing things. He brought out the puzzle Tricia brought him.

Nick Rhodes arrived at the University Inn at 12:35 p.m. He had a new Lumina rental car. He was just a-grinning. It was good to see my woodworking neighbor. He followed me to Carrboro. He was hungry, so I called Kelly. No answer. I figured the phone was unplugged, or she was grocery shopping.

I ordered us an extra-large Model T pizza, half hamburger, half pepperoni.

Nick and Coby worked on the *101 Dalmatians* puzzle while I went to get the pizza. It gave me the opportunity to return the videos we rented the day before as it was right by Model T's.

The pizza was ready when I arrived. It was huge.

I took it back to H-103, and we attacked the scrumptious pie pretty good!

Coby was really enjoying Nick. We laughed, cut up, and just had a good time. Later, when Nick had left, Coby said, "Daddy, wouldn't it be something to have Nick and Dale here at the same time?"

After eating, we took Nick on a tour of Chapel Hill. He seemed to enjoy it. When we got back, Doug and Kelly came over and ate some of the leftover pizza. There was even some left over after they finished!

Everybody then started working the puzzle. Coby's medicine was slowly dripping in. I think it is leaking at the cap, but I will wait until tomorrow when the nurse comes and checks.

All the gang finished the puzzle. Coby put in the last piece. I videoed it, and then we just sat around, laughed and talked. Kelly and Doug had to leave. Doug has finals this week. He really liked his shoes that Nick delivered.

Nick had to go and get some guys at the airport and go to Raleigh. Coby and I watched TV, read, did his medicine, and went to bed. Matt Casselberry called, and we talked about the NFL draft. He had gone to Muenster to run earlier. I was there two years ago, judging a chili contest.

Then off to sleep until 4:50 a.m. for Coby's medicine.

Day 66
Monday, April 27, 1992

Coby's medicine seemed to drip better until 11:00 a.m. when it was a slow go. I called the service. Hopefully, I will see them around three o'clock. Coby got up about nine, had a treatment, ate a scrambled egg, bowl of cereal, and eleven pills that he takes twice a day. He showered, got dressed, and we were off to the hospital for school.

Before school, we had to go by the lab and get some blood drawn. This will be about twice a week for a while. Routine for blood. Then to school we went.

"If there is anyone with a car out front, please move," the operator spoke over the intercom.

I knew we were back on schedule.

When Coby was finished with school, we headed to PT. We found out Karen had had her transplant and was doing fine. Coby and I were really excited about her good fortune.

I know our turn must be getting closer.

Coby had a good workout, and then we went home for the home care nurse to look at his IV. She installed another one, so Coby had two IVs at once.

I forgot to write about Saturday, when Kelly, Coby, and I were going down Colombia Street. We were stopped at a red light and Coby rolled down the window and asked the guy by us if he had any Grey Poupon!

After the nurse left and the antibiotics were given, we went to Toys "R" Us in Durham. Coby was going to get the Lego electric train he had been wanting. We also needed to pick up some Pulmocare at the Drug Emporium right next to the huge toy store.

The pharmacist that waited on us graduated from Plano in 1983, just ten miles west of where we live in Texas. She wished us luck, and then we went to eat at Chili's. Coby ate well, so well it is scary. I hope he can keep feeling this good up until the transplant and, of course, afterward.

We got back home, Coby worked on his train, and then I had him do a treatment. He took his IV and was then off to bed.

I set the alarm for 4:50 a.m. EST to put the saline and heparin out to warm, and then I went to bed.

Tricia called, and I knew something was bothering her, but I didn't press the issue. Maybe not much longer. After all, it is getting closer.

Day 67
Tuesday, April 28, 1992

I woke up at 4:30 a.m., so I went ahead and put the medicine out. I went back to bed, hoping and praying the medicine would flow just fine. Sure enough, it did. I was relieved. I set the alarm for the approximate time it would finish. I had a flashlight by my side so periodically I can check to see if it is dripping. Sometimes when Coby moves his arm into a certain position, it will not run. Luckily, it is doing fine now.

After the Primaxin, which is given every six hours, it is time for the home pump with tobramycin every twelve hours. The home pump is a plastic ball about the size of a tennis ball with a latex balloon filled with the medicine. The pressure of the inside of the plastic forces the medicine in, so there is no drip to watch. It takes the balloon about an hour or more to deflate.

Afterward it looks like a fishing cork.

Everything went fine. All drugs in now, and it was time for a breathing treatment. We weren't quite as rushed today because there was not school or therapy. After the breathing treatment, Coby took his handful of pills. It was ten o'clock. Every twelve hours this is done. He had breakfast, scrambled eggs, then started his homework, and then to the train. At eleven, the dripping Primaxin starts. I sure hope it drips.

We decided to go see *The Babe* with John Goodman. I checked the paper for the time, 2:55 p.m. at the plaza. Funny, my hometown movie was named *The Plaza*. I went for a run and then got ready for the movie. Coby had written Hollie a card, I stamped it, and off we went to the show.

It was a nice day. Coby made the comment of how nice it would be to grow up in Carrboro. "It is so pretty," he said. It does look like the small-town USA the movie screen tries to portray.

Coby is walking more than before the hospital stay. We arrived at the theater, bought some popcorn and a coke, and watched the movie. It was very good. Both of us enjoyed Goodman's performance.

Coby learned what I had always heard about the legendary Babe Ruth. It was a touching film.

Afterward to home we went. I made tuna the way Coby likes it, and he finished assembling the train.

Tricia called and told me about the pool incident that happened on Sunday. She is lucky the lid of the filter did not hit her when it flew fifteen feet in the air and landed on the other side of the driveway. The metal band had slipped with the O-ring, and the tank was not sealed properly for the pressure when the pump was on.

The pool people came and helped her get everything rectified. I could tell she was relieved. Also, the brakes on the Cougar had to be fixed, and the battery went out.

Pool and Cougar, 45; Tricia, 20

Roseanne Rosanna Danna was right. It's always something.

That answered my question of what was bothering her Monday night on the phone.

After talking with Tricia, we finished the routine medical chores, and Coby went to bed. He talked about *The Babe.* He really liked the movie, and we both thought Goodman deserved an award for his performance. An Oscar would be nice.

We read some Dr. Peale. I set the alarm, listened to Larry King on the headphones, and fell asleep.

Day 68
Wednesday, April 29, 1992

I laid back down after disconnecting the tobramycin at seven o five. At eight o'clock, a lawnmower was coming right by my window.

The apartment is below the ground, and the windows are ground level. I thought a Stephen King book had me. I dozed a little while, and then Coby woke up coughing.

"I need a treatment, Dad," he said.

"You got it," I answered.

Treatment, pills, breakfast, Primaxin drip, shower. Coby was ready for school.

Joyce Jackson called from Kaufman, and it was good to hear from her. Ron, the O_2 man, it's his week to deliver. Stan and Ron alternate weeks on the truck. Michelle called. "See you tomorrow," she said in her sweet Southern voice.

I shaved and showered and then loaded up Coby, his books, and his oxygen tank, and off we went to UNC Hospitals.

Oh my gosh! I lucked into a parking spot. So far, so good.

Coby wants to try and see Karen.

"Maybe we can," I told him.

When we entered the hospital, an open elevator was waiting.

Man, a parking space and an open elevator all in the same series. Man, ain't life great so far today!

After Coby's school, we got in the elevator to go to PT. Karen Saul's—who had her transplant last week—boyfriend stepped in the elevator from the fourth floor. Coby and I think he looks like Travis Tritt. He said Karen was doing fine. Coby wanted to see her after PT.

PT went well. Coby went thirty minutes on the treadmill and did better on the bike. I took him to see Karen afterward. He could look through the glass window in the door. He told me she was all tubed up. She waved at him, and he got excited about seeing her.

He also made a comment about all the tubes, "Man, I don't know." I told him it would be worth it when it was all over.

During Coby's PT time, I talked with Mrs. Nelson. Jo Beth, her daughter, had just moved into Ramsgate from New Orleans. She had been turned down at Stanford, Minnesota, and St. Louis. "Mainly because of her one lung," her mother said. Dr. Egan feels he can help her. In other words, there is not another option, just like with Coby. Other people doing what they've got to do.

Life is a ride, for others also.

After seeing Karen, Coby and I went home. He ate and played with his train. I ran, came back, and checked on Coby. Kaaren next door was sunbathing. Coby was glad.

I showered and was going to the store. When I got back, Coby was asleep for three hours. The treadmill had caught up with him.

Apparently, Tricia had called while I was at the store and talked to Coby.

He woke up, watched *Unsolved Mysteries* while he ate, and was feeling good. We watched the Country Music Awards and went to bed. Coby could not fall asleep, so we talked and laughed. Finally, we fell asleep. The alarm went off at 4:50 a.m. EST.

Same routine.

Day 69
Thursday, April 30, 1992

I heard a knock at the door. It was Michelle and Rose from Biomed. She was checking on Coby's IV. They are not going to change it unless necessary, and both Coby and I were happy about that. After she and Rose left, I did his treatment, and then we got ready to go to UNC Hospitals.

I dropped the $670 rent check off at the office. Shannon, the manager, was just a-grinning. She was about to get the weekend off for the first time since April 7. I kidded with her a while about it. I bought a paper so Coby could do the crossword later.

I went back to the apartment and started Coby's eleven o'clock meds. We had to go to the lab, so we left a bit earlier than usual. Coby and I pulled into the lot just as I looked and saw that a car was leaving the space I needed.

I couldn't believe it. Two days in a row! I parallel parked the van, and off into the big medical complex we went.

They drew his blood with no problems. I pushed him to the elevator, and lo and behold, there was one open and waiting! This is unbelievable. A parking space and an open elevator? And two days in a row. I sure hope the lungs come today.

I was sitting in the waiting room, and Carol Hadler and Pat Thomas stopped in. Carol was telling about how David Brinkley is going to speak at the graduation on Mother's Day. He is a UNC graduate. After PT (another thirty-minute walk), we stopped at Spring Garden Bar and Grill. It was nice. No smokers at this particular time. Coby got to sit and eat on a barstool.

He said he was Norm on *Cheers*.

The service and food were good. The time of day we were in, prices were cheaper. We really had a good time. After we ate, Harris Teeter was our next stop. We bought a few things, *The Simpsons* magazine being one of them. It was beginning to rain, so we went home for the rest of the evening.

I put the TV on CNN, and the Los Angeles riots were going on. What a mess. The looting, arsons, and all were really disturbing to Coby. I thought I was watching a video of the sixties. Coby said it reminded him of another country fighting in the streets.

"Now other countries are watching us," I said. It was really unbelievable, but deep down I felt like something like this was going to happen sooner or later. It just so happened the Rodney King issue was used to set things off. There is just too much frustration in the world right now.

Coby said God wants him to be an actor, so he was really disturbed about the incidents that were going on in the City of Angels. I told him we would be sure and watch *Arsenio* because he was sure to have some comments on the terrorism.

I did the routine medicines, watched the final *Cosby* show, and the reruns of *SNL* on the comedy channel.

Tricia called. She's 14, pool 27.

I think the pool is working on her patience. I told her it should be better for her after the PMS—pool maintenance syndrome.

Molly called, and everything is about the same. Jeannie called and reported on their flight for Monday. We watched *Arsenio*, and sure enough, Mayor Bradley was on the show. It was very good, I thought. After Coby's medicine, he went to bed. I watched CNN a little more and went to sleep after setting the alarm for 4:50 a.m. and praying for peace.

Day 70
Friday, May 1, 1992

A new month, so I changed the SI calendar when I got up. *What a nice swim cap*, I thought. Coby is still wanting a *Playboy* magazine. "When you are a teenager," I told him. He counted the days down to eighty-eight.

We got up, turned on CNN, and saw there were more deaths. Coby did a treatment, pills, ate, IV meds, cleaned up, and he was ready for school.

UPS delivered a package from Jonelle and John Williamson. It was Shaklee supplies.

We got in the van, put on Travis Tritt's "Here's a Quarter" tape, and headed to UNC.

This was unbelievable. Three empty parking spaces when we arrived. I feel this could be the weekend for the lungs. When we got to the elevator, I pushed the Up button, and the door came open. No waiting, three days in a row.

Call the *Guinness Book of World Records*! Coby and I have set a new mark.

While Coby was at school, the chaplain stopped by, and we had a nice chat about the LA mess. He is from eastern Los Angeles. If the weather is nice, Coby and I are going to the park to play basketball.

After Coby's school and before his PT, we went to the coffee shop and got him some fruit punch. When we got off of the elevator going from the coffee shop headed to PT, Coby spotted Dr. Wood in front of us. He turned in the direction of PT. As we got to the PT hallway, the doctor had done a 180-degree turn and was coming toward us.

"Just the guys I am looking for," Dr. Wood said. He asked how Coby was feeling and listened to his lungs. He seemed to be pleased. He asked Coby if he would be interested in trying their prototype machine. Coby agreed to give it a shot.

Dr. Wood told us to page him after PT.

Coby went thirty minutes at a faster rate, bicycle, and then we called Dr. Wood. He brought the machine. Coby tried it. Also,

Connie Arnold and Annie Downs. Coby filled out a questionnaire and agreed to use the machine at home for a week. He really got some mucus up. I was impressed.

We then went home and got our basketballs and headed to the park. It was nice just being out. Coby says it is so pretty here quite a lot. He is correct; it is really nice. I wish Tricia and Casey were here with us.

It was time to do Coby's meds, so we went home. The phone was ringing, and it was Doug saying he and Kelly would bring some hamburger casserole over later. "Why not?" I said.

Coby ate before they came and then ate when they came.

Tricia called, and Casey hyperextended her elbow in gymnastics, but she will be fine. Tami and Bud's pool was gunited today. *They will love the pool, as will their kiddos,* I thought. We watched TV with Doug and Kelly, did Coby's stuff, and went to bed.

"No school or PT tomorrow," Coby told me before he went to sleep.

"I love you, Dad," Coby told.

"I love you too, big man."

Day 71
Saturday, May 2, 1992

After doing Coby's medicine this morning, I went to wash. The laundry room is not too crowded at seven in the morning. I came back, checked on Coby, and then bumped the laundry and went for a run. It takes forty-five minutes to dry, so I run as they are drying.

It was starting out to be a beautiful day. I hope the regional track meet is as nice back home in Texas. When I returned, a young gal was walking her dog. It was the pretty girl who had had a lung transplant in November. She was going to UNC, had to have a transplant, and then came back to finish school. She looked great. Ceclor, an allergy medication, messed up her lungs. She does not have CF. She is a pretty girl. She told me she is in better shape now than ever before.

I folded the clothes and went back to the apartment.

Coby was rearranging things. I then did a treatment on him, fed him, and then he took a shower, and we headed to Pittsburgh, North Carolina, to Connie Arnold's yard sale. The housing addition she lives at was having a giant yard sale. Coby loves that stuff. It was a pretty drive.

Ellen, the transplant coordinator, was leaving. She pointed out Connie, so off we went. Connie gave Coby anything he wanted. Some lady gave him some smiley-face cups. They were yellow. He had not spent any of his money yet.

Connie told us about a place down the road that had cows and other animals and shops, so we went there after. It was the Farrington Farm, a really neat place. The cows have a broad white stripe around the middle of their bodies that circles them.

We ate at their café. It was a nice place. Someone was having a wedding in one of the gardens. The flowers and shrubs were nice and colorful. We then came back to the apartment. I sat outside in the sun and wrote outside our apartment. Coby was tired but felt fine.

Later I went to the video store and rented two tapes, *Boyz n the Hood* and *Hot Shots!* We had seen the latter, but not *Boyz n the Hood.* Coby wanted a hot dog. I fixed us some, and then we watched the video.

Later in the night, about midnight, Coby was throwing up those hot dogs. I felt a little queasy also.

I cleaned him up and then went and washed his sheets and towels. It was not very crowded at midnight. I finished and got to bed around 1:30 a.m. and slept until the morning alarm went off at 4:50 a.m.

Day 72
Sunday, May 3, 1992

Coby and I both stayed in bed until 10:00 a.m. I mixed up some blueberry muffins, cleaned the van, and then Coby and I took a stroll to the elementary school then hung around the apartment. Talked to Tricia and Casey. Jeannie, Mother, and Daddy are flying in tomorrow. Tricia and Casey next weekend. I will be ready. Maybe this week they will come—the lungs, that is.

Day 73
Monday, May 4, 1992

After Coby's early medicine, while he was still asleep, I went to run. It was a very nice, clear blue morning. When I returned from running, I did some stretches and showered. Coby got up at 9:15 a.m. I did the usual medical treatments, fed him, and then he showered.

Paula from Biomed called and said she would be out around four o'clock. After the eleven o'clock drugs, I took the needle out. It had been in for eight days. It was getting irritated from the powerful drugs.

We then went to UNC to get his blood drawn then go to school and PT. After leaving him at PT, I left to pick up Jeannie, Mom, and Daddy from the airport. They had a good flight and were excited about being here and seeing us.

We loaded up their bags and started back to Chapel Hill. They made the usual comments of how nice the trees and flowers were, which is very correct. We arrived at the hospital, but there was no place to park, so I took them in the back way and went back outside to keep an eye (which is all I have) on the van.

I then decided to take their bags out to Carrboro. Then we'd have it all taken care of by the time everyone got to the apartment. Jeannie went with me.

When we got back to the hospital, Coby was finishing up on the cycle. We all loaded up and went to Ramsgate. The nurse called and was going to be later than she had hoped. Mother checked out the apartment and thought it was nice.

That's good because I did not want to move.

The nurse finally came and restarted Coby's IV without problems. We ordered pizza, ate, and then went to the campus for a walk. It was getting cooler, but it felt nice. Everyone but Coby and I went to bed. Jeannie on a pallet on the floor by Mother and Daddy's bed. I did my usual nightly nursing procedures and went to bed.

Tomorrow no school, but we have to go to clinic at 2:30 p.m.

Tricia called and had broken up a fight. A normal Wylie Middle School day.

Day 74
Tuesday, May 5, 1992

Got up and ran, did Coby's stuff, and then took him to clinic. Afterward Grandma, Poppie, Jeannie, Coby, and I went to Elmo's at Carr Mill Mall and ate. Not bad. We rode around a while and then went home. Coby told me when he went to bed that when he got his lungs, he was going to run, just to see what it felt like.

I hope he can run soon.

I feel he is going downhill steadily.

Tricia called and said everything is about the same.

Day 75
Wednesday, May 6, 1992

The weather is still cool. Stan the Man called. He and Ron delivered the oxygen while Jeannie, Coby, and I went to the hospital. Grandma and Poppie let them in, and they had a good visit. After PT, we came back, picked up Grandma and Poppie, and took them to the hospital lobby to show them Coby's picture. We then went to Durham and ate at Darryl's. It was very good. I had the cajun shrimp.

We went back to Ramsgate after getting a honey-baked ham and settled in for the night. It was still pretty cool.

Jeannie and Mom did the laundry. I will be taking Jeannie to the airport in the morning. We will miss her. Maybe the next time she comes, it will be to see Coby with his new lungs.

Tricia called. I cannot wait to see her and Casey on Friday. I told her I wouldn't mind moving here permanently. She said it was okay with her. That's what I like about her, mobile.

I need to start looking at the playbook, but it does not seem to be that big of a deal right now.

Day 76
Thursday, May 7, 1992

Very cold and rainy morning, but we got Jeannie to the airport on time. We came back and started Coby's tobramycin and then went back to bed.

Got up and got Coby ready for school and PT. Drove up and got a parking spot, luckily, of course. Mom, Dad, and I walked around while Coby was in school. They were overwhelmed, like everyone else, about the size of the hospital.

Then PT. Jo Beth, the girl from Louisiana, was off today. She is really sick with only one lung. Her mom and dad have really been through a lot. After PT, we went to the university mall and got caps for Wayne and the boys. Daddy got a Carolina cap, looks good.

Came back home after stopping at the store. Doug and Kelly are coming over tonight, and Coby is looking forward to seeing them.

Tricia called, and they are ready to see us. I am ready to see them as well.

Doug helped Coby with his math, which I really do appreciate. Coby wrapped Tricia's gift with a newspaper, and it turned out nice. I hope the weather starts getting better, but I really hope Coby gets some new lungs fast.

Day 77
Friday, May 8, 1992

Casey called this morning and said she cannot wait to see us tonight. We are ready too. Coby slept well, got up. Treatment, ate, medicine, shower, school, and PT. The weather is about twenty degrees warmer, it seems. Should be a good weekend.

I picked up Tricia and Casey about nine at the airport, and it was very good to see them. Coby was very excited when we entered the apartment.

Day 78 and 79
Saturday and Sunday, May 9 and 10

This weekend went too fast. I knew it was going to be swift, but it was just too quick. We stayed around the apartment and just enjoyed being together. On Saturday we went to Farrington Farms. It was nice. We saw two new sheep and a new calf.

Everyone seemed to enjoy going.

Casey and I played basketball Sunday at the park. It was a beautiful Mother's Day.

After taking Tricia and Casey back to the airport, we took the scenic route back to Carrboro. We went around Jordan Lake, and it was really nice. I thought it would take some of the loneliness out of the airport trip.

Day 80
Monday, May 11, 1992

It was a beautiful morning. When I started loading the van up with Coby's school stuff, Kaaren was already sunbathing in the yard.

Daddy and Mother went to school with Coby, during which time we took a walk around the football stadium. There were men disassembling the graduation stage from the day before. David Brinkley spoke to four thousand graduating seniors. One was his daughter, the paper read.

When we got to the PT department, I found out that Susan Nutt had passed away last night. She was the girl from San Antonio who had graduated from UT. She was close to twenty-eight years old. Her mother had said she was a very bad risk from the start, but they had to try.

I really did feel for this family, but I told Coby that we must go on.

"There will be failures and successes. They will learn from Susan," I told him. "She will not die in vain."

May God be with Susan's family.

After Coby did his six-minute walk, he went thirty minutes on the treadmill. He seems to be doing fine, but I am not letting my guard down. When we returned to Ramsgate, I went for a run while Mother and Daddy stayed with Coby.

I ran into Michelle at the office. She was doing great. She had her new lungs put in about six weeks ago. She could talk without running out of breath. It was good to see her after hearing the news of Susan's death.

God is working to keep me up. He knows when I need a lift. Around seven o'clock, we all took a stroll. It was very nice and enjoyable. Maybe tonight will be the night.

Tricia called. Things are fine.

Day 81
Tuesday, May 12, 1992

No school or PT today, so we are going to Duke to show Grandma and Poppie the campus. We took them to the Dean Smith Center yesterday. They seemed to like it.

Grandma fixed Coby some blueberry muffins after his treatment, and then we went to an Army Navy store. Coby loves those stores.

We then headed for Duke. We parked inside the gates of the football stadium, walked into the Cameron Center, and looked inside to see where the Dookies play basketball. It was neat to see Coby excited about being there.

Grandma and Poppie enjoyed seeing the landscaping around the campus.

We spoke with a couple of boys who were graduating this Sunday. One was going to teach English in France. The other one, who was a manager for the basketball team, was going to medical school at UNC. We then went back to Ramsgate and ate.

Grandma and Poppie were going to leave in the morning on the six o'clock flight, so they were getting their things ready. It was nice that they could be here, and we will miss them when they leave.

Day 82
Wednesday, May 13, 1992

I got up to get ready to take Mother and Daddy to the airport. Daddy said he heard thunder. It figured because the last two times I took someone to the airport at this time of day, it would always be storming. We got to the van, and it was pouring down hard, so it made it more sporting. There was no traffic at all on the way to the airport, so we arrived at 5:30 a.m. I let them out and then parked the van.

Mother was at the ticket counter, and the same two women were working the desk just like the other two times I had been here. They got their boarding passes, and we headed to Gate C8. I waited until about twenty minutes before they were scheduled to take off and then went back to do Coby's medicine.

It rained most of the way back to Carrboro. When Coby got up, we went through the usual routine. Coby was whistling and singing all the way to UNC Hospitals. He went to get his blood drawn and then to school. Coby decided during PT that he wanted to go to Northgate Mall in Durham, so after I worked out, we did. We ran into DeAnne Thompson, her husband, and her daughter. Coby bought, with his own money, a Durham Bulls cap and ball. We are going with the support group next week to the game. He also bought a small Buck pocket knife. He wanted yellow, but black was fine. We then headed back to Ramsgate. I had taken his medicine with us so I could start it at the mall. When we got into the city limits of Chapel Hill, the beeper went off. We could not believe it.

We were ready, but not both of us at the same time.

I just drove straight to the ER since we were already close. Coby said, "Well, if I knew this, I wouldn't have eaten at the mall." He looked pretty intense.

It was a strange feeling, one of uncertainty.

I told him that if this was for real, Mom and Casey could get on the last flight for tonight, and that seemed to help. I pulled into the ER parking lot and went inside. Coby waited in the van. I got to a phone and called Ellen, the coordinator. It was a false alarm.

It happens.

I went back to the van and then to Ramsgate. We were somewhat relieved, but also disappointed. It will be wild, though, when the time comes.

I went to wash, and I was thinking I could call Doug and Kelly if the call came while our clothes were in the washer. They could come get them and put them in H-103. I would give them the extra key. Tricia called. Coby talked with her, and she said she didn't have to stay for jury duty, so she worked in the yard. She is a player. We then watched a little TV and went to bed.

Day 83
Thursday, May 14, 1992

After doing Coby's medicine, I went to run. I would rather run in the morning anyway. I thought, how nice it is going to be when Casey and Tricia get here in a couple weeks. I got back to H-103, and Coby was still asleep.

Michelle, the Biomed care nurse, called and would be out this afternoon to change his IV dressing. I woke Coby up to get him ready for school and PT. He seemed to be in a great mood. He is probably physically fit for the transplant. I really do not know about mentally.

That goes for both of us.

Coby is going to do a research project for school that will keep us busy for sure. After PT, we stopped at the grocery store and bought some things for tonight. Doug and Kelly were coming over to watch *The Simpsons* and help us finish the honey-baked ham.

Coby and I read some Vincent Peale when we got home from the store. Doug and Kelly did come over, and we had a good time watching TV and talking. Before Doug and Kelly came by, Shannon Burleson, our apartment manager, stopped by. She had never met Coby. She told me later in the hallway that he was so cute and a neat kid to talk with. She said to have him come to the office and visit.

Looks like he hooked another one.

After Doug and Kelly went home, we watched *Arsenio* because Oprah was going to be on his show. Then we went to bed.

It was a good night.

Tricia, Trisha, Molly, Grandma, and Poppie called.

Day 84
Friday, May 15, 1992

Went running again after doing Coby's medicine. Feels good just to be alive. I know Coby's new lungs will give him the same feel. He told me he was going to run just to see how it feels!

I returned to H-103. I started Coby's breathing treatment and took a shower. After getting cleaned up, I clapped on him. I then gave him his pills and mixed up some blueberry muffins.

He showered, and then we went to school.

We were in the elevator when a woman asked me if I was from Texas. I was wearing the "Somebody in Texas Loves Me" T-shirt. She was from Dallas, and her boy was on the sixth floor. Her boy got sick with a bowel obstruction. I learned all that going five floors in the elevator.

After Coby's school, he went thirty minutes on the treadmill and thirty minutes on the bike. Connie said they would increase his resistance on the bike.

He is doing great, Connie said.

Afterward he threw up tons of mucus. We then came home, and Michelle was here, waiting to change Coby's dressing. Then Doug and Kelly came over for pizza and to go to the Tar Heel baseball game. It rained, so we watched *Silverado* on video instead.

Tricia called, and then after Doug and Kelly went home, we watched *Carson* and went to bed.

Not a bad day.

Day 85
Saturday, May 16, 1992

After doing Coby's medicine, I went back to bed. I slept until 10:00 a.m. I must have needed it. I never sleep that late. We got up, and I did Coby's medicine and mixed blueberry muffins. We sat out in the sun awhile and then watched *Superman II*. Doug called and wanted to know if we wanted to eat some chicken he was cooking outside. We did, and then we went to a UNC baseball game. The baseball team came back and won big in the tenth inning against Cal Northridge. Coby had a good time.

When we got home, Tricia called and said it rained there most of the day. We watched the last *SNL* of the season. Woody hosted the show, and we then went to bed.

Day 86
Sunday, May 17, 1992

Did the normal medical routine stuff. Coby wanted to go see *Lethal Weapon 3*, so we did. After the movie, we went to Whim's, and I bought some running shorts. We then came home and went for a walk. Coby and I threw his boomerang at the elementary school. He enjoys afternoon strolls. We always stop at the mini-mart and get some kind of drink. Usually Hawaiian punch for Coby.

Came home, six o'clock meds, then dinner.

Mother and Wayne called and said it was raining a lot. We finished watching the Bulls defeat the Knicks. Jordan had 42 points. Bulls, 110; Knicks, 81. Coby is excited because there is a two-hour *Unsolved Mysteries* special. He has had a good day. He cut out all the coupons we use. Just thirteen days 'til Tricia and Casey. I am ready. Did the laundry, then Coby's treatment.

Day 87
Monday, May 18, 1992

Got up after Coby's a.m. medicine and went to run while he was still sleeping. Looked like a good day in the making, weatherwise. When I returned, Coby was still sleeping very peacefully. Sometimes it is as if there is nothing wrong with him. Then he moves around and stirs up the mucus. He coughs so hard the veins in his neck stick out, and his face becomes red, and then he throws up.

I hate CF, but I love Coby.

I went ahead and shaved my two-day-old beard then showered. I ate some pineapples and strawberries and then wrote *20/20* about donor awareness. Coby woke up, had his treatment, then his pills. He didn't feel like eating due to all the liquid he takes while taking his medicine, so I tube-fed some Pulmocare. He wants to eat at Spring Garden after PT. He should be pretty hungry then.

June, the Biomed nurse, called about supplies. Coby visited with her awhile. We then watched some *Geraldo* and then went to school. I went to my writing spot on the seventh floor, in the waiting room. There was a young black woman crying as she was telling the chaplain something. I decided to go to the fifth-floor waiting room where I was all alone. After school, Coby had another great day at PT. He is really working hard.

We ate at Spring Garden afterward. Shelly was our waitress again. She remembered Coby and that he was waiting for lungs. Coby really likes going there. The food is good. We then drove to the park and played with his boomerang. It was still, not much wind. It felt like it might rain to me.

We went home and sat outside our living-room window. I read the story he had to read for school. Kaaren stopped by, and we visited about all sorts of things, movies, etc. Coby was doing impressions. Kaaren was laughing at everything he did. After a while, the weather got cool, and it began to rain. We went inside and started his medicine. I vacuumed and went to Bob's down the hall and told him about the Memorial Day get-together the ladies were planning for next week. "Bring your own food to the clubhouse," I told him.

I came back. Coby watched *Cheers* and then showered after his IV finished. He ate, then we finished reading his assigned story.

Tricia called. Another day closer.

Brenna finished second and third at State.

I did Coby's treatment and pills, and off to bed he went.

I was clapping on him and thought, *It is very hard to believe we are here. But even harder to believe he has a disease. He is so much fun.*

Oh, Tray called him earlier. Coby is feeling so much better it is scary. He is even doing stretches on his own. He is reading on his own. I just know the lungs are going to work out.

Day 88
Tuesday, May 19, 1992

After doing Coby's medicine, I went back to bed because it was raining. I was lying in bed because we did not have school today. The phone rang. It was Sam Terry checking in on how things were going. While I was talking to Sam, Coby got up. After we hung up, I started Coby's treatments.

When we finished with all his medicine, we got ready and went to the library to work on his report about sheep. I told him to look forward to going, and let's make it fun. We had a good time looking up the information. He worked hard.

I made copies of the *Britannica* and magazine articles, and we headed home.

We stopped and had lunch at the Pizza Hut buffet. I got some Ben & Jerry's Ice Cream (cookie dough), and then we went back to H-103 and did the notecards for his report. All he has to do now is interview the Ramses keeper, and he will be finished. We finished the cards at 5:15 p.m., and I went to run before *Cheers* came on. I came back, showered, and watched *Cheers*.

The gymnast man called back about Casey, so we have a date for that: June 5.

Coby then watched *Trading Places*, then treatment, then bed.

Tricia called. Just eleven more days, and she and Casey will be here.

Katy did good on her operation.

Ken stopped by and put freon in the Cougar for Tricia. I will miss him a lot next year during football season.

I received my Gordon Wood book today. The first thing it says about being successful is having a good mental attitude. It made for good reading.

It is a day closer to the lungs. I know God is with us.

Jeannie and Mother called, everything the same, rain.

Day 89
Wednesday, May 20, 1992

I fell asleep around 2:30 a.m. EST. I wrote some, but mainly I just could not fall asleep. Stan the Man called around 9:30 a.m. He will be making an O_2 run about 1:30 p.m. The office will let him in. He is also going to leave another portable oxygen tank for tonight's Durham Bulls game.

Coby got up. Same routine. He started coughing, so I looked around for a spit-up pan. I find myself looking around to make sure one is always near, either here at home or when we are out and about. We left for school. As we were singing "Two of a Kind," I just looked around at the tree-lined road and hillsides. It is still hard to believe we are even here.

Of course, it is still hard to believe Coby has cystic fibrosis.

He went on to school. I waited at the seventh-floor waiting room. Pat, the chaplain, stopped by, asking how things were going. "Fine," I always say. After school, PT. Not bad on the treadmill, but the cycle was not too good. Coby's legs were sore from stretching, I think. Anyway, we made it through another PT day.

Coby then went to the lab and got stuck. I had gone earlier and dropped off some scripts at the pharmacy. I will pick them up on Friday, so we are now free to go. Coby wanted a baseball bat and ball so I could pitch to him at the park. We went to the university mall, and it was raining when we got out, so we just went back to Ramsgate.

I talked with Kelly. She thought she would not go, so Coby and I would just meet the others at the stadium. I called to make sure they were playing, and they were.

I called Jo Ann and Jo Beth Nelson to let them know the game was still on.

We decided to ride together because Ray was going to ride with them. They went with us. Coby got dressed, wearing his Durham Bulls cap he had bought, we picked up the Nelsons, and off we went. The sky was beginning to clear up, and it was nice to not worry about the rain. Only the smokers now.

The stadium was easy to get to, downtown Durham. I was looking for Susan Sarandon but could not find her. I let Jo Beth and Jo Anna out at the front and then went to park.

I parked on the street behind the left-field scoreboard. The stadium was neat to look at. It was the color of the Denver Broncos, orange and blue. It holds five thousand fans. The outfield wall was nothing but advertisements for Bull Durham cigarettes to AC repair. They were all colorful.

The big bull on the right field fence was fun to see. His eyes lit up, and he blew smoke out of his nostrils. He bellowed like a charging bull. There was food, beer, souvenir stands everywhere, and Coby loved it all. We sat just behind the Bulls bullpen, so we could see the girls in heat at the fence.

There were Susan Sarandons all over the place.

These guys will put their phone numbers on a baseball and give it to the gals. They were mainly a group of college kids, all with a beer in hand. They would not have known if the teams even made it on the baseball field or not.

It was a pretty good education for Coby, and he really got a kick out of it all.

The Bull mascot came in the stands, talked to Coby, and autographed Coby's program (signing it "The Bull"), and then Coby pulled his tail. Everyone got a kick out of the bull cutting up with us. It is a fun atmosphere, just too much boozing for me.

There was hardly any smoking, I could not believe it. The game went to the top of the tenth, 0–0, but it was time to get Coby home for his medicine. We loaded up and went back to Ramsgate. We saw that Salem won 1–0 as we watched the sports while doing Coby's treatment. He wants to go back. We will when Casey and Tricia get here. It is pretty interesting.

We went to bed.

Ken Ard called. It was nice hearing from him. I will really miss coaching with him. Maybe we will coach together again at some other place.

Day 90
Thursday, May 21, 1992

Coby got up in a good mood and had his normal routine of medicine and breakfast. We went to school and PT. Afterward we went to the ballpark, and I pitched to him in the batting cage. It was sunny with a nice, gentle breeze. The temperature was around seventy-eight to eighty degrees.

We both took our shirts off. It was a lot of fun seeing him hit the ball. He tried so hard to go long, but about twenty minutes with rest in between is about as far as he can go.

We then went to the basketball courts. We had them all to ourselves. He watched as I shot around at each goal. We then went home and sat out in the sun with Kaaren and a friend of hers. Coby really enjoys talking with her. She tells us about the Northeast. We tell her about Texas.

We both got pretty red. I then went and bought a BBQ grill made in New Braunfels, came back, and cooked burgers. Coby enjoyed his burger, he said. Keenan called, Tricia called, and Molly called. I called Trey Wallace and Jon Peters. Peters said I will love working with Coach Brooks. I have the receivers. I have always loved catching the ball, so it should be fun.

I guess we got too much sun. Coby fell asleep earlier than usual and then woke up vomiting. That is usual for him. A lot of mucus.

I could not go to sleep, so after Johnny Carson, I read some of Coach Gordon Wood's book and went to bed, prayed, and fell asleep.

Day 91
Friday, May 22, 1992

Got up after Coby's meds, ran, and then washed our clothes. Coby did not have school today due to teachers' meetings, so we only had to go for PT. Not too bad a day there. We then went to the batting cage at the park. I cooked outside when we got home, made some kabobs.

Coby really liked them a lot. Got a video, *Adventures in Babysitting*. He wanted to watch it again. We then watched *20/20*. Mainly, Coby was staying awake for Johnny Carson's last show.

Kami called. Tricia called.

Johnny Carson came on and put on a pretty good show. I have been watching him since I was twelve. It does not seem like thirty years. Coby and I fell asleep on the couch during the Letterman show. I got him up about two and put him to bed. I then fell asleep after setting the alarm for five to set the meds out. Then for six, then for seven.

Day 92
Saturday, May 23, 1992

We just stayed around the apartment. I fixed more kabobs on the grill outside for Coby.

Tricia called. Just one week away.

Casey slept most of the day. She was at an all-night gymnastics party.

In the late evening, Coby and I went walking to the pool. He put his feet in the water. "Felt good," he said later. We went back, watched *SNL*, and then went to bed.

Day 93
Sunday, May 24, 1992

Slept 'til ten after doing Coby's medicine. Ran, then lifted at the clubhouse. I mixed some muffins up, and the nurse came by and stayed about an hour, changing Coby's dressing.

We then went to Harris Teeter (grocery store). Coby had cut some coupons out, so we used them accordingly.

Day 94
Monday, May 25, 1992

We slept late.

John Elzner called.

We went to the clubhouse with other CFers awaiting transplants. I then fixed turkey fajitas and met with Susan Nutt's family. Jo Ann Campbell told me later in the day that Susan worked so hard on the treadmill she fractured some ribs.

These CF guys are tough.

I have a lot of respect for their fight and the courage they display.

I am so proud of Coby. He visited with everyone and was very nice.

Doug and Kelly came over and talked about their camping trip. They had a very good time. We stayed up and watched Jay Leno's first show.

It is different.

Day 95
Tuesday, May 26, 1992

Clinic today.

It is raining and unusually cool here for this time of year, or so I have been told.

Coby had a good clinic visit. It would be nice if the lungs would come in now. Physically he is in good shape. After clinic, we came back to the apartment and ate. I later went to get a haircut, went for a run, and then cleaned up.

Coby rearranged the closet for Casey's stuff.

He finished his math, we got ready, and then we went to the Campbells from New Jersey's apartment. We had spaghetti, and it was good. We had a nice visit. The Campbells' (Jo Ann and Gordon) son has been waiting here since November.

Gordon is a teacher, and Jo Ann is a respiratory therapist. They have two more sons, one who also has CF and an adopted child. Gordon flew helicopters in Viet Nam. They were living in Mineral Wells when their oldest son was born. Dr. Kramer treated him in Dallas. They both said they should have never left Texas.

After leaving the Campbells, we returned home so Coby could watch a movie he wanted to see.

Tricia called. It was raining. Sounds like she has everything secure to leave for North Carolina on Saturday. I am not surprised. I am lucky to have someone like Tricia who can handle things. Again, she is a player.

Esther called. Not much longer 'til school is out.

Day 96
Wednesday, May 27, 1992

After Coby's medicine, the Biomed nurse called, and then Ray from the oxygen company. I just went ahead and got ready for school.

Coby had a better day on the bike today in PT. We then went to Harris Teeter and bought him some more kabobs. I fixed them for him this afternoon.

As the fire was getting ready, I ran. After eating, I washed clothes. Tricia and Molly both called and said it was raining. Coby talked to Tricia for a long time. I know he would like to be at school tomorrow for the last day, but he seems to be adjusting fine.

It is really nothing new for him.

Anyway, he is now an eighth-grader. I just know, after the lung transplant, he may never miss another last day of school again. I know it will be soon. I pray everything will be fine for Coby. He is such a neat kid, even though he is mine.

After Coby went to bed, I watched the finish of the Bulls game. They demolished Cleveland. I then watched the Texas Rangers in extra innings over the White Sox. I checked on Coby before brushing my teeth, and he was sleeping sound with the radio playing.

Day 97
Thursday, May 27, 1992

Michelle got here at 6:45 a.m. I had been up since 5:00 a.m., when I set Coby's meds out to bring them to room temperature. Michelle was here to draw blood before the tobramycin was infused, then after the infusion, to get a urine sample from Coby. She left around nine o'clock, and we visited while waiting. Michelle had also brought Coby a sausage biscuit from the Big Mac's. She is very nice.

Coby couldn't go back to sleep after the last blood stick, so I went ahead and did his treatment. It looks like winter outside, but it actually feels nice.

We got ready after Coby's treatment. He coughed a lot and threw up his breakfast.

Nothing new.

We had school, then PT. We went out to eat for the first time since last week. We ate at Spring Garden, came home, and read some Texas history. Doug called and talked with Coby. He and Kelly might come by later tonight.

I told Coby when it was 3:30 p.m. he was now an eighth-grader. It was very hard to believe. I could still see him going into the Hartman Elementary School. The building is now gone, but I can still visualize seeing him.

What a great memory.

Casey is now going to Wylie Middle School… That's scary.

Day 98
Friday, May 29, 1992

Woke up to a dreary, rainy day. Mrs. Taylor called and moved Coby's schooltime to eleven. We read history from twelve to one and then went to PT. We then came home, ate, and cleaned the apartment. *20/20* was on TV, along with Ross Perot and the Bulls game. Coby went to bed and started coughing. He threw up everything.

It is very hard for him to gain weight.

Tricia and Casey are just twelve hours away.

Elbert Gowans called. I am hoping for the lungs this week.

I couldn't fall asleep after Coby went to bed. I tried reading, listening to headphones, and finally, about 3:30 a.m., I fell asleep. I do not know why it took so long.

Day 99
Saturday, May 30, 1992

I got up and did Coby's meds at five and six. I was pretty alert, considering I didn't sleep much. I got Coby up at 10:30 a.m., did his treatment, and then we left for the airport to pick up Tricia and Casey.

When we arrived, it was raining, so I parked underneath, just outside the baggage pickup door. When we got inside the terminal, I looked at the TV showing the arrivals. The two had just landed.

We hurried to the elevator, made it past the metal detector quickly, and headed to Gate 15. Sure enough, the plane had just taxied up to the walk tunnel. Coby and I were not there one minute when they walked out of the tunnel.

We were all pretty happy to see each other. We got the celebrated hugging out of the way and headed to the baggage claim. After loading everything in the van, we started for Carrboro in the rain. We spent the rest of the afternoon putting away Tricia and Casey's stuff and then went to Durham to eat at Darryl's.

We then came home and watched the College World Series. Texas pounded Oklahoma. Tricia and Casey went to bed pretty early.

Well, Casey went to bed, and Tricia fell out on the couch. Overall, it was nice being together again.

Day 100
Sunday, May 31, 1992

After doing Coby's medicine, I went back to sleep until about ten or so. Tricia fixed blueberry muffins. She and I later went walking; running starts tomorrow. We then came back and went to Harris Teeter. Lunch at home and then to the show to see *Sister Act* with Whoopi Goldberg. It was a lot of fun.

It was then time for Coby's medicine. We went home, hooked him up, and then went walking toward the elementary. Coby likes that a lot.

While out, we went to the Carrboro mini-mart. When we returned to the apartment, it began to get cool but felt nice. Tricia and Coby started the Dallas puzzle. Casey and I went and played tennis. She is beginning to get stronger with her strokes. We played with the lights on for a while and then headed back to H-103.

It is nice knowing they are not having to leave in the next day or so.

Back at H-103, Casey read some Dr. Peale aloud while Tricia and Coby worked the puzzle. It is nice not having the TV on. We are winding down now with Coby's treatment and Casey playing *Super Mario*.

I like shooting the ducks on *Duck Hunt* (Nintendo).

It has been an interesting one hundred days.

I hope the next few days will bring some new lungs for Coby.

Day 101
Monday, June 1, 1992

The start of another month in North Carolina started with a beautiful, sunny, non-sweaty day. Tricia went to run, and I waited in case the supply nurse called. When she returned, I ran.

We all then went to school and PT. While Coby was in school, Casey, Tricia, and I walked over to the Athletic Field House, hoping to see Coach Hemphill, but he wasn't in.

We returned to Coby at PT. Casey got her a Bomb Pop.

Coby had a good workout and even went twenty minutes on the bike. We returned home, and I made the kabobs Coby enjoys so much. Tricia washed while the food was being prepared.

After eating, Casey and I went to the park to play basketball then returned to the apartment to play tennis. Doug and Kelly came over and played Taboo which was a lot of fun.

Coby seems to be coughing a lot, but lime green mucus is coming up. Usually not a bad sign, and his appetite is good. After his 5:00 p.m. pill, he threw up quite a bit.

I know the lungs will be here soon.

Day 102
Tuesday, June 2, 1992

No school. No PT. Good thing. Coby did not have too good of a night. He was up coughing and throwing up a lot. I got up, wrote the show *60 Minutes*, and then we all just took it easy until we decided to go and eat at Spring Garden. We arrived at two o'clock, and Shelly was working. It was good that she could meet the rest of the clan.

It was then time to go and meet Ramses, the mascot of UNC. He was going to be sheared. We met Mrs. Taylor at the YMCA and then followed her and her twin daughters to the Hogan Farm Lake.

It was a classic old farm with grain silos, old barns, and about a hundred dairy cows. It was time for the afternoon milking, so we got to see the process of the cows one by one walking to the automatic milking stalls and then exiting once the milking was completed. Twelve cows were milked at once, twice a day.

Mr. and Mrs. Hogan were great hosts. Mrs. Hogan had brought a card table with chips, cokes, and sprites with ice. We were under a great shade tree enjoying a slight breeze.

I felt at any time Ernest T. Bass would show up, chunking rocks!

Mr. Hogan was very nice, answering questions Coby had prepared beforehand. Tricia had suggested bringing Coby's tape recorder to record the questioning and answering about Ramses, the UNC mascot.

Coby did very well. He told me later it was easier than he thought it would be. Mr. Hogan was a nice first interview. The farm had been going since 1930, and the Hogans have had all the Ramses. This was number fifteen.

The shearer showed up after the interview. It was nice watching the process.

Coby and Casey got to pet Ramses before and after the shearing. His horns still had blue paint from the fall. Mr. Hogan told Coby if he happened to be here during the football season, he could go to a game with Ramsey. Coby thought that would be fun.

I thought maybe a checkup could be scheduled around a game so Casey and Tricia could also go.

It was time to go to give Coby his medicine, so we left for H-103.

Tricia and I took a walk then went to the store. Nurse Casey stayed with brother Cobo. It is really nice having them here. It would be even better if we could get some lungs soon.

God knows the right time.

Til tomorrow. Day one-oh-two was fun.

Day 103
Wednesday, June 3, 1992

Tricia and I got up and ran after doing Coby's medicine. We got back and did the usual treatments on Coby. Casey and I went to play tennis. She is improving.

We had to leave earlier today because Coby had to have his blood drawn for an electrolyte reading. He then went to school and PT. We stopped at a music store in Carrboro to check on a piano or keyboard to rent for Casey. A man was wearing an Ernest Tubb T-shirt and told us to check at another place, as he does not rent out.

We went home and snacked. Casey and I played more tennis and went swimming.

The support group was getting ready tonight for pizza, so we got ready and went to the clubhouse. It was a lot of fun, especially seeing Michelle and Karen doing so well post-op. We all visited. It seemed that we had all known each other longer than 103 days.

I guess because we all have lived similar lives, battling CF.

The meeting disbanded around nine o'clock. Tricia and the kids fooled with the puzzle, and I watched Jordan dismantle the Trail Blazers, to take 1–0 for the series.

We all then went to bed.

Day 104
Thursday, June 4, 1992

Woke up to a rainy Carolina day. Coby went to school and PT as usual. Afterward it was back home to wait on the home care nurse. She arrived and changed Coby's dressings. We ate at home and then went to the university mall to get Coby some shorts.

Coby bought Casey a tennis racket so she wouldn't use his.

We then went home and watched the UT Horns lose their attempt to stay in the college world series, and then off to bed.

Day 105
Friday, June 5, 1992

Tricia and I got up and ran. When we got back, Tricia and Casey went swimming. Coby slept 'til eleven o'clock. He had a good night's rest.

Then off to PT; no school today.

Coby went twenty minutes on the bike. We then went home and ate.

Today is the day Casey goes to gymnastics. It will be a good change for her. I hope she likes the class.

Well, Casey went to gym. Of course, it was different, but maybe it will do. They are not as disciplined here. I told her she would just have to adapt. Players do.

She will go on Monday, Wednesday, and Friday from six to eight thirty.

Day 106 and 107
Saturday and Sunday, June 6 and 7, 1992

This weekend we went to Farrington farms, farmer's market at Carrboro to eat, sunbathed with Kaaren, swam, played tennis with Casey (she is improving), ran, and walked. It is getting hotter. It is hard to believe we are all here just waiting for lungs.

Tricia talked a good while to Michelle about her transplant. It is amazing how she does not have to struggle to breathe in between words while talking. Coby sees the results of Michelle and Karen, and that makes him ready.

I just hope he doesn't have to struggle much more.

The coughing, vomiting, struggling to breathe…it will be nice for him not having these daily normalities for a CF patient.

Casey and Coby are having fun, playing a Nintendo game. It is nice seeing them together and enjoying each other. Tricia told me she asked Coby if he and she could make it up here without Casey and Daddy. His answer was, "We won't have to."

That is what I like about Coby. He has a good attitude.

Tricia is sleeping on the floor next to me on Ron's mattress. The bed hurts her back. It is nice having her and Casey here.

Day 108
Monday, June 8, 1992

Tricia and I ran, swam, got the kids ready, and then we were off to school and PT. Coby has the six-minute walk today. He did very well, his teacher said, on his presentation about Ramses. He then went to PT and did well on his walk.

We came home. I cooked outside and took Casey to gym. Tricia did waternastics / water aerobics with Jo Anna and Helen. Then the rain came, and it poured all night.

Esther called and said Debbie interviewed for the Newman Smith job. She is a good one.

I read about Ken Ard's leaving in the Wylie paper. I will miss him. My prayers go with him and his family. I am beginning to get ready for football. I am ready to work with Coach Brooks and the partially new staff.

Day 109
Tuesday, June 9, 1992

When I got up to do Coby's medicine, it was raining. I just went back to bed and didn't bother Tricia about running. The weatherman called for rain all day.

When we all got up, I did Coby's treatment. Tricia prepared corn for Coby. He is on a corn kick…wants it all the time. Tricia and I went to the movie store around noon and rented *JFK* and *The Fisher King*. We watched *JFK*, got pizza halfway through it, and then finished the movie.

This is what I heard in 1977 at a McDonald's in Denton. What a country.

Tricia talked with Tina Sorrells today. Everything is about the same back home.

Tricia and Casey went to the pool with Helen and Jo Anna.

Coby talked to me about going home and how he wishes whites and blacks could just get along.

As he was talking to me, I thought about what a neat kid he was and how lucky I was to have him as a son. He is one hell of a player. He and I both are ready to go home, but we both know we can't go without the lungs.

I hope it will be today.

Tricia finished another puzzle. She is back to cross-stitching.

The kids went to bed after *SNL* reruns on the comedy channel. Tricia watched The Fisher King, and I wrote a little. Man, that Fisher King is wild.

Day 110
Wednesday, June 10, 1992

I finally fell asleep around 3:30 a.m. Don't know why I couldn't sleep, don't matter. Today is Coby's last day of school for a while. That means just PT.

When Tricia and I came back from running, Ron, the O_2 man, called, "Delivery today." Shannon would let them in while we are gone.

Coby had school and then PT. I saw John Blanchard in the blood-collecting waiting room. He was with his wife, five-month-old son, Gabriel, and a friend. Gabriel was being sweat tested for CF. I visited with them a while and then went to PT.

Coby said a donor came in last night. The lungs were not good, but they used a heart.

It is getting closer; I can feel it.

Connie said Dr. Roop was coming in from Plano for a transplant. It will be fun when he gets here.

We then went to Ham's and ate, then to a camping store, and Ben & Jerry's. Back home, and Joe Stone called and said we are going to throw the ball a lot. Since I am a receiver coach now, I am glad for that.

I took Casey to gymnastics then called the Blanchards. The sweat test was negative. I was glad to hear that. Although I didn't say anything to them, some CF patients have a negative test. Strange disease.

I went and got Casey, and then we all watched *Father of the Bride* with Steve Martin. Everyone then went to sleep. I watched the Trail Blazers even the series at 2–2 and then looked over my offensive playbook. I am writing questions about terms I do not understand yet so it will be easier when I meet with Coach Brooks.

I went to bed at 3:30 a.m. Everyone was sleeping fine, it seemed. I listened to the headset awhile in bed, hoping the lung call would come in.

Day 111
Thursday, June 11, 1992

After doing Coby's seven o'clock meds, I fell back to sleep until 10:30 a.m. I got up, and Tricia and I went walking to the Carrboro park. There were school kids having picnics for the last day of school. It was cloudy but enjoyable.

On our way back, a lady stopped her Saab and asked us how to get to Durham. I told her. She had North Carolina plates and the accent to go with it. That is something. I feel like this is home. Strange feeling.

We went to PT and then home to eat. It is raining a little.

Tina called about Km. Tricia and Casey went swimming while I was lifting weights.

Standard night. No lungs yet. Tricia and I watched *Cape Fear*, good movie.

Day 112
Friday, June 12, 1992

Friday morning started out with a run, then PT, and Coby had a good workout. It is beginning to cloud up and rain. We just went to the apartment and hung out: reading, Nintendo, puzzles…just waiting for the lungs.

Day 113
Saturday, June 13, 1992

Our plans were to go and see *Wayne's World* and get Casey a keyboard, which we did. We ordered a pizza at Model T's. Doug and Kelly came over and did a puzzle and played Taboo. We all had a good time.

Tricia and I silently watched the moon from our bedroom window.

Day 114
Sunday, June 14, 1992

It was raining when I did Coby's medicine. I went back to bed, got up later, and did his treatment. Patsy Tallant called before she went to church. Tricia and I went walking to the university lake. When we returned, the kids played us some songs on the keyboard. We just hung out at the apartment and watched *Boyz n the Hood.* It is a well-done movie about street life in the hood. It just shows more shortcomings we have as a country.

Cooked burgers out and then watched Da Bulls come from behind and win their second straight NBA title. Jordan made MVP again. He is one heck of a competitor. Mr. Hogan called Coby and wants to visit with him. It is 11:30 p.m., and I am going to bed now.

Maybe lungs tomorrow.

Day 115
Monday, June 15, 1992

Typical morning treatments and workouts, getting ready for PT. We loaded up and headed toward UNC Hospitals.

Parking is a problem since the Pizza Hut trailer is taking up parking spots. The fast-food line inside the hospital is being worked on, so pizza is being sold in the parking lot next to PT. I have just been double parking and checking every so often to make sure I do not pick up a fifty-dollar ticket.

Coby worked pretty hard. We stopped by Ben & Jerry's Ice Cream on the way to H-103 and picked up some strawberry ice cream. Tricia fixed a meal, and then she and Coby started a puzzle. Casey went to gymnastics.

Trey Wallace called with some horrible news about Trace Sampson. He dove into a pool at Kara Ford's house and broke his neck. He had a six-hour surgery, and the results will not be known for about two weeks, when the swelling will be down. The surgeon feels good about the operation, Trey said. He has had some adversities the last few years. A BB in his eye, and now this.

His faith will be tested, along with that of his family, but I am sure they will come through.

God does not give people things that, I believe, they cannot handle. My prayers are with him and his family. It is starting to storm. Clinic tomorrow.

Day 116
Tuesday, June 16, 1992

I believe it rained all night. We all got up and got ready to take Coby to clinic. It would be Tricia and Casey's first Carolina clinic. Later Tricia would say, "Clinics are all the same." She has never gone to clinics much. I think there is still a slight stage of denial.

Me, I treat it like I am still in the hospital business.

We had to wait about an hour for Dr. Wood to see us. When he did, he was pleased. He reupped some scripts while deleting others. He also called someone about Coby's G-tube, about completing the button. It was scheduled for Thursday at 10:35 a.m., and a Dr. Lacey would look into the procedure.

After clinic, we ate at Model T's, came home, and it was beginning to storm again. We just stayed in.

Kelly came by and brought the kids' gifts from the Whitts, Doug's parents. Earrings for Casey and a Jordan cap for Coby. After she left, Tricia and I went walking and then to the store. I thought about Trace and his neck injury. I am going to write him soon.

Went to bed after Coby's treatment.

Maybe lungs tomorrow.

Day 117
Wednesday, June 17, 1992

I got up after Coby's morning medicine and went to the Chapel Hill Tire Company in Carrboro to have the van's tires rotated and balanced. The noise I have been hearing was diagnosed as a worn-out speedometer cable. No damage should be done to the van.

I then came home, washed some clothes, and Tricia was still groggy. She can't seem to get going. I really hope the lungs come in while I am still here so Tricia will not have to go through the process alone. I worry about when I am gone that Coby will get in one of his crying moods and want to go home, although he hasn't in a long while. I know she thinks she can handle it, but it is difficult from 1,200 miles away.

I know God has us on a schedule, so I should not be so concerned.

We got dressed and went to work out. There was a parking spot because Mike and Andy are off today. There is still a lot of activity around the Pizza Hut wagon, but I made it to the parking spot without wounding anyone.

Jo Beth, who is in the hospital, was back working out today. She looked a little tired but was doing all right, her mother said. That is who knows best anyway.

After the workout, we went to the mall and got Coby some batting gloves and then came home for a sandwich. Casey and Tricia went to the pool with a new friend we met and her mother.

Coby and I stayed in H-103. Later Tricia and I played tennis, and then I took Casey to gym.

I came back for the support-group meeting with Ellen and Will. They updated us on some procedures, reported that Karen went home, and Michelle is going home. They stayed two months after their surgeries.

Hopefully, ours will be soon.

After the meeting, Tricia and I went to get Casey. Picked up Coby a pizza and came home. Nick called and said the pool was yucky and that he may be here next week. Betty had called earlier and said the A/C motor in the house was out.

Just more hurdles.

It is nice to have Nick and Betty checking on things. I am not worried.

Coby did his usual throw his guts up, got a treatment, and then we all went to bed.

I couldn't sleep, so I put the radio on Larry King. Tricia went to the couch. Said it was better than on the bed or on the floor. PMS time.

My mind wondered about when the lungs would arrive and about Tricia being with Coby.

It seems I should stay, but I am afraid I will lose my job.

God knows what is going on, so things will work out.

Day 118
Thursday, June 18, 1992

Tricia and I got up and ran. I put the towels Coby upchucked on in the washer. Went back to H-103, showered, and then put the towels in the dryer. I put some gas in the van, went back for the towels, picked up Tricia and the kids, and then went to get Coby's button.

When we got to the hospital, I let them out front and then went to park the van. When I let them out, a yellowjacket got in the van. It was buzzing all around. I put the passenger-side window down, and it flew out. I was glad.

After parking the van, I went to the second floor on Gravely. I found them in the waiting room. We met the doctor, and he, along with his partner, decided to wait to fool with the button until after surgery. Sounds good to me.

Coby needs no complications right now.

We then went home and returned to the hospital for PT. Coby was tired but still wanted to go hit some baseballs at the park later. We stopped at Ben & Jerry's to reload our ice-cream supply and then went home to wait on the nurse to check Coby's IV. It has been in for six weeks.

Dr. Wood could not believe it.

Coby and Tricia are doing the puzzle. I am doing this, but Casey is running steps. We are still waiting on the nurse.

There was some kind of communication screwup. The nurse never came.

I got a laugh out of Casey who kept telling how many hours and minutes late the nurse was. We just stayed around H-103, and I took Casey swimming.

On our way back, we chased a cat away who was trying to get a young bird who had left the nest too soon. Casey chased the cat while I put the bird in a tree.

Casey said I was a hero. I said I just don't like bullies.

Regular routine with Coby and then off to bed.

Our saying lately is, "College town, anything goes!"

Day 119
Friday, June 19, 1992

Everything is about the same, except Coby has to be at work out at 12:30 p.m. We then went to Ham's to eat. Then Tricia and I played tennis. I just cannot seem to move like I used to because of my slipped disc. The quick movement and I do not mix anymore.

As we were playing, the sky darkened, and it started lightning. Casey came and said the nurse was here, so we headed back to H-103. It came one heck of a storm, hail, and the works. The hail stopped long enough so I could get Casey to gym. After she got back, we played basketball in the house. She and Coby were on a team against me.

It was fun with the tiny tikes.

I think of the fun we have, and I cannot wait until Coby gets some new lungs so he can really have a time without worrying about the O_2 tube. Of course, they won. 0–2 today. Just not my day in tennis or Little Tikes basketball.

Interesting, the nurse has a son at the University of Texas at Austin.

Day 120
Saturday, June 20, 1992

We got up early, for us. Tricia and I went to the farmer's market and bought some blackberries, which, we later found out, were bug-infested, but we took care of them. We stopped at Muffins and More and then back to H-103.

I did Coby's treatment, ate, and then loaded up and went to the Carrboro park to play baseball and basketball. It is fun seeing Coby excited about hitting the ball. Again, it is nice to all be together. We stayed about an hour, then went home and swimming, and then to the Northgate Mall in Durham.

The kids spent some of their money, and it was pretty busy, it being one day prior to Father's Day. On our way back, we stopped at the home of the Durham Bulls so Tricia and Casey could see where they play. There was a youth league going on, so we watched for a while. We then headed back home, and Tricia and I went to Harris Teeter to shop for groceries.

We came back to the apartment, and Kelly had called saying she had spaghetti. She and Doug came over with the grub, and we all ate and watched a Sissy Spacek movie. We put a puzzle together also, and it was a fun night…just laying back.

Day 121
Sunday, June 21, 1992

Woke up to a cool, stormy Father's Day. It was sixty-three degrees and actually felt pretty nice. I didn't go to sleep until around 3:00 a.m., not sure why, so I was a little sluggish. Since we couldn't go to the park, we decided to go and see the movie *Housesitter* with Steve Martin and Goldie Hawn at the new plaza. It was funny. We came back home, and I watched Tom Kite win the US Open in golf. It was good to see him win his first major after twenty-one years on the tour.

Tricia went to wash and took Casey swimming while Coby and I read the assigned Texas history reading. Afterward Tricia and I went for an hour walk in the cooler than usual night air. When we got back, I called Patsy Young in Alpine, Texas, to let her know what was going on with us. Doc was in Dallas. Coby and Casey played me again in basketball. Coby made the winning shot. He was exhausted.

He and Casey had me Dad's Day cards. I am a lucky guy to have both them and Tricia. Oh yeah, and of course, Katy, the dachshund, back home.

I have a strong feeling that this week the surgery will be done. I told Coby, and he hugged me. I told him that I am excited for him. He just kept holding me.

I just know it will be successful.

It is 11:45 p.m. Everyone is in bed. I am sitting on the couch, looking around the room. Posters cover the walls. It looks like we have lived here forever.

"We love you, Coby. Remember, we love you. Get well" are all some of the computer printouts his family and friends have sent. There is a Michael Jordan and Bugs Bunny poster, Coca-Cola in Japanese, UNC posters, a beach with palm trees, and of course, a *Wayne's World* poster. This room was so much of Coby's happy place as his mother and I have felt for years. I am not ready to lose him.

I know God will provide what Coby needs. I know I must wait the time with patience, which I will.

Day 122
Monday, June 22, 1992

After doing Coby's medicine, Tricia and I got up and made sure Casey had all her stuff ready to go for the day. She was invited by the Rousseauis' daughter, a girl Casey met in gym, to go horseback-riding and spend the day. After she left, Tricia and I went walking and then came back and got ready for Coby's school and PT workout.

After the workout, we stopped at Spring Garden, and then Tricia went to Talbot's, a women's clothing store at Carr Mill Mall. Annie Downs from PT was there, shopping. We then went to H-103 and laid out with Kaaren.

I helped Andy Campbell's dad, Gordon, move a piece of furniture from his truck into their apartment. I then went to run and lift. When I got back, Mazzon called. He got a job with Naaman Forest. He had talked with Spann, and he signed with Northwest. It was time to get Casey, so Tricia and I left while Coby was talking with Hollie Whitcomb from back home. When we returned, Whitey Jordan, a UNC football coach, called me and invited me to their high school football camp the next day. I accepted.

After I hung up the phone, Coby's IV of seven weeks was bothering him, so I removed it. He will get another one tomorrow. We all went to bed early.

I just know it will be soon.

Day 123
Tuesday, June 23, 1992

I got up and called the nursing service. They would be out around noon to start another IV. I then got ready and went to the football camp. I parked outside the practice field and waited for a break to talk to Coach Jordan. Break came, and I introduced myself to him. He acted like he had known me for years. He told me to wander around, ask questions, just whatever I wanted to do.

I watched different coaches and learned some different drills. It was also good to know I had been doing some of the same drills already. I really enjoyed watching Coach Jordan work with the boys. He was funny but firm.

I was watching the receiver's coach work when a man came up to me and introduced himself as Mack Brown. I knew, of course, he was the head coach. He visited with me for a long while, asking about Coby and my family. He then introduced me to Cappie Jordan, Coach's wife, who was extremely nice. I visited for another thirty minutes or so, talked with Coach Hemphill, the recruiting coordinator, and then went home.

They all want to meet Coby, so I am bringing him back to the six o'clock session to visit.

I went back to Carrboro and reported my schooling. The nurse had come and put Coby's new IV in. Everything was flowing just fine. Spann called and told me about his new job. He seemed pretty pleased. They just got a good coach, so did Naaman with Mazzon.

Casey, Coby, and I played some baseball outside the apartment in the yard. Tricia lay out in the sun awhile. We ate at home. At six, we went to the afternoon football session to watch the workout. We got there a little early and just looked around. One of the fields was being resurfaced with Astroturf. It looks like a highway surface, pretty hard. Players started showing up, and then the coaches. Coach Hemphill came over to visit, and Coach Jordan followed. I walked over to another drill. I looked back after a few minutes and saw Coach Brown visiting with all three.

I walked over, and we visited for another fifteen minutes or so. It was just like Coach Brown had nothing else to do but visit with us. All the coaches were very nice to us. Coach Tim Brewster, the tight end coach, came over and introduced himself. We stayed until it got pretty cool. Coby did not want to leave, but it was getting time for his medicine.

We went home, through the usual routine, and off to bed.

Maybe lungs tomorrow.

Day 124
Wednesday, June 24, 1992

Tricia and I got up, ran, and then washed. We went to school and PT. We went to eat at Model T's, but it had closed down. There went some good pizza.

Casey is beginning to be bored, but if we were at home, she would be. I was sitting on the couch, watching her play Nintendo, and began thinking who must have been in the apartment a year ago. Why, I do not know. I know this was the furthest thought in my mind a year ago. That we would be waiting on a new set of lungs for Coby.

I wrote another letter about donor awareness I am going to send to other shows, *Good Morning America*, etc. I was thinking if

I wanted to be a head coach or a college assistant, how CF has controlled so many decisions Tricia and I have made over the last few years. I also think of Casey's life being affected, but mainly how she and Coby have had to adjust.

I really admire Coby's courage in making the choice to have a double-lung transplant.

I don't know if I could do that.

I believe his courage will get me through anything, along with the faith I have in God.

I left a message today with Mr. Musgrave's secretary. The notion hit me that he may know someone in the media who could help us with awareness. I know he will return my call.

Nick called tonight, and he will be here tomorrow on business.

Casey had gym, so Tricia went with me to pick her up. Actually, Casey walks into the van by herself!

Anyway, when we arrived back at H-103 and opened the door, Mr. and Mrs. Bob Hogan, Ramses' keepers, were having a nice conversation with Coby. They stayed for a good while, and we all had a good time.

Mr. Hogan had brought some old paper clippings about UNC sports, his father's class of '51, etc. They also invited us out to fish. During the Hogan stay, Ron Shultz called to tell us about Nelda Spies passing away. That bothered me. She was my first secret pal at Wylie in 1981. Cancer ended her life here on earth. Her husband is left with two young kids.

Life is one hurdle after another, it seems.

Ron also mentioned his dad was diagnosed with lung cancer in the upper lobe. He is being treated with radiation. The Hogans left, and I then called Doug to tell him about Nick's visit. I did Coby's treatments and then went to bed.

Day 125
Thursday, June 25, 1992

I woke up, did Coby's medicine, and let Tricia sleep in. Casey was even sleeping later than usual. I started to get ready to go and work out when the phone rang.

It was A.C. Musgrave. I had had a feeling it was when the phone rang.

I caught him up on what was going on with Coby. I told him about how there was not much lung donor awareness. He understood.

He wants me to fax him Coby's poem, and he will see what he can do. He also told me Coby is on the regular Wednesday-night prayer list. Of course, it happened to be Wednesday when I called. He also told me Lynette just had a baby girl, her third child, in Los Angeles.

He was leaving this afternoon to join Mrs. Musgrave, who was already out in the City of Angels. I thanked him and then got ready for school and PT. After leaving Coby at school, Tricia, Casey, and I went to Ellen Cairns' office at the Burnett Womack building to fax Coby's poem to Mr. Musgrave. We went to 108 on the first floor, and Ellen happened to be at her desk. She agreed to fax the information.

I went back to the seventh floor while Tricia and Casey went to the college bookstore. I had a feeling my birthday tomorrow was on their mind. Mainly Coby and Casey. They love buying gifts for Tricia and me.

I went to the school floor and had about a twenty-minute wait. I then took Coby to PT. Tricia and Casey came in about twenty minutes into Coby's walk, and yes, they had a sack with something in it.

After PT, we went by Revco to get Casey some muscle ointment for a strained muscle in her leg. We returned to the apartment and snacked because Nick was coming over from Raleigh after his meeting, so we would wait and eat with him then.

When we got home, the kids gave me my birthday presents. They gave me some Carolina shirts plus a birthday cake made at Harris Teeter. It was a football field with players. White cake with white icing, of course.

Nick came as well as Doug and Kelly. We had pizza from The Hut, and it was a nice visit.

Mother called and wished me a good birthday and told me about Vita Hamm talking with *The Maury Povich Show* about Coby.

We went to bed, feeling the call for the lungs would be soon.

Day 126
Friday, June 26, 1992

Well, I am forty-three today. I just wish Coby's lungs would be my present.

After doing his IV, I took the needle out because it was infiltrated.

Casey had already left with her little friend from gym to go horseback-riding.

I spoke with the nursing service, and they would be out at three or past.

We went to the hospital for school.

No parking place, so I just watched it while I was double-parked.

Tricia took Coby to school. At PT, Connie said Dr. Roop would be there Monday at one o'clock for exercise. Afterward we ate at Ham's with the Nelsons and a friend of theirs who is cousin to Chip Beck, the pro golfer. We then left for home.

The nurse came. Couldn't hit a vein, so we will wait til Monday. If unsuccessful, a central line will go in. By the way, there was a lung transplant attempt Thursday night. The patient was in the OR, but they found a spot on the lung and aborted the surgery.

They are pretty thorough around here.

At least there was some movement. We were going to watch the football camp this afternoon, but it was raining. Doug and Kelly stopped by, and then Tricia and I went to get Casey. Not a bad day except for Coby's IV. I just know his veins will be up Monday.

Maybe the lungs will be here this weekend, and we won't be worrying about veins.

Day 127
Saturday, June 27, 1992

Mother called this morning and said that *The Maury Povich Show* might call me Monday. They want to know some information. Maybe this will be a chance for awareness.

We were all pretty lazy today, although we did go see *Batman* at the Ram Triple Theater. The *Batman* movie was dark but all right.

Afterward we went back to H-103, and I cooked pork chops out. I went for a walk after eating and then visited with the Nelsons. I gave Coby a treatment and went to bed.

Hoping for a call.

Day 128
Sunday, June 28, 1992

Did the usual morning thing with Coby's treatment. We went out to eat, came home, and watched the Dream Team beat Cuba by seventy-nine points. Looked pretty good, seeing all those guys playing on the same team.

We then watched the track trials from New Orleans.

No lungs for anyone yet.

Made a Ben & Jerry's run. Strawberry already out.

Day 129
Monday, June 29, 1992

We got up and ran and lifted. Casey is going to another little girl's house for the day. It is not far from the hospital.

We arrived first at the hospital today and found a parking spot. Dr. Roop was working out for the first time today with Coby. It was good seeing him again. He was pretty weak.

Connie and the treadmill will get him in shape. Andy was pretty sick today, but he made it. Mike was wearing his Seahawks jersey, Jo Beth her North Carolina T-shirt, and Ray strolling with the soaps.

I almost forgot, Cassie, Dr. Roop's wife, was waiting in the parking lot. I told her this was the crazy part, the parking. After Coby worked out, we ate at Spring Garden. Matt, the waiter, told us he was in a tryout for a CF commercial at UNC. He should find out tonight if he gets the part.

After Spring Garden, we went home to wait on the nurse. Hopefully, she will hit Coby's vein. I hear Kaaren's music. She must be sunbathing.

Tricia and I went to wash, and sure enough, Kaaren was outside in the sun.

I am writing, Tricia is reading, and Coby is putting puzzles together.

Oprah is on with sons-in-law dating mothers-in-law.

Life is a ride.

I went and got Casey from gym. On my way over, I think of how far Coby and I have come since arriving. I really want to be here when the lungs come in.

I pray to be here.

Coby and I both cried yesterday, talking about it. We just have to rely on God's strength.

Day 130
Tuesday, June 30, 1992

Well, today Coby is off from UNC. He wanted to go to the South Gate mall in Durham. We went after Tricia, and I ran. It was a good day.

Casey got some clothes, Coby some shoes and shades, as we ate at Spinnakers. It was nice all being together. I just want everyone together having fun.

I know we will soon.

Day 131
Wednesday, July 1, 1992

Well, July first has made it. I couldn't fall asleep until 3:00 a.m. I think of how much I will miss not seeing Coby. I have never been away from him for more than a week. Once, when we lived in Alpine, and he was in Children's at Dallas. Tricia and Casey stayed with Jeannie and Sonny at the time.

I think of how much Coby and I have gone through being here, the transitions of a different hospital and meeting new people. I then refocused on why we are here.

Get lungs.

I finally fell asleep then got up at 8:00 a.m. to do Coby's medicine.

Didn't run today. The oxygen man and medicine man were both coming by, and I did not want to miss them.

We went to PT, and Coby had a good six-minute test walk. Dr. Roop is still struggling, but he will be fine. Jo Beth working hard, Ray watching soaps, everyone else was off. After PT, we went to Elmo's to eat and then home. Tonight is support group.

Don Hart had called earlier and wanted to see Coby, so I went to the hospital and picked him up after taking Casey to gym. Don stayed with Coby while Tricia and I went to the support group. There were fifty people at the meeting. It was a good get-together as each transplant recipient spoke about how they were coping.

It was good for Dr. Roop and his wife, Cassie. It seems they are going through a transition adjustment.

I thought back to Coby's and my first night arriving here: the ambulance, arriving at night, Wayne Wheeler, the ambulance attendant giving Coby a Duke keychain, the room that needed painting, Coby's crying because he wanted to go home (I wanted to do the same but didn't), the needle sticks he went through late at night...

I am very proud of the quick adjustments Coby made and how he has done everything asked of him.

I remember the anticipation of the unknown, not knowing if he would be a transplant candidate or not, and then the relief when he was accepted. I remember the ICU trip, Coby telling me how much he loved me…

My mind really was wandering.

The meeting was over. I went and got Casey, came home, took Donald back, and then Coby, Casey, Tricia, and I watched the Dream Team beat Argentina. Michael Jordan was MVP.

We then went to bed.

Gee, I love all these folks.

Day 132
Thursday, July 2, 1992

Tricia and I went running after doing all Coby's stuff. Pretty humid.

I called a media agency in Dallas for awareness. Tricia rewrote a letter I had composed to *Good Morning America*, and we then went to PT.

We ate at Chili's and then went to DSG sports store. We came back home, washed, and went swimming. Tricia and I visited Jo Anna Nelson. The two of us stayed up late talking.

Maybe lungs tomorrow.

It seems like February 21, 1992, was just yesterday.

Day 133
Friday, July 3, 1992

After doing Coby's medicine, Tricia and I went walking. It was overcast. The PT department took today off for the fourth, so we were just going with the flow. Casey is going skating today with a little gymnastics friend then off to the gym.

We are going to the Hogan house later today for a visit.

Tricia prepared spaghetti, so we just ate at H-103. I called Mrs. Hogan and asked when a good time to come out would be. She said Mr. Hogan was stretched out for a while, and five o'clock would be a good time.

When we arrived at the Hogan Farm, the first thing in sight is a huge Magnolia tree. I followed the driveway to the back of the house. Shade trees, flowers, old barns, and, of course, a basketball courtyard. It is a very pretty place.

Mrs. Hogan came to the back door and asked us in. It is a beautiful, very old farmhouse, two stories, with wood-paneled walls. It was Mr. Hogan's great-granddaddy's house. Mr. Hogan is around sixty, I suspect. The dairy farm has been in operation since 1930. Mr. Hogan was not there when we arrived but got there shortly with their grandson, Daniel. He is a very good-looking, blue-eyed brownder.

He had brought some match cars. I asked if Richard Petty, the number 43 car, was in the collection. He looked quickly, but no. "He is racing his last race tomorrow," Daniel told me.

Mrs. Hogan brought out a chocolate chip cake. Dots of chocolate chips!

It was very tasty.

Coby had Breyers with his. Coby and Tricia then took a tour of the house. Mr. Hogan and I had a good visit about old ball players around, people who had played for UNC and come out to fish and hunt. This is one of the best places in the state to fish and hunt, and Mr. Hogan gave me a key to the place.

"Anytime, come out," he said. He has really taken a liking to Coby.

Daniel went outside and got the water hose and was shooting the window glass Mr. Hogan had his back to. Coby, Mr. Hogan, and Tricia went out back, looking around. All of a sudden, water started dripping on Mr. Hogan. Daniel had shot the water under the eaves, and it dropped right on Mr. Hogan's head. He moved the couch and went outside to see exactly where Daniel had shot the water. Mr. Hogan checked out the spot.

I picked up a basketball and asked Daniel if he could shoot this thing.

He said, "I will play you in a game."

Daniel said he would be UNC, and I could be someone in the ACC.

"Okay, how about Duke?" I asked.

"Yeah!" he yelled.

We had a good time, playing his rules, of course. He is quick and is going to be a good one someday.

After a while, Mrs. Hogan, Tricia, and Coby came out of a barn with an old aluminum Coke chest. Coby was excited. Mrs. Hogan just gave it to him.

It is really something how they have just accepted us in their lives. It is really nice to meet such kind people so far from home.

We visited for a good while. Mr. Hogan had to take Daniel to his house up the road, and when he came back, he took us to his shop. It was cluttered but had a lot of neat stuff, even some of the old Ramses' horns from mascots in the past.

Coby found an old prop. Turns out, Mr. Hogan is a pilot also. They are both interesting people. Mrs. Hogan's dad was sheriff of Orange County, so she was raised in Chapel Hill. Dorothy Sloane was her name.

After touring the shop, we sat down to visit underneath a shade tree. Mr. Hogan pointed toward the shop and showed us a groundhog that comes out every day. It was pretty neat, and I told him I had never seen a groundhog.

We ended our visit. The Hogans told us to stay in touch and to come back. I am very glad our lives have crossed paths.

CF may have one plus. It has let us meet some of the world's nicest people, people like the Hogans.

After bringing Tricia and Coby back to H-103, I went to get Casey from gym. It was beginning to lightning and looked like another rainy night. We watched the Dream Team and then went to bed.

Oh yeah, Steve had a false alarm. He was in the OR, waiting for the green light, but he got a red.

Day 134
Saturday, July 4, 1992

Well, it is the country's birthday, July 4. Festivals are happening here, just like all over the states. Even President Bush is in Faith,

North Carolina, for his fourth celebration. He played softball with the locals. Earlier in the day, he was at the Daytona Speedway to see Richard Petty's last race.

A year ago, Coby was in Presby at Dallas.

We were getting him ready to go to Destin, Florida.

I got up and ran and lifted. It was pretty warm, but not like back home. When I got back and cleaned up, Tricia was preparing things to take to the picnic. We transplant candidates and families are having a get-together at one o'clock.

We watched Steffie Graff win Wimbledon over Monica Seles. Andrew Agassi defeated John McEnroe to play Goran Ivanisevic for the men's final tomorrow. I loaded up the little smoker I bought with all the other necessities for the get-together and put them in the van.

We had a good turnout. Most everyone was there, except Dr. Roop. I am concerned about him and his wife. They seem to be having a transition problem. I hope they adapt.

I visited with everyone, but I mainly hung around the smoker to cook. Eventually, the topic of waiting came up. I guess it is good that the celebration ended up being a support-group meeting.

Casey and Coby went back to H-103 and watched *Terminator 2*. I watched Leighann's niece. She is nine and wanted to go swimming. Leighann is from South Carolina and is waiting for a double-lung transplant.

The day went by, and it was time for everyone to go home for medicine or because they just got tired.

Later in the evening, we went to the UNC Hospitals parking lot and watched the fireworks display. It was fun.

Back to Ramsgate for some *SNL* and then to bed.

I never went to sleep.

I listened to an all-night oldies station out of Florida through my headset. I never could get sleepy enough. I don't know why.

Day 135
Sunday, July 5, 1992

Tricia and Coby slept until eleven. Casey and I watched Delirious with John Candy. When everyone got up, we just snacked around.

Casey went over to a little girl's house for a couple of hours. We all then went to see *A League of Their Own*. It was a very good movie. Penny Marshall seems to have the touch. I was thinking of contacting her about doing a movie on these transplant candidates. After the movie, we came home and just took it easy. Tricia and I went for a walk.

I was hoping the lung call would come.

Day 136
Monday, July 6, 1992

Did Coby's medicine, then ran. We hadn't planned anything but to eat at Spring Garden after Coby's workout. Dr. Roop seemed to have a better workout, but he is really sick.

For a Monday, Coby was strong working out. His clowning around on the treadmill got everyone laughing. I made the comment, "Coby needs lungs to slow him down!"

He was walking backward on the treadmill. Connie and Dr. Roop were laughing out loud. I know it is a false security of how well Coby is doing because he is on IVs. If the IVs were removed, he would be very sick in three or four days.

After eating at Spring Garden, we went back to H-103.

Tricia and I laid out by the pool for a while and then went back to the apartment to watch *Cheers* with the kids.

Kelly had called and was coming over for a while. She stayed for about an hour, and I asked her what was going on in Wylie with Mr. Whitt. I had received a card in the mail, and it said he was going to be fired. She verified the letter. After twenty years, the board fired him. No reasons yet.

Wylie is going to be a lot different, but time goes on.

Day 137
Tuesday, July 7, 1992

Coby is off today. He wanted to go to Franklin Street to shop. After the nurse came and changed his dressing, we headed for Franklin. I had gone and got a haircut, showered, and was ready for the strip.

We stopped into a Bugle's first and had a bagel. It was the first bagel I had ever had. It wasn't bad at all. We were about to leave when this man behind us asked if we were strangers just passing through. I said, "No, we are just strange!"

After a chuckle, I told him our reason for being here. He introduced himself as David. I noticed he was reading a book about *SNL*. It was the scripts from 1977. I asked him if I could see the book, he agreed, and I showed Coby the manuscript. David asked if Coby liked *SNL*. I told him we were all big fans.

After visiting awhile, we decided to continue our Franklin Street journey.

David gave Coby the book, said it was meant for him.

I couldn't believe it.

He also did a numerical reading of Coby's birthday. We said our thanks and left out.

We stayed on Franklin Street about three hours. It was what Casey and Coby wanted to do. We went into a jewelry store and left Coby's "Peace" necklace to be fixed.

Kami Moore was going to be at our apartment around six to eat pizza, so we left for home. She was in town to take her nursing boards. She stayed about an hour and a half. She had a new hairstyle, and she seemed very happy to be at Charlotte.

Tina Sorrells called Tricia and told her about Mr. Whitt then some very sad news about Cheri Cox. It seems she has an inoperable brain tumor. After Tricia and Tina spoke, I called Coach Shaeffer who verified the news about Dr. Cox.

I told the kids we must pray for her. She has been very good to our family. She helped implement Coby's homebound school. They prayed for their elementary school principal.

Wylie is really going through some changes, proving life is a ride.

I was told by Keith Meyers that we are picked next to last in the district. It will be fun to prove them wrong.

Day 138
Wednesday, July 8, 1992

We found out this morning at the mailbox that the lung transplant drought is over. Jo Anna said the transplant team did a single lung last night, and everything was fine.

Coby told me this was his week.

I hope so.

He told Tricia he did not know if she could do everything and wanted me to stay. It would be nice if it would happen soon.

We took Coby to school. We had to park in the front lot because of the road construction going on by PT. Coby had a horrible workout, just wasn't feeling good.

I know we are living on borrowed time. The lungs, I hope, will be here soon.

I was going to call Ellen Cairns, the transplant coordinator, when Coby was having PT. Just so happened, she was there at PT. I visited with her about Coby's morale. "He is a little down because I am leaving in about twenty days," I told her.

We went straight home from PT. Tricia cooked. Coby fell asleep and took a three-hour nap. He felt better.

Sam Terry called and updated me on the Wylie chaos.

Tricia and Casey went to the support group's watermelon supper at the clubhouse.

I stayed with Coby while he slept on the sofa. He woke up, so I went and got him some melon. I have a concern about him. I feel he is getting weaker. I know God knows his timeframe, so I tell myself not to worry, but it is hard.

"The melon is good, Dad," Coby said. *It is nice to see that smile,* I thought. Coby seems to be throwing up more lately.

The disease is the pits.

Casey and Tricia came back from the melon feast, and we finished the night just about the usual way. I was glad the transplant drought was over. Usually, things happen in threes.

I just hope Coby is second or third this week.

Day 139
Thursday, July 9, 1992

Esther called, talking about the news article in the *Dallas Morning News* concerning Mr. Whitt. Spann then called to talk about it as well. Then Mother called, wondering if I knew where in Florida John Elzner was. It seems he may be in Destin with Jared, but nobody knows for sure. His dad has had a heart attack, and the family is trying to reach him.

I called Kim Howell at the dive shop in Destin, and she is having a deputy sheriff check the campgrounds.

Tricia and Casey went to meet with a reporter about the support group.

We got ready and went to school and PT. Coby had a better day in PT today but still didn't feel too good. After PT, we ate at Elmo's Diner, and then we headed back to H-103.

Tricia and Casey went to the pool while I stayed with Coby.

I want to spend all the time I can with him. Tricia and Casey came back from the pool, and the kids started playing Nintendo, so Tricia and I went for a walk. We returned, and the kids said Doug and Kelly were coming over for a while. They stayed about two hours. We visited about the Wylie mess.

Kaaren stopped over and watched a little TV with us. Everyone left, the dreaded night came, and no lungs again.

Maybe day 140 will be the day.

Day 140
Friday, July 10, 1992

Tricia and I went running. My back seems to be getting worse, but I figure if Coby can put up with not breathing, I can sure get my butt up and run for those who can't but would if they could. It was pretty humid, but we made it.

Casey wanted to run, so I went around the apartment complex with her. We then went back to H-103 and got ready for Coby's school and PT.

When we returned to the apartment, Coby had filled his pan up with vomit…a typical morning for him. We got ready for PT and school.

I gambled on the parking space and lost. Someone was parked in the spots for PT. I let Tricia, Casey, and Coby out and then waited for a parking space to open up. Sure enough, in about fifteen minutes, one became available.

It was nice to have Tricia here today to take Coby up to school. It is heck by oneself, but it can be done.

During Coby's workout, I started to feel like crap. I thought I was going to faint. I had a chill and just became weak. I managed through. I figure if Coby could go through a workout like he does, I could make it.

We went to the university mall to see a LEGO display and then came home.

Later that night, Casey went with the transplant bunch to eat pizza. Coby did not want to go, so Casey went with Jo Anna and Jo Beth.

I took an antihistamine and went to bed at midnight.

Day 141
Saturday, July 11, 1992

I woke up feeling better than when I went to bed. It was a day I did not care for though. We have got to go and get our plane tickets to leave in a couple of weeks for Casey and me. On the drive out to the airport, I thought of the many times Coby and I had picked up and taken people back to the airport. Coby and I stayed in the van while Tricia and Casey went in to get the tickets.

Coby and I talked about the first night we saw RDU. He pointed out where the ambulance was parked. Man, we have been through some stuff since then. We talked about how he is going to have to be strong for his mom. The days he doesn't feel like working out, he must push himself too. I have gone every step with him as I can, but he has got to work out on his own. I told him to think about anything that will help him get through the workout.

He agreed.

But he also told me he wishes I would stay.

I told him, "Let's hope the lungs come in soon." To pick up morale, I asked if he wanted to drive to Raleigh today and see the capital and NC State. He wanted to, so we did.

When Tricia and Casey got in the van, they said we have to leave July 25, 1992, Coby's birthday. The next day is Tricia's and my anniversary. Two weeks.

Please come in, lungs.

We went to Raleigh and saw the capital, Meredith College, an all-girls Catholic school, Peace College, State, St. May's, and the fairgrounds. I thought it was interesting seeing the tribute to the confederate soldiers that died for North Carolina in front of the capital building.

On our way back from Raleigh, we stopped at Cary Towne Center in Cary. We also ate there, and Coby ordered a *Wayne's World* video. We went back to H-103 and took it easy for the rest of the night.

Day 142
Sunday, July 12, 1992

Tricia and I got up and went walking. We didn't see Shirley and her husband outside smoking, so I guess they were at mass.

It is pretty hot already, even though it is only 8:00 a.m. When we returned to the apartment, we did the laundry. Actually, we took the clothes to the laundry room but had to wait because all the washers were being used.

Tricia and I just sat under the shade, by the pool, waiting for a washer to open up. We were just talking about how we couldn't believe we are North Carolina when Gordon Campbell walked by with his dog. Gordon is Andy's dad from New Jersey.

"I was going to call you later," he said. "Mike is at the hospital, waiting to see if it is a go," he explained.

"Well, that explains why his mom and dad were not out here smoking this morning," I said.

Also, his dad was supposed to return to their home in Pensacola this afternoon. Tricia and I got pretty excited. I then looked up and saw Casey just a-running toward the laundry mat.

I knew she knew something.

Jo Anna had called and told her about Mike. It was around ten, and this all started to happen around midnight. I was afraid it wasn't going to be a go because it seemed like a long time.

Gordon told us when Jeannette, one of the coordinators, called last night and asked for Mike Booth. Mr. Booth told her that he wasn't there, that he was in North Carolina. It seemed that Mr. Booth's body was in North Carolina, but his mind was in Pensacola. Lack of sleep will do that sometimes.

Anyway, he figured out where he was, and they are up at UNC, waiting for the word right now.

When Tricia and I got through washing, Casey had received word that it was a go.

Mike was going to get his lungs! Ironically, they were coming from Florida. The reason it was taking a while to find out if the surgery was a go was that a big thunderstorm was delaying Dr. Egan's plane from landing. We decided we would go up to the hospital waiting room to see Shirley and her husband, so we loaded up and went.

I let Tricia, Casey, and Coby off in front of the hospital and then parked the van. As I was walking up to the entrance of UNC Hospitals, a station wagon pulled up behind me. I turned to look, and it was Dr. Egan. He and another man got out of the car. They had a cooler with them.

It donned on me that it was Mike's lungs.

Tricia couldn't believe it. She told me later she figured there was a back way they brought the organs in. Dr. Egan walked by, spoke to us, and said he was going to work.

If Chris Farley was there, he would have said, "Awesome!" We then went to the second-floor waiting room. We visited awhile. Ellen was there and Bob's wife, another lung patient from New Jersey.

It was time for us to leave, so I went and got the van. When I pulled out of the parking lot, I thought, just a few months ago, when Coby and I first came and he was in the hospital, we would probably be out looking around—either going to the Dean Center, football stadium, or visiting Franklin Street. We did not stay in one place for very long.

Those are memories he and I will never forget.

We seem to have come closer than we already were.

I got the family, and we went back to Ramsgate. Tricia and I went to the video store and rented a couple of movies, *Aladdin* and *Brighton Beach Memoirs*. I thought of the donor's family and asked God to be with them during this earthly loss.

I also thought of Shirley and her husband smoking one after another in between the buildings, just outside the ICU.

Life is a ride.

It was about 2:00 pm. The surgery may go 'til midnight.

I prayed I will be here for Tricia, waiting, and not in Texas.

We kept tabs on Mike's condition all throughout the afternoon. Everything we heard was good. It is pretty neat how everyone is pulling for Mike out here at the complex. Even people who live here and are not here for medical reasons have become interested about how the transplant candidates are doing. All these people waiting to be transplanted are a real inspiration, not only to me but to others as well.

Just six months ago, I did not know any of these people, and now my prayers go out to them and their families. Everyone is pulling for each other. "It is like a subculture," Andy Campbell's dad described it.

We decided to go back to the hospital and see Mike's family in the waiting room. The kids really wanted to go. It was around 8:00 pm when we arrived. We got to the waiting room, and Mike's dad, mother, sister, Jo Anna and Jo Beth Nelson, Andy and Gordon Campbell, and Allen were all there visiting.

They said they were told Mike should be out around ten thirty or eleven and that everything was going fine.

I told Andy there will be an empty treadmill tomorrow. He smiled. I feel Andy will be soon. He and Mike had just bought John Mellencamp tickets for next week, but Mike will be in the hospital. It seems Mike's presurgery workouts are paying off, since his vitals are doing so well.

We left for H-103, all a bit more positive than when we woke up this morning. When I had let Tricia and the kids out, Ben Butler, one of Coby's nurses on seventh, was coming out the door. He stopped and visited and said Ruth Ann was still getting married and that her new husband would be doing missionary work for at least a year.

Coby and I will never forget her.

She was the nurse who helped us the first night we came into UNC Hospitals on February 21. She was supposed to be getting off, but she helped Coby and me settle into our room. It was very hard for Coby at first, but he adjusted fine. We both had each other, and it helped to have a nice person like Ruth Ann Wheeler, with her smile and compassion. Like I said earlier, we both will never forget her.

Coby and I were doing his treatment, Tricia was putting Casey to bed, and a knock came from the other side of the door. It was Ellen, Bob's wife. She just came from the hospital, and Mike was out of surgery and into ICU. Everything was still going fine.

Thanks, God.

Day 143
Monday, July 13, 1992

Tricia got up earlier, ran, and then walked with me. My back was feeling better, but I am not pushing it. We talked with Mr. Booth, who was outside smoking. Mike was doing great, and they were to see him at eleven o'clock.

Suzi, one of Casey's gym friends, called Casey and asked her over for the day. We will let her off on our way to UNC Hospitals. Coby went to school and then PT. He had a pretty good workout, not as good as some but not that bad.

Andy was having a hard time. Jo Beth seemed fine, and so did Ray. Coby wanted to eat at Ham's, so we obliged. I still am aching all over. My eyes feel like I have a fever. It must be the flu.

I changed Coby's dressing, and we watched *The Addams Family*. It was then time for me to go and get Casey from gymnastics. When I arrived, they were finishing up their workout. Casey had a good time and even got to go on a jet ski.

Suzanne's father is a big soccer guy and is an assistant coach for the Lady Heels. We came home and then started working toward bed.

I took a Benadryl to try and get cleared up.

Last word we had about Mike was that he was doing fine.

Ron Shultz called. Same old mess back home. Loy Dorsey called, and he is now coaching in Paris, Texas.

Maybe the lungs will come tonight.

Day 144
Tuesday, July 14, 1992

After starting Coby's treatment, Tricia and I went walking. My back is better, so I might start running tomorrow. The Booths were not outside, so they might be inside sleeping.

I went to the weight room. Coby's nurse was coming by this morning, and I wanted to finish up before she got there. Gordon Campbell came up and said Mike was put on kidney dialysis around two this morning. Hopefully just a small setback.

Coby doesn't have PT today, but he does have clinic at 2:30 p.m. I'm beginning to get down about leaving him here, but I guess I must go.

I pray that the lungs will be here today or before I go.

We went to the clinic to see Dr. Wood. He told Coby he had been in Chapel Hill too long. "We are doing the same home medicines, just waiting," he said. On the way home, we stopped and got some bagels for Coby. We finished watching *Top Secret*. Coby loves those types of movies by the Zucker brothers.

Casey and Tricia went to the pool. Jo Beth came by and watched Cheers with us.

Kelly visited for a while until Doug was finished with school. He did his one-ring call signal. Coby loves it. He calls from a payphone, and when he hears the alert signal on the other end, he hangs the phone up. Kelly then calls him right back.

Twenty-five cents saved again. Pretty clever. Gig 'em, Doug!

We found out that Mike is doing a lot better and is not on kidney dialysis. I told Jo Beth someone was going to get called by morning. It would be the third in seven days.

Kaaren and her boyfriend, Gavin, visited for a while. Coby made them laugh. It was around midnight when Coby went to bed.

Tricia and I stayed up and watched *Shining Through* with Michael Douglas and Melanie Griffith. It was over around 2:45 a.m.

My cold, or whatever, is a lot better.

Oh, earlier in the day, Dr. Roop's wife, Cassie, called. They seem to be adjusting a lot better.

Day 145
Wednesday, July 15, 1992

Today is the mower men day. Every Wednesday, since Coby and I moved in, they have come to mow rain or shine. The mower men start at 8:00 a.m. It seems they are coming right into the apartment because of us being below ground level.

The phone rang. It should be the O_2 guys coming today. Tricia came and said it was Ron from ASAPSA (oxygen guys). Before she hung up the phone, Jo Anna was on call, waiting. Lola from South Carolina was at the hospital in the holding room, waiting to see if she was going to get some lungs today. She would be number three in seven days.

I was hoping Coby would get that slot.

I hope it is a go for her. She almost went home not long ago because the waiting was getting to her. She is up here all alone. Her husband is working back in South Carolina. They had to sell part of their land to come up with $100,000 for the double-lung transplant. Just another example of doing what you have to do.

I got up, clapped on Coby, and then went to the weight room. I am making myself go. I must whip this cold. I don't know what keeps Coby going. I guess just the will to live.

Casey and Tricia are making chocolate-chip cookies. Casey and I looked at the mixing bowl and fought over the egg beaters.

Coby left a note for Ron, the oxygen man. He wrote on the note to have some cookies, "even though you're not Santa!" Ron will get a kick out of "High Flyin'," as he calls Coby. We are off to school and PT.

It is time to fight for a parking space.

Sure enough, when we arrived, there were no spaces available in which to park. Tricia, Casey, and Coby went on up to the seventh floor while I double-parked. Finally, a space became available. Someone without a sticker to park got in and drove off. She was real mobile. Probably parks in handicap spaces at shopping malls because she is better than the rest of us.

I got up to the seventh after parking. Tricia said Lola is still waiting to hear if it is a go, and Mike is doing well. I said a silent thanks to God; he hears.

Coby was struggling on the treadmill, but he went the thirty minutes, at one point six miles per hour. He sat down and threw up his guts. He kept on throwing up so much, in fact, it was like he had a stomach flu or something.

Of course, it is CF.

He was so tired afterward Connie sent us out without doing the bike. We went home so Coby could rest. Tricia fixed supper, and then I took Casey to gym and went to the support group meeting. Tricia, Coby, and I went. The topic was bronchoscopes. It is the dreaded exam post-op procedure that takes place every few months at checkups.

The same old bunch was there, except for Mike and Lola. They were in the ICU and waiting room, respectively. I looked around the room at the faces, including Coby's, of the hopeful lung recipients. They were listening to every syllable Jeanette said.

Rejection and infection have the same symptoms, she explained. I was thinking we may have to move around here, but that is something time will tell. I have been in a lot of locker rooms before games and felt the intensity.

It is nothing like the intensity I felt with this group.

They were truly attentive. It reminded me of the days when I used to work in emergency rooms, when a doctor would talk about a loved one's condition. They always listen with wide eyes and closed mouths. Everyone was getting more relaxed. I thought of the courage each and every one had. They all are definitely a special cut of people.

Coughs are heard throughout Jeanette's presentation, but no one is offended. Not even the group of people from the church. I think they are just as impressed with the determination of these young people as I am.

I look at Coby's coughing and fighting to breathe, but he is determined to get his lungs before Casey and I leave. His fight keeps me going.

Jeanette finished. Questions were asked, and she updated everyone on Mike and Lola's condition. We left, I went and got Casey from gym and then watched the video "The Right Stuff" with Coby. I fell asleep around 2:00 a.m., listening to my headset and thinking, *Are we really here waiting on new lungs for Coby?*

I thought back thirteen years ago when he was born, the times we lived in Alpine, the trips we made to Disney, T-ball, etc. I just know he will be fine once he gets his lungs.

Day 146
Thursday, July 16, 1992

Coby slept well, but his stomach was upset. Must be the flu. He went to school for the last time in a couple of weeks. He was not having a good workout, so we sent for the doctor.

Dr. Thomas came and looked him over. "Looks like a virus," he said. I thought it would be nice if these CF kids wouldn't have to fight other nuisances.

You would think CF would be enough.

He sent us home and told us to Gatorade him for the rest of the night. We did what the doctor ordered.

Day 147
Friday, July 17, 1992

Coby seemed a little weaker, but he felt fine. I took Casey over to Suzi's for the day. Tricia, Coby, and I went to UNC for Coby's workout. He got on the treadmill and went ten minutes. Dr. Thomas stopped him and sent us home to rest until Monday. We did again what the doctor ordered.

Coby wanted a couple of videos for the afternoon. In between movies, Tricia and I did the wash. We were walking back from the laundry mat. I told Tricia, "How fast a summer can go by. It seems like Coby and I just picked you and Casey up from the airport yesterday."

Now, in just seven days, Casey and I are going back. Tricia said Andy's dad said the same thing. I told her it is going fast because time means so much more to us now. We want to do so much with Coby and Casey once this is all over. We just do not want to take things for granted.

I love them all so much.

I really do not want to leave Coby up here, but maybe he won't have to wait much longer.

Mike and Lola are doing fine. Casey and I played with William, a little kid at the apartment, after she came home from gym.

We watched *Shark Week* on Discovery. Tricia was still sick. I laid awake listening to my headset, wondering if I should stay or what. I know God will direct me his way, not mine.

Day 148
Saturday, July 18, 1992

Coby seemed to sleep pretty good. I did medicine. He jumped a little when I did the saline flush. I imagine the IV is about gone.

He slept until about 11:00 a.m. He is pretty weak from the constant regurgitation. His arms are beginning to bruise because of the IV sticks.

We stayed at home all day, except for when Tricia and I went to Harris Teeter for groceries. Late in the afternoon, we went and picked blackberries at the Hogan farm.

Coby and I had a good talk under the shade tree. We talked about where we have been, what we have been through. He said he thought he would get his lungs a week after we got into our apartment.

Coby also said that he was glad that he decided to get a transplant. He just wishes it will happen while I am here. He said he loved me and knew I would be thinking of him.

I have grown up a lot and learned a lot while being with Coby up here.

Life is definitely a ride.

Doug and Kelly are having car trouble, so I went to get them. They visited a while, and I took them home. I took out Coby's IV. I feel a central line coming on.

Day 149
Sunday, July 19, 1992

We stayed home all day. The nurse couldn't get an IV, so tomorrow we should find out about a central line. Coby seems to be getting sicker. I know God will take care of him.

I just hope Coby doesn't have to suffer much longer with these lungs.

He wants to eat, but almost everything he eats he throws up.

Casey spent the afternoon at Jo Anna and Jo Beth's apartment. The Nelsons are dog-sitting the Booths' dog while Mike is in the hospital. Casey takes it for walks.

We watched a movie and then went to bed.

I was hoping "the call" would come today, but it didn't.

I did get a call from Nick to tell me that some syringes were found in our driveway, outside the fence. The police are running a check on it. Also, Chesley Bogan called, and he is in Asheville, North Carolina, heading this way. They should be here sometime early afternoon.

This is Casey's and my last week before we go back to Wylie. I am planning on spending every available second with Coby. I really am mixed about leaving. I do not want to leave him.

Day 150
Monday, July 20, 1992

Not much different than any other day, starting out. Jo Beth called and said they are doing a transplant. It started at ten last night. It is one of the ladies from our support group who has COPD. The stream continues. I will just be glad when Coby is added.

Coby does not have school this week, so we did not leave for his workout until 12:40 p.m. He had a good workout for being sick with a virus. I am more amazed at his courage.

We had to wait on the doctor to examine Coby, so Casey went home with Jo Anna and Jo Beth.

The doctor felt better about Coby, and I did too. We don't know about the central line yet, but Dr. Thomas said he would get back to us. We left and ate at Spring Garden. It was time to take Casey to the gym when the phone rang. It was Chesley, and they were at Carr Mill. I gave them directions and then took Casey to gym. When I returned, Chesley and Joyce were at H-103.

We had a good visit. Chesley and I went and rented them a room at the Red Roof Inn and then went and got Casey. They stayed a little while longer and then went to their hotel room for the night. We would see them tomorrow.

I called Jon Peters to check in, and everything is the same.

Day 151
Tuesday, July 21, 1992

Esther called this morning and said the school board had reinstated Mr. Whitt. Wild and crazy small-town politics, I guess.

The Bogans came by, and we went to the mall in Durham. Coby seemed to have a good time, especially when we found the Michael Jordan sweatsuit he wanted for his birthday at Dillard's. We all just strolled around the mall.

We went back to Carrboro, stayed home an hour and a half, and then went to the university mall in Chapel Hill. Coby got pretty sick at the mall. He threw up all over himself, but we got him cleaned up. We then headed back to H-103.

Joyce and Chesley stayed for a couple more hours. We had a good time talking about the Biltmore mansion. Chesley talked to Coby about coming to Yellville, Arkansas, next spring to go canoeing and camping. Coby and Casey are really wanting to do that more than anything.

They were leaving early the next morning, so they headed back to their hotel room. It was nice that they could come and visit.

Day 152
Wednesday, July 22, 1992

Jon Peters called last night and said that coaches didn't have to report until Wednesday instead of Tuesday. Tricia called American and had Casey's and my flight changed. This way, we will be here for Coby's birthday and Tricia's and my anniversary.

We went to PT. Coby struggled but made it through. Dr. Wood stopped by, and the decision to have a central line placed in Coby was made official. Dr. Lacey would be getting in touch, but Friday looks like the day.

Tricia decided to get a cake made by Harris Teeter on our way home Thursday night.

Doug, Kelly, and Kaaren are coming over Thursday to celebrate Coby's thirteenth with us. We went home and just watched TV the rest of the day and night. Casey went to gym, Kelly came by, a big storm hit…

Still no lungs.

Day 153
Thursday, July 23, 1992

I had a talk with Tami and congratulated her on the girls' basketball job. She said, "I must be crazy!" I know she will do fine. I will miss her with the sixth-grade PE.

Coby got up, we did his treatment, he ate, and then took a shower. He threw up everything he ate for breakfast in the shower. He got out, and I just turned the shower on to wash away the vomit and mucus.

Mucus was stuck on the surface of the tub. The water finally loosened the grip the deadly mucus had on it. Down the drain the slime went, green in color, of course. I thought of Dr. Prestridge telling me one time that the mucus could be stretched thirty feet before breaking.

It is hard to believe a little boy's body can produce that much mucus constantly. That is why I know the new lungs will help him so. Of course, the vomiting is not new to Coby.

He just keeps on going.

Scott Brown called from the First Baptist Church in Wylie. He said all his dad's side of the family are from the Carolinas. He was checking in on Coby. Trace was about the same, but his spirits were good.

Coby went to PT but really struggled. He got through the treadmill but took all his scheduled time doing it. He usually gets both treadmill and bike in in an hour and a half. It took him an hour and a half to do the thirty-minute treadmill.

We went home, and he slept for a couple of hours.

Kelly, Doug, and Kaaren came over for cake. We are going to be at the hospital at seven thirty in the morning to get the central line put in.

I hope to get the lungs tonight and just do everything then.

Kaaren had bought a Dream Team T-shirt when she went to Washington, D.C. Coby was excited about the shirt because Jordan was on the front.

Day 154
Friday, July 24, 1992

Jo Anna came by about 7:10 a.m. and picked up Casey. Tricia, Coby, and I went to the hospital's day operation for the placement of the central line. Waldron Garrison spotted Coby and visited with him awhile.

We checked in to the day-op, and Coby fell asleep in the waiting room.

Ellen Cairn stopped by and wanted to know how he was doing. Michael Booth is doing fine, along with the other two women. Mae Nelle passed away this morning. She was in pretty bad shape going into the surgery. Her prognosis without the transplant was less than a year. I feel for her family. She has a fine-looking fifteen-year-old son. They are from South Carolina. My prayers for comfort go out to them.

It is 10:00 a.m. Coby is still sleeping in the waiting room. The doctor stopped by and told us it would not be much longer. The nurse called Coby's name about 10:30 a.m. They took Coby's temperature and blood pressure, and I helped Coby get into his gown.

Coby said he wasn't scared.

It was time for Coby to go to the pre-operating room. Tricia and I were able to go with him. The nurse put him in his bed, a hair cap on his head, hooked up his oxygen canula to the wall. The anesthesiologist, or gas passer, Dr. Sellmon, put in an intravenous line.

Coby did fine.

Tricia is beginning to feel uptight. I have confidence Coby will be fine. It was time for Coby to go into the operating room. I looked on the schedule board. He will be in OR Room 5.

Tricia and I both kissed him and told him we loved him. He said the same.

I walked away, looking back at him as they carted him away to room number 5. I thought how brave he was one day shy of his thirteenth birthday.

Tricia and I returned to the waiting room. It was very cold in there. Tricia read while I looked at magazines and our offensive playbook. Of course, time does not move fast enough anytime Coby has a surgery. After about an hour, a nurse came by and told us Coby did fine. He should be out into the recovery room in about fifteen minutes.

The nurse explained how we would keep care of the Hickman catheter that was now in place. Shortly, Dr. Lacey stopped by and said things went fine. We could see Coby soon, and that relieved both of us. We got to see him, and he was doing good, just a little groggy.

It was just a little time for recovery, and we were then able to return to the apartment. We just spent the rest of the day quietly around H-103.

Tricia took Casey to gym for the last time, and I stayed with Coby. He was beginning to get hungry. He was doing pretty good. Sore, but in good spirits. I went to get Casey, and the girls gave her a going-away party with gifts and a cake. Casey cried when she first came, and now she is crying because she is leaving.

Growing up can be tearful at times, she is finding out.

We went back home and took it easy, hoping the lungs would come in.

Day 155
Saturday, July 25, 1992

Coby is thirteen today, ten years older than what we were told after he was diagnosed with CF.

We are playing the day by ear about what we are going to do.

Esther, Jeannie, Molly, and Nanny called, wishing him a happy birthday. The Nelsons stopped by with a pillowcase that had Ramses on it, painted by Jo Beth herself. Everyone at PT and those awaiting a transplant signed the pillowcase. Coby really did enjoy it.

The Campbells sent a T-shirt and an autographed book from Andy's aunt. Doug and Kelly were to come by later. Coby just wanted to eat at Ham's, so we obliged. He was taking TYLENOL with codeine, so he was a little drowsy. I thank God for letting him have a thirteenth birthday.

Tricia and I are very lucky to have Casey and Coby. I love them all so much.

It will be nice to get everyone back home.

Casey surprised Coby with a Ben & Jerry's T-shirt. He loved it.

Kelly and Doug gave him a Nike T-shirt. Coby liked them all.

All in all, Coby had a nice thirteenth.

Hollie called, and she had sent him a bracelet and Mickey Mouse ears with his name on them from Disney. He had tried to call her yesterday but could not reach her. He is still on me about getting him a *Playboy* magazine. We'll see.

We watched the opening ceremony of the Olympics. It was wild.

Day 156
Sunday, July 26, 1992

Today is Tricia's and my seventeenth anniversary. They've been good. The only thing I would change would be for Coby not to have CF, of course. We just stayed around, hoping the phone would ring and that it would be the hospital with lungs.

Casey put a hickey on my face. I was mad at her for doing it. I might be feeling the pressure of having to leave Coby.

We watched *Superman III* and then the Olympics.

Day 157
Monday, July 27, 1992

Today is nephew Dale's birthday. He is thirty-three.

Coby went to PT, threw up his breakfast before we left.

Casey and I are leaving tomorrow. Coby told me he did not want me to go. I really thought we would have the lungs now.

He saw Dr. Bogart because of the constant vomiting. I hope they will give him glucose at home.

We watched the Olympics. It was pretty low at the apartment. It was raining outside. I told Coby I would be in Wylie, but my heart would be in Carolina.

Mike Booth is having rejection. I pray he will be fine.

I still worry about Tricia being here, but I pray to God to take care of her and the Cobe.

Day 158
Tuesday, July 28, 1992

Coby was up a lot during the night coughing. He is becoming dehydrated. I talked with the doctor by phone, and he wants us to bring him in. This is the day I have been dreading, going home without Coby and Tricia.

We took Coby to the clinic where they decided to rehydrate him. It was about five hours before we were to leave for the airport. The doctors told us that if Coby was going to get to go to the airport, he would have to be better than he was doing.

Coby only weighs fifty-one pounds.

He began crying a little because he wants to go see us off. It was very hard for me to see him stressed. He doesn't want me to leave.

I don't want to leave either.

Tricia and Casey went back to the apartment to get ours and Coby's things. I stayed with Coby; we had a good talk and cried and laughed together. He fell asleep for about an hour.

I just watched him and prayed.

It seemed time was just standing still.

Tricia and Casey got back with some food. Coby ate and was feeling better. The nurse came in and said he would be able to go to RDU airport with us. We left, and it was a miserable feeling. I dropped Coby, Casey, and Tricia off with the bags and then went to park the van. Tricia was getting the tickets.

An attendant came out and said a prayer for us. It was nice.

It was time, and Casey and I had to board. It was tough for all of us.

Coby hugged me, told me he loved me, and said to "party on, Dad!"

I told him the same.

I hugged Tricia and told her I loved her and to kiss Coby for me daily. We went down the tunnel, and I looked back. They both waved.

I hope the next time I see Coby, he will have received his lungs.

It was a good flight. Sonny and Jeannie picked us up. We stopped at the store on our way home. When we got home, Casey showed me all her new stuff and her school accomplishments. It was nice seeing her excited; she is a trooper.

Wilbanks called, Mark Mazzon and Keith stopped in, Spann called, and Nick and Betty had left a cake.

Football meetings start tomorrow.

Tricia called, and I talked with Coby. It seemed different, my not being with him. I will never forget the last 158 days.

God, I miss Tricia and Coby so much already. I asked God to give me strength and kissed Casey on the head.

I know he will.

Day 159
Wednesday, July 29, 1992

The coaches started today. Kyle Story, offensive coordinator, and Warren Swann, defensive coordinator. Everyone was very nice. Oh yeah, Jimmy Brooks, the head coach, also. The training was not a surprise.

Everything is going to be fine, though, once we get into the swing of things.

These guys have really got the place looking nice. I have been thinking of Tricia and Coby all day. I know their routine. I called Casey about ten, and she was fine. Mother and Daddy were coming at noon to be with her. Casey had called Lyric to come swim.

I called Casey again at noon, and Mother answered the phone. Casey was in the pool with Lyric.

Coby had called and talked with Casey about a Nintendo game.

We dieseled the practice fields today. I got home around seven o'clock, cleaned up, and went and got Casey from gymnastics. She seemed glad to be back.

We stopped at Sonic, picked up her lime slush, and headed back to Wylie. I called Tricia and Coby when I got home. He was still vomiting, but not as much. Michael Booth was doing better. Tricia met Dr. Egan. He doesn't come by much, but I think he likes Coby. Tricia said Coby missed us. I talked with him, and it felt good to hear his voice.

Everyone worked good in work out today, he told me.

Esther called and said Dr. Cox is not doing well. Our prayers go out to her.

I feel the lungs will be here soon.

Day 160
Thursday, July 30, 1992

I woke up before the alarm went off. Casey was waking up also. We talked awhile. I then got up and got ready for football. When I arrived, we listened to Warren Swann, the defensive coordinator, explain the defense. He did a good presentation.

Coach Brooks would pitch in as well as Kyle Story. They are good folks, I can tell.

I came home at lunch, and Mother had it ready. Jeannie was there with Brianna and Jeremy. Casey was having fun being the big sister. Mrs. Whitt called and is going to bring lasagna and cookies later today. I went around to the supermarket and was looking for donations for a new water machine for the boys called "the Cow." It would be nice to have.

After work, I went to Plano and got my airplane tickets. I then came home and mowed the yard for the first time this season. I called Coby, and he sounded a lot better. He may go to the apartment tomorrow. He had a magnesium deficiency caused by too much throwing up. He is feeling better and did his workout. Tricia said things were better with him. Mike is doing fine.

I talked with Rock King today. He started his own business. John called, and he was doing about the same. Archie called.

I am planning to start my workouts tomorrow, Nordic Track and the weights. It is beginning to rain now, strange weather for this time of year.

Dr. Cox is not doing good at all. The doctors had to perform surgery to relieve pressure on her skull.

It really feels strange being here.

I don't know how long I can go without being around Coby. I know God will take care of us all that believe.

Day 161
Friday, July 31, 1992

Casey stayed with Jeannie last night. I got up and did the NordicTrack and then went to the field house. I was the first to arrive, so I lifted weights a bit. Kyle Story, the offensive coordinator, came in and said he had driven through a big rainstorm.

Everyone finally eased in, and we got started talking offense. Kyle presented the scheme, with Coach Brooks adding in at times. I will have the receivers including the tight ends. I am looking forward to a new position.

At times, during the morning session, I would check my watch and guess what Tricia and Coby were doing in North Carolina.

Lunch arrived. Jon, Joe, Keith, Wilbanks, Warren, Kyle, and I went to Steak Kountry. We had a few laughs and then went back for the afternoon work. I straightened up the training room and then went home. I will go get Casey from gym around 5:30 p.m.

I called H-103 in North Carolina to see if Coby got out of the hospital. Coby answered the phone. He was tired but doing okay. He did the six-minute walk but had to stop at times. He told me he had never stopped before. I told him he was just weak from the throwing up, but he would get back in shape soon.

Tricia said everything is about the same. Andy's mom and girlfriend are there from New Jersey. I called Miss B. Casey, she, and I are going to eat at Tia's tomorrow night. It will be my first Tex-Mex food in six months. I picked up Casey and then took her home to clean up.

Afterward we went to Walmart for a few things. We then went home and called Tricia and Coby so Casey could talk to them. Casey was pretty tired, so we watched some of the Olympics and then went to bed.

Maybe the lungs will be tonight.

Day 162
Saturday, August 1, 1992

Another start of a new month, and Coby has been at NC for 162 days.

It seemed unbelievable.

Casey and I got up, watched a little TV, and then I got ready and went to a coaches' meeting with Sam Terry residing. All coaches were present, and we met in Coach Joe Stone's classroom. We stapled some forms first, and then Sam gave us picture dates, Booster club meetings, etc. The meeting took about an hour. I met Rhonda Precord, whom I would be working with in PE. It seemed strange not seeing Ard, Spann, Mazzon, Salerno, but things are a-changin'.

Afterward I went home. Casey and I went to Nick and Betty's so Casey could dive. We visited a while, went home, and got ready for physicals. Casey went with me. It was nice seeing the boys again. Some were bigger, and some were the same size. Some of the boys said they had missed me. It made me feel good, but sure, they did (sarcasm).

Physicals were over around 6:00 p.m., so Casey and I went to Tia's to meet Miss B. It is beginning to storm. Lightning was flashing everywhere. When we got to Tia's in Plano, it was raining pretty hard. As we were walking in, I was looking for Miss B, but I couldn't find her.

Just then, I saw her standing up at a table, so Casey and I didn't have to wait for a table. It was good seeing her and good eating enchiladas. After eating, we walked around the mall, talked with the Chapmans and Coach Smith from Bonham.

Casey and I went home and watched the Cowboys. I called Tricia and Coby. They and Kelly went to the mall and ate at Spinnaker's.

Coby seemed to be breathing heavily, but overall doing fine, Tricia said.

I fell asleep watching the Cowboys get beat by the Oilers.

I prayed for the Carolina bunch when I woke up and then went back to sleep.

Day 163
Sunday, August 2, 1992

Casey and I were pretty lazy. But we did finally get up and go to Eckerd to pick up the pictures she took. We then came back home, and I took Casey diving at Nick and Betty's. We visited a while. Casey and I went home. I called Brian Chaney about the driveway leak, and he said he will fix it Monday. Tricia called and wanted to know where PULMOCARE was. I told her where.

Miss B and her sister Julie were coming swimming, and then Casey was going to spend the night with Miss B in Plano. I will get her tomorrow night from gym. It is raining very hard. I am wanting to call Coby and Tricia, but I am going to wait until later.

Casey did go to Miss B's, and it stormed hard. I watched a little of the Olympics and then put my football stuff in a folder. Spann called, asking about Coby.

I called Coby and Tricia. Things are about the same was the report. I sure do miss them; it is very lonely without them here, especially with Casey gone.

Day 164
Monday, August 3, 1992

Since I was here alone, I got up and did the NordicTrack around six o'clock. Showered, got ready, and then left for the field house. I left the back door unlocked if Brian needed to get in the house. When I arrived at the Field House parking lot, everyone was there except for Kyle and Wilbanks.

We loaded up in the van and headed for the Dallas Convention Center. I thought of Tricia and Coby. Tricia was probably getting up and putting his medicine out. Hopefully, he was resting.

We arrived at coaching school in downtown Dallas at Reunion Arena. We stood in the registration line, and I got my coaches' pass. I found Warren and Sam at one of the exhibits. We just looked around, and I talked to some of the people I know. Looked at the Aqua Lift. Hopefully, we will get a couple, maybe three.

It was getting time for us to leave, so we met in front. We stopped at Tia's and went back to the Field House and talked football. Afterward I got a lift in.

When I came home, I called Tricia and Coby. They had a good day, except for the oxygen tank. It broke, so she and Coby went to get two new tanks at PSA. Stan, the O_2 man, saved the day. Tricia said she is putting a lot of PULMOCARE in Coby. He is trying really hard to eat. Tricia also said Mike Booth may go to the apartment soon.

I got a letter from Carol Adler, Coby's social worker. She is leaving to go with her husband to Japan. Coby will have a new social worker. When I told Coby, he said he imagined he would see her soon. Carol was very nice and a lot of help when Coby and I first arrived at UNC Hospitals. She wished us well. I almost cried when I hung the phone up with them today. I miss them so.

I made myself get on the NordicTrack, and it helped a little. I think of how Coby walks on the treadmill, pushing himself. He inspires me.

I then showered and went to get Casey. She started crying because her balance beam routine was not going good. I told her I was having to learn a new system and was telling myself I could do it. She said she was trying also. I think we both are just missing Tricia and Coby so much.

I feel like I am pushing a boxcar or something sometimes.

We stopped at Sonic and got a couple of lime slushes then sang on the way home. She took a bath when we arrived and called Megan to come over tomorrow.

Mother and Daddy will be here, so they should be fine.

We watched a little TV, and then Casey went to bed. I laid down with her and had her do the Dana Carvey imitation of John Travolta. I like for her to go to sleep laughing.

I need to go over some football stuff, and then to sleep I will go. Dang, I miss them.

Day 165
Tuesday, August 4, 1992

I was first to arrive at the high school parking lot. Joe got the van. We loaded up Coach Brooks, Jon, Joe, and I went to coaching school. When we arrived, the others had been following us in their cars. We stayed for the regional meeting then went to eat. Afterward we headed back to Wylie.

When I arrived, I called Dr. Reidmiller's office to talk about Casey's braces. Mother was washing, and the machine broke. I called Mr. Ellis, the repairman, who will be here tomorrow. I then went to see Mr. McAdams who said things were fine. He even gave me an annual dedicated to Coby. The first annual ever at WMS.

I went back to the field house. From there I went home and mowed the yard until the mower broke. I had talked with Tricia earlier, and Coby was having some chest pain.

I feel it is mucus, but I told her to take him to the ER if he continues to hurt. Sure enough, I called her after mowing the yard, and she had taken Coby in for films and an exam. While they were there, the beeper went off. Coby said Tricia went nuts.

It was a false alarm.

After talking with Tricia, I studied football, Mother and Daddy went to bed, and Casey was at Megan's for the night.

Ronnie Johnson, Kyle's dad, and Esther had called earlier. I am getting up at 4:40 a.m. to go to the FCA breakfast in Dallas. Then I'm coming back to give my receivers' presentation for the coaches.

Please, God, be with my family.

Day 166
Wednesday, August 5, 1992

I did get up early, 4:40 a.m., for the FCA breakfast in downtown Dallas. It was a good breakfast with a good speaker. God knew I needed the lift.

I wish Tricia, Coby, and Casey could have heard the speaker. They would have loved him. He did a great Barney Fife impersonation from *The Andy Griffith Show*.

After the breakfast, Jon, Keith, and I walked to the convention center. On the way, we stopped at the train station to go to the facilities. A homeless man was in the restroom, washing up. It was a bad thing to see, people with no place to go.

When we arrived at the convention center, Joe Stone and I went to a trainer's lecture. It was good for me to get reacquainted with things. We then attended the general meeting to vote for THSCA, officers and such.

After the meeting, all the staff went to Hooters for lunch. Coby was right, the Hooters are nice. We then went back to Wylie for the afternoon coaches' meeting. I went to the house to change clothes. I saw Casey. No braces until November.

I then went back to the field house and listened to Jon give lineman drills. I then gave my receivers' presentation and training room talk to the other coaches. During my talk, the phone rang, and Joe answered.

It was Tricia.

I did not have the feeling the lungs were in. Sure enough, they weren't.

Tricia told me Coby was put back in the hospital because of chest pain. The mucus he is throwing up is dark green, which means the infection is getting worse. Mucus plugs were clogging up his breathing passages.

Tricia seemed a little disturbed, but I knew God would help her through.

I thought about how we must get some lungs soon.

I told her I would call them later to see how things were going. She hung up, and I said a silent prayer before putting the receiver down. Coaches were talking football. It seemed I was in a different world.

When my presentation was over, Coach Brooks talked to us about practice. When he was finished, I lifted a while, showered, and then went home. It was time to get Casey at gym.

Casey was in a better mood today when I got her. I told her about Coby. She knew. She had called Jo Anna Nelson. She remembered her number. I know she misses both Tricia and Coby. *Somehow, we will manage,* I thought.

We stopped at Sonic and got our usual fresh lime slush then headed east for Wylie.

Casey called Coby when we got home. Then I spoke with Tricia. The usual stuff was going on. Nurses Sue Baker, doctors, and therapists coming and going…the normal chaos. Coby has a perfect view of the Tar Heel I helicopter out front.

Doug and Kelly were there visiting. I talked with Coby a little. He wanted to know about Hooters, of course. When I was through talking, Casey and I watched some of the Olympics and then went to bed.

I thought maybe the lungs would come in while he is in the hospital.

Day 167
Thursday, August 6, 1992

Sam met with all of us male coaches today. He went over policies and stuff. When he finished and left, I felt I had been in a race. Coach Brooks asked me if he did his football meetings like that. We ate lunch at Hutchison's BBQ.

Mom and Dad took Casey to gym, and I got her at 7:45 p.m. We spent all the afternoon handing out shoes, shirts, helmets, and other equipment. I spoke with Coby. Kaaren was visiting. He seemed to be in good spirits.

Mike may go home this weekend.

Day 168
Friday, August 7, 1992

I had the day off from the Field House, so Casey and I went to Kaufman. I got a haircut at Archie's and my car insurance taken care of by Eva Trail (Hetmer). Casey and I stopped at Walmart in Rockwall on the way home. I got some hanging file folders for my field house drawer.

I took Casey to gym and then went back to the field house and worked on getting my files straight.

I picked her up from gym. We then went home and watched the Olympics and the Cowboys.

Tricia called. Coby was not doing so good. They decided to give him a pint of blood. The lung infections were using his blood up fast. Tricia called later, around 1:00 a.m., and Coby was sleeping. I felt she just needed to talk.

I know the feeling.

1,200 miles from home, and your child is going through a blood transfusion.

It is a little scary.

I thought after she hung the phone up, those days when Coby was getting evaluated, how lonely it was in those waiting rooms, praying Coby would be all right. It sure is not like going to the mall, as Dr. Wood told Coby about the transplant.

Day 169
Saturday, August 8, 1992

I got up and worked out. Casey and I had planned later to go and get me a golf hat, go by Eckerd, see Trace at his house, and eat at Schlotzsky's, then get Katydog, and then finish the day in the pool.

Casey also wanted me to cook hamburgers outside. We did it all, just as we planned.

I spoke to Tricia and Coby this morning. He seemed much better. I talked to him later, and I could tell he was tired.

He might go home tomorrow if further tests seemed all right.

Casey and I finished the night watching Olympic track. They were fun to watch. The US men and women did well.

I am very proud of Casey. I know she misses her mom and brother.

Mrs. Ewing braided her hair for me. Julie and Tami said just to call. It is nice to have so much help.

Day 170
Sunday, August 9, 1992

Casey and I got in the pool early. We then had a Sunday school lesson and then went and put up my weight chart for two-a-days. It shows how much weight the players lose. Hello, August.

Then to Tia's we went. Back home to the pool again. In between the pool and Tia's, we went back to the Field House, and all the coaches were there, doing last-minute preps for workouts. Joe said his son, Matt, had to get five stitches because he cut his foot. Jon Peter's daughter, Janie, was up there with him.

I am worried about Casey's knee. I hope it is not bad. She hurt it at gym, just standing up from a sitting position. I talked to Coby. He seemed a little better.

I hope the day is soon for the lungs.

I saw Coach Lancaster from Farmersville. His little girl has cystic fibrosis also. She is doing fine, though, and does not even do breathing treatments. Mainly with girls, it is intestinal problems. His wife's family lives in North Carolina. Her father is a preacher and might visit with Coby.

Life is a ride, that is for sure.

Casey is saddened by the closing of the Olympics. I am glad she enjoyed watching the twenty-fifth.

Tomorrow football. I feel like a weight is on me. I know it is worrying about Tricia and Coby, but I also know God will not give me anything I cannot handle.

Bob Costas is closing out the games. I feel he will get an Emmy; he was so polished.

Day 171
Monday, August 10, 1992

The first days of two-a-days have finally arrived. I will admit, I am glad. I'd much rather be with Tricia, Coby, and Casey in Chapel Hill, though. We got off to the usual confused-but-not-too-chaotic morning practice. I was lost, but that is nothing new.

I know God will get me through.

We had two practices this morning, and that was all. I think the kids will like it better. It gives them more time off to recover. The coaches were through at five. I lifted, came home, and took a swim. It is just Katydog and me tonight. Casey is with Jeannie.

I miss her not being here.

I called Coby and Tricia, and Coby had had a pretty good day. He is still throwing up some, and I imagine it is the medicine. He has clinic tomorrow. He also gets to pick up his *Wayne's World* video at Cary Town Center.

Kaaren and Gavin took Coby and Tricia to Circuit City, and Coby bought a CD player. Tricia said she gets up and does his medicine, and then she cannot go back to sleep. That is when my trouble with sleeping started as well.

After talking with the Carolina bunch, I studied some offense and then read a little.

I prayed to not make him go much further without getting his lungs.

I am concerned, but I also remind myself God will handle everything. I just need more patience.

Day 172
Tuesday, August 11, 1992

It has been two weeks since Casey and I left Tricia and Coby. I really hope it is not much longer.

I got up this morning and skinny-dipped at 5:30 a.m. It was nice and refreshing. I then got ready and went to the Field House. I was the only one there.

I got the ice ready for the a.m. workout. I am feeling comfortable with each workout. The more I see the system, the better I feel. I have enjoyed working with Kyle. I went to the middle school between workouts and picked up Casey's schedule. I talked with Mr. McAdams. I visited with Dr. Cox's daughter, Courtney. She is really getting pretty. She said her mom was doing better. I heard it was the contrary.

Had a pretty good afternoon session. The boys worked hard. We should surprise some folks. We got one of the Aqua Lifts today. Phil and I went downtown to James Wright's barbershop to see if he could help us get more donations. He would try, he told us. One man gave five dollars right then. Just $685 more.

It's a start.

Meyers and I went to Old El Paso and had supper. We had a good visit.

I also met Mazzon's girlfriend who seems nice. I also saw his new explorer; it was nice also.

I came home, called Tricia, and she and Coby both have a virus. They went to clinic. Dr. Wood changed some things and told Coby everyone wants him as a patient.

Coby has always had an effect on folks.

I know he and Casey have had an effect on Tricia and me.

I will get Casey tomorrow at gym. I am ready to see her.

Day 173
Wednesday August12, 1992

I hit the pool around 5:45 this morning. It helps me to get going. Today's workout was pretty bad. I said the third day we did not rise from the soreness. The boys seemed really tired.

James Wright called. He has raised some money for the Aqua Lift. Jon Peters and I went to Steak Kountry in the afternoon and at lunch. I went and got Casey from gym. Jeannie had bought her a lot of nice clothes and school supplies.

When we got home, Julie Black from next door brought some cinnamon rolls. They were great. Julie is Coach Black's wife. I talked with Coby and Tricia. They got the *Wayne's World* video today. Coby had already watched it.

Mother and Dad are coming tomorrow. They will help Casey get to and from places.

I pray each day will bring the lungs. I just hope Coby is not too scared. He tells me every night he loves me. I miss him so terribly much.

Day 174
Thursday, August 13, 1992

We had a freshman-only practice today because the new coaches had new teacher in-service. After the workout, Joe, Matt, Jon, and I went to Purdy's for lunch. We returned and dieseled the playing field. The varsity and JV came on the fields from 5:00 to 7:00 p.m. It would be our last workout in shorts. Pads tomorrow.

I got home too late to call Tricia and Coby.

Day 175
Friday, August 14, 1992

I got up at 6:30 a.m. and went swimming. It was raining but felt good.

I called Tricia. Coby was still asleep. She was missing the first day of in-service. I told her to hang with it. She felt different, she said. I went to school, but it was a strange feeling.

Tami was now at the high school; there were new teachers who were in junior high when I first came to Wylie. I went to Tricia's room, and it was strange not seeing her there.

Life is definitely a ride.

Lance Campbell, Keith, and I went to Maria's for lunch. We had a two-hour workout, a one-hour break, and another two hours after that. Then we ordered pizza. It was nice, the whole staff together watching football film.

After everyone left, I stayed and helped Jon get the uniforms ready for the next day. It was about midnight when we finished.

Jon and I got a slice of cake each and Dr. Pepper and then went up and sat on the press box. We looked at a full moon and just talked about different things. It was an uncharacteristically cool August night. We were through with two-a-days, and it was only the middle of August.

After leaving the field house, I went home. Megan and Casey were still awake. Mother and Daddy were sleeping. I sent the two kids to bed, and I followed.

I really miss Tricia and Coby so much.

Day 176
Saturday, August 15, 1992

I got up and started getting ready for team pictures. Mother and Daddy were going to leave at nine to go back to Kaufman. I went on to school, and we had our team pictures then a scrimmage. Watermelon followed.

I went home, and Doug came by and picked up the suitcase with Coby's books and some clothes for Tricia. Doug and Kelly had been home visiting and were headed back to Carolina. I then took Megan and Casey to Chili's. They really like playing together.

I took Casey to Rusty Rosser's birthday party. I then came home and returned to the party at eight to pick up Casey. She was going to stay with Megan and go to church tomorrow. Patrick and John came over and watched the Cowboys. It was a good game.

I told John he would be taking Casey and me to the airport tomorrow. He laughed.

I know it will be soon.

Day 177
Sunday, August 16, 1992

The phone rang at 7:45 a.m. It was Tricia.

"They are going to look right now," she said. "Are you ready?" she asked.

"You bet!" I answered and asked her to put Coby on the phone.

"Hey, man, this is it! You ready?" I asked.

"Yes, sir!" Coby said. "Tell Casey I love her," were his next words.

I started tearing up.

After they hung up, I started getting things ready. I called for the 3:54 p.m. flight. John Hartley, Megan's dad, would take Casey and me to the airport because Jeannie was in Louisiana. He said, "Fine," when I called him.

Esther called. I am going to call her to make all the calls when we find out for sure. I talked with Mother, and they were coming over. Tricia called back and said the team was flying to Louisiana to look at the lungs.

Coby told me he would be Cajun Man. It sounded good.

After we hung up the phones, I started getting things together. It is finally here, I hope. I called Mrs. Draper, the preacher's wife. Special prayer would be started. I thought how nice it is to be around nice people.

Miss B called and said Coby told her his lungs would be here this weekend.

Mother and Daddy came over from Kaufman to stay with us while we waited. The telephone rang regularly, and people were stopping by wishing us well.

Tricia called and said the team was on their way to Louisiana later than planned. I changed our flight to the 8:10 p.m. We waited. I watched the PGA championship, keeping an eye on Coach Brooks' nephew, Mark. By 3:30 our time, I should know if it is a go. It was around four o'clock, and Coby said the lungs were not good.

It was a no-go.

Tricia got on the phone and said it was pretty low there. I could feel it through the telephone.

"Well, the day ain't over yet," I told her, staying positive.

I told her I would call her back. I needed to cancel Casey's and my flight.

I called American Airlines for the third time.

I was disappointed, but I felt for Coby. The emotional ride he must have taken would probably floor me by now. John Hartley had brought Casey and Megan over. They decided to go back over to Megan's to eat.

I didn't have much of an appetite. Mother and Daddy went back to Kaufman, and it was pretty lonely.

I showered after Doug called from the airport and told him it was a no-go. He would not be picking Casey and me up tonight.

I sat on the couch and dozed off. It was time for me to go get Casey because it was time to take her grocery shopping. I went and got her, and we headed to Brookshire's. We saw James Wright and Mary Bolton, his wife, with their three kids.

James insisted on me taking $25 for groceries. I tried to get him to keep it, but he wouldn't. I thought I will just get a haircut there sometime. He is very nice.

When Casey and I returned from grocery shopping, we went over to Julie's so she could roll Casey's hair. We stayed about thirty minutes or so. We returned home, and Tricia was on the recorder.

"We are going again!" she said excitedly.

Molly was also on the machine. Tricia had called her and said they were going out to South Carolina to look for some lungs and to call her as soon as I could.

I called American Airlines first and got the first flight out in the morning. I got a hold of Tricia on the phone, and she said this was a first time, going out twice to harvest lungs in one day. Coby was doing fine, although he was going to have to reprep, which meant more GoLYTELY.

I talked to Coby and told him, "Hey, this is bigger than the Super Bowl."

He told me, "I know, Daddy, but I've got a lot of cheerleaders."

We would call later and find out if it was a go. I called Molly and Archie. We decided Archie would take us to the airport because he was off on Mondays. He was coming to the house to stay the night until we left in the morning.

I went to bed about one o'clock or so. Tricia called.

It was a go!

Coby talked with me. I told him I loved him. He cried a little but was fine.

I told Archie after hanging up what was going on. I called Jeannie and then Dale. I also called Esther, Mother and Daddy, and Brother Draper.

I laid back down and watched the clock.

Day 178
Monday, August 17, 1992

I got up at 4:00 a.m. and got in the shower. Archie came in and said Tricia had called and said things were fine.

Casey got up and got ready, and Archie took us to DFW. Casey told Katydog the news about Coby, and Casey said she wagged her tail.

I had talked with Mr. McAdams earlier. We decided that if I had not called by seven in the morning, I was on my way to North Carolina. He said his prayers are with us.

Dale met us at Gate 21A, and Archie stayed until we went down the boarding ramp. We took off at 7:00 a.m. I prayed things were still going fine.

What a ride. Six Flags doesn't have a ride like this, not even Disney.

I looked at the date, August 17. One plus seven equals eight, divided by two equals four, my number.

Coby knew it was going to be this weekend, just like he told Miss B.

The flight was rough at times because of a thunderstorm, but we landed on schedule. When Casey and I walked through the unloading ramp, we saw Doug there, waiting. He looked tense, so I asked him how things were going.

We went down to the baggage claim and left for UNC Hospitals.

We parked at PT and went to the second-floor ICU waiting room. Tricia, Jo Anna, Gordon, Bob, and Ellen were all there. It was nice seeing everyone.

They had finished the right lung and were halfway through finishing the left.

Doug and I went to the apartment to get the van because Gordon took Coby and Tricia to the hospital. When I got back, the doctors came out and said everything looked good.

Tricia cried. I was numb.

I'm just glad Coby had the opportunity. We would get to see him in a couple of hours.

I said prayers for the donor's family.

Jo Beth came by before going to PT, then Leighann and Chris. After seeing Coby was resting, we went to the apartment to shower and then returned to the hospital.

When I saw Coby, he, of course, was tubed up.

His color was great! He opened his eyes and squeezed my hand.

I knew then we did the right thing by coming to Chapel Hill 178 days ago.

Mother called when we got back to the waiting room. Jeannie and Dale were coming in at about seven o'clock.

It was getting close to 7:30 p.m., so Casey and I went out and waited. The Tar Heel I helicopter took off, so Casey got to see it leave for the first time.

Jeannie and Dale came driving up, honking the horn. Definitely from Texas.

I hollered, "Are y'all lookin' for Ramsgate?"

When they parked, we went to the second floor. It was time to see Coby. They both got to see him, and Jeannie cried. Dale looked numb, like I was. Coby still looked good.

We stayed for a while, and then we were leaving. The nurse stepped outside and took his mask off. It was our next-door neighbor, Kevin Brady. He would be Coby's nurse for the night. He said he would be home around eight in the morning and would give us the report.

We headed to the apartment. While Coby was sleeping, we thought we'd do the same.

Tricia stopped and talked with Kevin's wife and Jo Beth. We talked with Bob and Ellen, then went to bed.

Dale and Jeannie stayed at the Holiday Inn for the night.

I thanked God and slept real good.

Day 179
Tuesday, August 18, 1992

We got up and called the hospital. They said we could see Coby at 10:30 a.m., so we left. We had a lot of calls at the apartment and the ICU waiting room as well.

Coby looked good. He was breathing on his own. They had removed the ventilator.

People were coming in and out all day. We would see him at the times allowed and then go back to the lobby. We all went to eat. While we were gone, they put Coby back on the vent because of a mucus plug.

He needs to cough, they said, because his lungs are really wet. It was a small problem, and it should work out, they said.

The color of his fingers still looked good.

Between visits, Dale and I went to football practice. Coach Brown said he was happy about Coby's lungs. We watched a while and left for the hospital to see Coby again. Doug and Kelly came by and got to see him.

He was using hand signals to communicate. It was great to see him so active.

It was time for him to sleep, so we headed to the apartment.

When we got home, the phone was ringing. It was Sonny, Jeannie's husband. His dad had just passed away. Sonny seemed upset but said he was fine. I really felt for him being home alone. Jeannie and Dale would be leaving on the first flight in the morning to head back to DFW.

I prayed for Sonny.

Knowing Kevin, our neighbor, was at the hospital with Coby made things better.

Day 180
Wednesday, August 19, 1992

Jeannie and Dale left early, although Jeannie got confused about the time change. She forgot. But they called us from the plane and said they had made it on time. Dale got to the airport in eleven minutes. It is normally a twenty-five-minute drive for me in the van.

Tricia and I met Carrie at the steps of the apartment. Coby had a good night, she said.

We went to the hospital after phone calls. We got to see Coby, who was sitting up.

He hand-signaled to me about Larry Bird retiring. He was watching ESPN on the TV. He is really being strong. He had been up an hour and even walked a little with all the equipment he is attached to.

The physical therapy he had done before the surgery was paying off.

He signaled that he was ready to get back to bed, so we left to go back to the lobby. He is being a player.

I am so proud of him, and I told him so.

Day 181, 182, and 183
Thursday, Friday, Saturday, August 20–22, 1992

Every day Coby seemed to be getting better. He had his flat days and then up days in three days. He would gradually increase his walking distance. He told me he would like to get the catheter out… soon!

His voice was coming back. He is coughing up mucus. One nurse said that he is the first transplant patient that she had who could cough up the mucus. Coby has been sitting up longer each day, and his color looks really good.

People from home have been keeping the phone operator busy. Their thoughts and prayers are appreciated.

We have met some nice people in the waiting room. One of my favorite things was going on in the waiting room—black gospel music. A black family was harmonizing in the waiting room. We also met a lady named Telrot. She was waiting for her daughter to come out of surgery. Her daughter was having her large colon removed. She had colitis.

She reminded me of the lady that played Sidney Portier's mother in *Guess Who's Coming to Dinner?* She and her sister were very nice. We later met her other daughter.

We also met a family whose father had had a heart transplant right after Coby received his lungs. He was in the room next to Coby. He is from Mt. Arie, the hometown of Andy Griffith.

Everyone seems to help each other in the waiting room. There is the one old boy that answers the phone when a volunteer or Casey does not get it. He takes good notes. His fiancé was involved in a car wreck.

Saturday in the morning, Ray Schiender from Ellington, South Carolina, arrived. He is a Vietnam vet who walked three hundred miles for Leighann Woodsen, a lung transplant candidate who is in our support group. Ray is not walking only for donations for Leighann but also donor awareness.

He is a special man. He has only one leg.

It was an emotional scene when he met Leighann for the first time in front of UNC Hospitals. I had told Tricia that I feel, since Coby's lungs came from South Carolina, that Ray is responsible for bringing the awareness.

The VFW of Chapel Hill presented Ray with a proclamation that August 22, 1992, would be Donor Awareness Day in Chapel Hill.

Tricia and I both gave TV interviews about Coby. We were on the eleven o'clock news. I was touched by the hard work of Ray and Leighann's people. Leighann is a go-getter. When she gets her lungs, I can see her running for office in South Carolina.

Later that day, Tricia and I went to the Tar Heel inter-squad game and spoke with Bruce Hemphill. The TV reporter that did our interview was there. She was surprised we knew Bruce, since we were from Texas. Coby had not such a good day but was improving.

He will be leaving the ICU soon.

Doug and Kelly stopped in for a visit. Coby was ready for us to leave so he could get some sleep.

Day 184
Sunday, August 23, 1992

Tricia spoke with a nurse this morning. Coby was having some temperature. I felt they would be doing a bronchoscope. Infections and rejections give the same symptoms.

Sure enough, when we arrived at the ICU, Dr. Detterbeck talked to us about scoping Coby. He felt there was not a rejection, but he needed to scope it out.

I felt a little pressure. I have never feared the surgery, but the post-op scares me. I asked God to be with Coby. Prayer always makes me feel better. It is a psychological workout for me.

Life is a ride.

Coby made it through his first post-surgery bronch. His throat was still swollen from the transplant ventilator trachea. Hopefully, Coby would not remember.

Dr. Detterbeck said Coby always does what he is asked. He will be on steroids for the next three days. Coby will sleep out the next few hours.

Casey, Tricia, and I went for a snack at the cafeteria; the snack bar is closed on weekends. We returned to the waiting room, and the family with the man who was crushed with sand was there. Things were the same with them.

Dr. Detterbeck stopped in and said Coby's scope looked good. They were going to treat him for rejection, though. Coby slept out most of the afternoon. He did not remember much about the bronch. I was glad about that.

Casey, Tricia, and I went to the apartment and drop-dead slept.

Maybe tomorrow Coby would be moved to the floor.

Day 185
Monday, August 24, 1992

Tricia called the ICU nurse when she got up. Coby would be moved to the floor this afternoon. We got ready and went to the hospital.

When we got there, Coby was up doing his walk with his entourage (nurses, techs, etc.) and all his attached tubes and machinery. He was one less chest tube. Three down, one to go.

When he returned to his ICU room, the nurse helped him in the chair.

It reminded me of yesterday when Coby was receiving a suppository behind the curtain, and he sang out, "Moon river!" like Chevy Chase in *Fletch*.

When we arrived, the nurse said we could stay as long as we wanted. Coby would be moving to the floor at two o'clock.

It was amazing. Just one week after his double-lung transplant, Coby was moving to a regular floor. We started loading things up. The time had come. Coby was masked up, as we all were.

Tricia was filming, and off to the elevator we headed. Our destination was room 4730.

Coby was singing, "I'm making a move, New York, New York." He was ready to get out of ICU. They were all good folks there, though. Will was waiting on the fourth floor. He had given Coby a Redskins cap earlier. We arrived, and Coby met his new nurse, Mary Beth. She and Cheryl helped Coby to the bed.

They took Coby's oxygen off, and he never put it on again until he took a walk later. One liter though.

People called. Doug and Kelly came by.

It was nice seeing Coby without a nasal canula.

Coby received a Ram cap in the mail from golfer Mark Brooks and a golf card. Brooks is the nephew of my new coach. He had just won the PGA championship. Coach Brooks, apparently, had him send it to Coby, who was pretty thrilled.

Things are definitely looking better.

Tricia, Casey, and I went back to the apartment for the night. Rose was the night nurse. We were all tired but really excited. I thanked God and prayed for the Andrew hurricane victims.

Day 186
Tuesday, August 25, 1992

When Casey, Tricia, and I got to the hospital, Coby had already had an x-ray in the department. Annie stopped by and said Coby would be walking around ten o'clock. He had a good night's sleep. At one, he asked Rose to put the nasal cannula on, only she did not turn the oxygen on. He never knew.

The mind does play tricks on us.

Cappie Jordan came by and left Coby a Carolina football media guide with a lot of the players' and coaches' signatures. She even came back later and brought a T-shirt Coach Brown took off and sent to him. It was the bowling T-shirt.

Coach will give the shirt off his back, literally!

School will start for Coby and Casey today. That is when Tricia and I would go eat and bring the kids something back. The rest of the day, we watched videos, walked, and did homework.

Coby did it all without the aid of an oxygen tank.

It was a miracle!

Coby was beginning to swell in his lower extremities and testicles because of the steroids. Coby said, "I am surprised about the extremities!"

We went home, but stopped beforehand to be with Jo Anna because Jo Beth was in the hospital. I got a Pepsi and peanuts. Hurricane Andrew had run Jo Anna's husband out of Louisiana to Quitman, Texas…home of Sissy Spacek.

Life is a ride for everyone, it seems.

Day 187
Wednesday, August 26, 1992

Things went about the same until around six o'clock. Coby started having abdominal pain. His testicles were still swollen, and he just felt miserable. I stayed with him. He slept off and on. I know he is in a lot of pain.

I can tell by his eyes.

I fell asleep and was awakened by his crying. It really is hurting him. He finally fell asleep.

I turned the A&M/Stanford game on so I would get sleepy. It worked.

Day 188
Thursday, August 27, 1992

Coby was taking an x-ray around 6:00 a.m. He wasn't hooked up to anything except for the last of four chest tubes.

When Tricia and Casey arrived, I went to the apartment to shave and shower.

Coby's stomach will seem to be fine, and then he'll get hit with another pain episode. The doctors made the decision not to let him eat until Friday morning to see how things are going. He sometimes acts as if the appendix is the problem. He had an ultrasound, more abdomen x-rays, and they showed a lot of gas.

Dr. Lacey drew out a lot of fluid from his G-tube. It looked pretty raunchy.

They are not giving Coby any medicine for pain for fear of hiding something in his stomach. The immunosuppressants may be hiding some issues, but we do not know yet. I talked with Mr. McAdams, my principal, and told him I was going to call him today about when I was going to return to school. I was planning on this Sunday, but I am not leaving until Coby is better.

At times he is feeling good, but when the stomach pain occurs, he really seems to hurt. The lungs appear to be doing great, but for some reason, the stomach just isn't. I can't help but wonder if the omentum they pulled up from the stomach part of the transplant might have something to do with it.

Time will tell.

I am getting more concerned than earlier about the stomach. I pray that this is only a temporary setback. I stayed with Coby again that night. This chair doesn't sleep too bad. I figure if Coby can go through what he has, I can handle some discomfort.

Coby is a brave young boy.

He has taught me a lot about dealing with adversity.

I love him so much.

Day 189
Friday, August 28, 1992

Coby was restless most of the night. The doctors came in early and ordered more films. I went with Coby to x-ray, and the tech was having a lot of equipment problems.

I remember how that used to make me mad.

Coby did what the tech asked of him. Coby was still in a lot of pain. He told me he needed some relief, and I told him they would do something about that today.

When Tricia and Casey arrived, so did the doctors. They decided to do an exploratory lobectomy. In other words, go inside and look around. They actually did not think they would find anything but wanted to answer some questions.

Coby was ready for some relief. They finally gave him some "pain remover," as Coby refers to it.

They came and took Coby to surgery at two in the afternoon. Casey, Tricia, and I went and stayed with him until they took him to the OR. We went back to room 4730 and waited.

We hadn't eaten, so Pizza Hut delivered right to Coby's room.

About two hours later, Dr. Lacey, the surgeon, called from the OR. He said things look fine. Dr. Detterbeck was performing the bronch as we spoke. Coby also had a rectal scope.

Good thing he was drugged during all the procedures.

I felt good and that things were fine, but for some reason, I was uneasy and did not know why.

Coby got back to his room at 7:30 p.m. and was doing fine. All the doctors talked with Tricia and me. Casey was in Jo Beth's room. Coby's lungs were working great. It would be a few days for the stomach not to be so tender. They thanked us for being patient.

I thought, *Man, you guys have given Coby another chance. You don't have to thank us for anything.* These guys made a great team.

Casey stayed with Coby while Tricia and I went to the apartment to get some clothes. She was staying the night.

Shirley Booth went with us to get her apartment ready for Mike to come out for the weekend. Tricia and I went back to the hospital. Coby was still sleeping.

I went and visited Dr. Roop on the third floor. We had a good visit, although he is very sick.

Casey and I went home. She was asleep before I got to the bypass one and a half miles. I put her to bed and munched on some Cheetos and sipped on a Mountain Dew while watching the news, high school football highlights, etc.

One heck of a day for Coby. I prayed for him and then went to sleep.

Day 190
Saturday, August 29, 1992

Casey and I slept through the 8:45 a.m. digital alarm and then finally got up. Tricia called and said Coby had had a good night. Morphined up, but good.

Tricia's mom called.

When we arrived at the hospital, they had just finished putting a new central line in Coby. He was pretty drugged out. Connie from PT came and did some exercises with Coby.

Then there was a portable chest x-ray. We would be getting Coby up later to walk. He is really sore from the exploratory surgery. He asked me why he was so sore, and I told him that they had stretched and looked around for a good while. I pushed the pain button to ease him a little, and he went back to sleep.

Tricia and Casey went to the cafeteria. Right now, I do not know if I am leaving tomorrow or not.

I want Coby to be doing better before I leave for the airport. I will make the decision tonight or in the morning.

Day 191
Sunday, August 30, 1992

Dr. Detterbeck made my decision when I'll go home. He said to wait a few days. That was easy.

I called Jon Peters, and he would tell Coach Brooks. Casey went to Suzi's for the day. Doug and Kelly came by for a while.

Coby got up three times. He is still very sore. Hopefully a better day tomorrow. No bowel sounds yet.

Day 192
Monday, August 31, 1992

Coby had to go to the x-ray department for a tube placement in his right lower lung. There is an accumulation of fluid there. He did fine. The reason for the fluid was the soreness of his stomach, so he could not breathe deeply. His lungs, otherwise, are doing fine.

We do not have to wear masks in Coby's room anymore. Only Coby wears one when he leaves the room. He is a player; he walked three times today. Dr. Egan and Coach Hemphill visited him today. Coby has developed a pretty good following.

Casey, after school, went home to Ramsgate with Jo Anna and Jo Beth. Casey is a player also, along with her mom. I am staying with Coby tonight.

I still do not feel that good about Coby's stomach problem yet. Not until he can eat and be fine will I be all right.

Also, I had to beat up my briefcase. It wouldn't come unlocked.

Day 193
Tuesday, September 1, 1992

First day of dove season in Texas. Coby got his tubes pulled out of his chest today. He said he was finally tubeless. He is getting stronger as the day progresses and even got to eat some Jell-O at lunch.

We walked five times, each a long walk. He even walked outside without an O_2 bottle. I think he surprised himself.

Casey and I went home early to sleep. People called, so I got to bed later.

Day 194
Wednesday, September 2, 1992

The phone rang at 4:25 a.m. I knew it was not any news I would want to hear.

Sure enough, Coby was having seizures because of the cyclosporine drug. It happens often with CF lung transplants. Tricia said Coby was banging the bed with his fists.

I tried to calm her. She had called the nurse, and people were everywhere, she told me. I could hear the loudspeakers through the phone, "Code 4 Anderson."

That is Coby's room.

I got a real sick feeling, so I laid down on the couch. Good thing Coby and I bought the long phone extension. Casey already got dressed and was ready to go. Then things got better, and we stayed home. Casey went back to bed, and I prayed.

I was afraid there would be more seizures. Sure enough, at 6:25 a.m., Tricia called again and he had had another seizure.

Casey and I left for UNC at once.

When we arrived, Tricia was totally wiped out. Coby was sleeping. The drugs they gave him were working.

Tricia just wasn't prepared for the seizures. I was not either.

The CT scan was ordered, so I went with Rosie the nurse, a resident, and Coby down to x-ray. We were waiting for the room to become available. I was watching Coby sleep when he started having another seizure, his third. It was really scary. I had seen people have seizures before. Just not my own child.

It didn't last but about forty seconds. Another Ativan was given, and Coby went back to sleep.

The technician came in and rolled Coby into the CT scan room. Coby was beginning to wake up during the exam. I put a lead apron on and talked him through the procedure.

It seemed to ease him when he heard my voice.

Training at Baylor Medical comes through once again.

The scan read normal. I was relieved then. That meant no brain hemorrhage. We went back to the room. Casey was touching him, and he rose, as if to speak. He was having another seizure, number four for the day. Casey was frightened. She thought she caused the seizure.

Dilantin was given to Coby. It is an antiseizure drug. Coby slept out the rest of the day. The doctors said all his levels are normal. It is just the CF transplant patients who seem to have seizure problems. Dr. Egan told me the week of the evaluation that we are merely trading some problems for other problems. A nurse was assigned to Coby the rest of the day.

I stayed the night and will probably stay each night for a while.

Tricia is apprehensive about staying. I do not blame her though. I prayed to God to help me be strong. It always helps. Coby did not have another seizure that night or morning.

Day 195
Thursday, September 3, 1992

I went to the apartment and took a short nap. I called Tricia around noon. Coby was taking a shower. He seems to be waking up. He was walking everywhere after the shower and was fired up, mainly because of the drugs he had taken.

Tricia and I went to eat at the K&W Cafeteria, and Casey stayed with Coby.

Coach Brown sent a balloon and stuffed Ramses that sticks on glass from the NC football team.

As night came, Coby became restless and started to have a headache. I stayed with him, and at 4:25 a.m., he had another seizure.

Day 196
Friday, September 4, 1992

I got the nurse Rhonda and a doctor. We all were surprised when Coby woke up from the seizure and told me he was tired.

It is a helpless feeling when he is seizing. Hopefully, he has no recollection of anything.

I did not call Tricia. I waited for her to call before she came up to the hospital. I told her about the seizure when she arrived. I assured her Coby would be fine.

Coby has definitely had a wild ride the last couple of days.

A blood test showed Coby's Dilantin levels were low, and that was what caused the seizure. His dose was, of course, increased. I went to the apartment and took a nap. Tricia and I went to eat. Casey stayed with Coby.

I realize I am not too fond of those seizures.

Coby walked everywhere. The IV poles have been disconnected, and he is free. He visited PT twice and walked some stairs.

Day 197
Saturday, September 5, 1992

It wasn't too great of a day for Coby's stomach. He slept when he could. We watched UNC beat Wake Forest. Mark Brooks took the Milwaukie Gold Tournament. Coby's spirits were good.

He walked around outside and saw the copter come back.

Day 198
Sunday, September 6, 1992

Coby had some Colace for his stomach. He looks good, just the stomach pain. Dr. Egan asked Tricia and I if we would visit a little boy in the PICU. He is seven years old and waiting for a double-lung transplant. He has pulmonary hypertension, and the family is very scared.

I know how they feel.

Coby got out on a pass and went to apartment H-103. His stomach was hurting the entire time. The doctors think it might be adhesions. I feel tired. I guess lack of sleep is catching up to me. I'll get back into my workout routine soon, and that will help my rest.

I am going to stay with Coby tonight.

Hopefully no seizures.

Day 199
Monday, September 7, 1992

It is Labor Day, and Coby seems to be.

His stomach bothers him quite a bit. Our plans today are to go out on pass again. The nurse took Coby to x-ray, brought him back, and drew some blood. Coby does not take his meds until the blood is drawn. I wonder how many times Coby has been stuck since he was diagnosed twelve years ago.

The lung bunch is going to have a get-together this afternoon at the Ramsgate Clubhouse. We have had one each holiday, Memorial Day, Fourth of July, and now Labor Day.

Kelly stopped by to visit before they release Coby on pass. It was time that we left for the apartment. Tricia prepared a chicken for the get-together. We left for the clubhouse. There were new candidates in attendance.

I talked with Shannon, the manager of Ramsgate. There are 188 units, and she has 186 filled.

That answers the parking lot overcrowdedness.

We stayed awhile, and Coby felt pretty good. People could not believe how well he was doing. I am still in a daze myself. We went back to H-103, and then it was time to go back to the hospital. I stayed with Coby, and we watched *Monday Night Football*. It was the Cowboys versus Redskins. Cowboys won. It looks like the Texas heat took its toll on the skins.

Coby had to have a pill to help him sleep. His stomach again. Who would have ever thought that would be what held him up? I pray for him to be relieved of the stomach pain and also to no longer have seizures.

I padded up the hospital chair with pillows and blankets and then dozed off. It was a day closer to going back to Wylie, I thought.

Day 200
Tuesday, September 8, 1992

About six in the morning, Coby awoke in a lot of pain. He couldn't get still. It was as if he was having a kidney stone. Dr. Blythe drained a bunch of mess out of Coby's G-tube. His stomach is just slow-emptying. I hope it corrects itself soon.

I talked to Tricia. Casey is not feeling well, possibly allergies. Coby was feeling better as the morning progressed. Tricia and I took Casey to the doctor. She now has a UNC Hospitals card, just like Coby. I spoke with Jeannette and Dr. Egan about Casey and me going home tomorrow. They felt it was okay.

It will be hard, but knowing they will be coming home in a few weeks makes a big difference.

Casey and I will be busy with school, gym, football, and all the other activities.

I stayed with Coby. It will be the last night with him for a while. Maybe just three weeks.

I told Dr. Egan I would think of everyone up here on a daily basis. I will never forget this place as long as I am on this earth. These are just good folks who help people. That is what it is all about.

Day 201
Wednesday, September 9, 1992

We checked Coby out on a pass and went to Ham's to eat lunch. It was nice seeing Coby walk down Franklin Street without oxygen or a wheelchair. We went to the camping store and then out to the apartment. I said bye to everyone, and then it was time to go to RDU airport.

It was sad to leave, but I knew Tricia and Coby would be home to Texas soon.

Casey and I called Coby and Tricia while we were flying. It was neat to do so. Jeannie picked us up at the airport and took us home after taking us to the grocery store.

School tomorrow. It was Farmersville week. We won.

During this time, things have been busy. Casey is going to school and gymnastics, and school and football for me. It helps time go by. A benefit for Coby was held at the Wylie Opry. Casey spoke because I was at football prep.

Tricia said Coby was getting stronger and sounded good every time I spoke to him. He was ready to come home, which he did in October. I flew to RDU to drive the van back. When we arrived in Wylie, the front yard was full of people! There was a huge "Welcome Home, Coby" sign, and folks were cheering when Coby stepped out of the van.

He was finally home. We would have been there sooner, but Coby had to stop and eat at every Cracker Barrel along the way. Due to the steroids, he was hungry all the time.

Casey had had a gymnastics meet, so she stayed with Jeannie and Sonny.

What a sweet reunion.

How fortunate we feel as Coby is the only one out of his transplant group that survived. Everyone, except for Jo Beth, was blessed with new lungs, but due to complications with infection and rejection, they did not make it.

They became family and always will be in our hearts.

Kelly and Doug found out before we left that they are going to have a boy.

This is why we are adopted Tar Heels.

Wednesday, March 24, 2021

I had not looked at these journals in over twenty-nine years. I do not know exactly why I kept a journal, but I know now that God had a hand in it, so here goes…

I think back to the first time I saw my son, Coby, in the incubator at Presbyterian Hospital of Dallas on July 25, 1979. To me, his chest looked different than other newborns, but I was a proud new dad to my first child, so I just took Coby as he was. Eighteen months later, Coby was diagnosed with the genetic disease cystic fibrosis.

Tricia's and my life had changed again. Not only did we have a newborn but we also had a sick newborn.

We were told not to let CF change our lives. Yeah, right. There is not another choice but to change, but I guess that was the doctors' way of consoling us. That is after they told me they didn't know if Coby would live another three months or three years. Nothing was certain.

The one certainty was that we had a newborn baby girl, Casey, who tested negative for CF a month after she was born. While waiting for the test results, Tricia and I licked on Casey a lot to see if she was salty-tasting like her brother and the other CF patients.

These journals are merely a piece of a huge jigsaw puzzle. There were twelve years before the transplant of Coby getting needle sticks, having surgeries and near-death episodes, being stared at and made fun of, and multiple hospital stays. Through it all, Coby kept his faith in God, a great attitude, and no matter how sick he felt, he made sure other folks were happy and felt special. Our trip to North Carolina proved that miracles can and do happen. God places people, places, and situations in our lives, and there is no stopping what he can do.

People ask about my family's story and ask how we did it. We did not have to do anything. Coby was the one who put up with CF, fought the good fight, and never gave up. My son is an overcomer and a player. He stayed his focus on the One that matters and kept that mindset his entire twenty-nine years on this earth.

The last time I saw my son, Coby, was December 23, 2008, at Baylor Hospital in Dallas. It was ironic because on July 1, 1967, when I was only seventeen, I started Baylor's School of Radiology Technology. Never could I have imagined that forty-one years later, I would watch my son take his last breath at the very same hospital.

Once again, God had lined things up for me early in life by making me an x-ray technician so I could understand and handle my son's disease later in life. I learned a lot from Coby. People always wanted to describe him as sick, as if that was all he was. However, Coby never let his disease define him. He told me that God gave him CF to see what he would do with it. It is an incurable disease, but if you ask me, Coby whooped it!

Because of a thoughtful family and a boy who made a giving decision, my son was able to live for over sixteen years with borrowed lungs. The donor family's loss was definitely my family's gain, and we are forever grateful.

Our family, friends, the folks from Wylie, and all the people in North Carolina helped our ride go a little smoother.

'Cause life sure is a ride.

Coby, I will never forget you.

About the Author

Todd Michael Gent graduated from Baylor Medical School of Radiology Technology in 1969. After five years of being an x-ray tech, he decided to go back to school to become a coach. Gent graduated from The University of North Texas in 1979 and became a football, basketball, and track coach while continuing to work summers and weekends as an x-ray technician. He recently retired in December 2018, after thirty-eight years of coaching and teaching. Todd Gent currently resides in Kaufman, Texas, with his wife, Tricia, a retired teacher and coach as well.

Todd has two children, Coby and Casey. Coby passed away in 2008 because of complications from cystic fibrosis. Casey graduated from the University of West Florida and has lived in Destin, Florida, since 1999.

Todd is a health enthusiast who enjoys sports, staying active, and is a big music fan.

Todd Michael Gent published his first book, *Hold Your Breath… Breathe* in 2020 and is currently working on other projects, including collaborating with his daughter, Casey, on children's books.

CPSIA information can be obtained
at www.ICGtesting.com
Printed in the USA
BVHW071250181021
619201BV00006B/167